A Tale of Sisters

Wanda Battle-Frazier

Scriptor House LLC

2810 N Church St Wilmington, Delaware, 19802

www.scriptorhouse.com

Phone: +1302-205-2043

Published by Scriptor House LLC

Paperback ISBN: 979-8-88692-109-0

eBook ISBN: 979-8-88692-110-6

Contents

It was one of the worst times in the town's history. No one could believe that such a prestigious and affluent community like this could ever fall victim to such heinous crimes, especially to their most influential resident, Charles Lambert, and with the murders of his daughter and son-in-law, and with the loss of his granddaughters, this case became one of the most highly profiled crimes in the town's history.

In the early eighties Seattle, Washington started experiencing a string of healthy African-Americans and Hispanic babies missing for no apparent reason. Captain Joe Morris and his A-Team worked long arduous hours in conjunctions with the FBI to find these perpetrators and bring them to justice. Billionaire and philanthropist Charles Lambert, a prominent executive in Seattle has always been a person of interest. He and his family have been constant targets of unsavory kidnapping attempts in the past. Some say, it was Lambert's unethical and immoral approach toward his rival business competitors that could have been motive for these crimes perpetrated against him. Captain Morris vowed to his longtime friend that he would not stop searching for his granddaughters until they were found. After a year of searching and surveillance, and hours of investigations, the FBI only recovered 70 percent of the stolen babies. Raylene Chambers, Robyn Richards, and Jessica Lovejoy were never found. Here are their stories.

Raylene
You'll Have Better Luck Playing Lotto

I am going to be twenty years old in a few months, and I have since learned to disconnect and desensitize my mind, body, and soul. It isn't enough that he invades my dreams. "Edify your mind with substance and not with all of that he said, she said shit!" I'll hear repeatedly in my conscious and subconscious. I'll do anything to have a normal life because this shit here isn't normal!

Anybody who is anybody is at the club on a Saturday night. They know where to go when they want to get their groove on and they know not to disrespect me or any member of the family. The Do Drop Inn attracts some of the most powerful and influential people in and out of the tristate area. Sports figures, politicians, doctors, lawyers, and entertainers from all walks of life visit the infamous club.

The night is going well, and Big Daddy is actually in a good mood until this stupid bitch tries to play me. "You will have better luck playing lotto!" I yell at her as I continue to kick her, "And don't you ever, for as long as you live, disrespect me again," while my fist is pounding her face. I'm not as hot-tempered as I used to be, unless I'm provoked. I was seventeen the last time I fought this hard. I'm frustrated and relieved at the same time. Frustrated because I let this bitch get to me, and relieved because I imagine she's Big Daddy. It depends on where you are sitting or standing, I'm told, whether a shoe, piece of clothing, jewelry, or a weave flows by you.

"Stop her before she kills her!" I hear Carly yell, but no one dared get in my way.

"Somebody go and get Big Daddy!" Amanda screams. "Raylene, you're going to kill her! Do you want to go back to jail?" I hear her say. I want to stop. I try to stop. I can't stop. I'm not in control anymore. I'm not myself.

After a few seconds, I feel a tight grip around my waist, and I'm being lifted high into the air. "That's enough!" he yells as he peels me off the half-beaten girl. I know what's coming next: the back of his hand across my face. I look toward the deejay for some kind of assistance but realize I'm on my own.

By the time she's able to stand on her feet, she yells, "Cornell, I'm going to sue your ass! And when I get finished with you, you nor your two-dollar, tawdry-ass hoes won't be able to work at a dog show!" she yells at the top of her lungs while bleeding and grasping for air.

"Bitch, you want more of me? Get your no-frills ass out of here before I finish what I've started!"

"Who you calling no frills, you black bitch!" she hollers back. I hate it when people call me that. I am either black, or I am a bitch, but I will be damned if I am going to be both! I head in her direction again when Big Daddy's round frame steps between us. Even with the ass whooping I know I'm going to receive, I still go after her. I want her so bad I start to drool. Big Daddy points toward the penthouse. "Get your stupid ass upstairs! Are you trying to get me sued?" I decide to obey and not push my luck any further. I'm in enough trouble already, and I'm well acquainted with his temper. We've met several times before.

"Okay, people, there's nothing left to see here. Drinks are on the house!" he says as a last attempt of damage control. Thursday, Friday, Saturday, and Sunday nights are the busiest times at the club, and security is doubled.

By the time we reach the penthouse, I could see the anger in his eyes. "Bitch, have you lost your fucking mind?" his voice booms. It does that whenever he gets angry or excited.

"She—" is all I could get out before I feel the sting of the back of his hand across my face. I don't dare cry. Big Daddy always says that is a sign of weakness, and I am not a weak person, but trust and believe, I want to. I try to explain.

"I don't want to hear it! Get your ass cleaned up and get back out there and get me my money!" he roars. "And if that bitch sues me, that's your ass!" which there is no need to say because I already know that.

"Yes, sir," I say as I muster up any inner strength I have left in me to move as quickly as I can. Anything can and will set him off and I'm not about to give him another reason to start beating on me again.

I've been in counseling for about two years now. The officials have me seeing this bitch-ass therapist, who is trying to make me believe I am in control of my destiny. She has lost her mind. "You have the power to change your future by changing your thoughts and your actions," she would say to me, which was a crock of shit.

By the end of the evening, Big Daddy advises me to get the girls ready because we are all going to leave for Atlantic City for the weekend. "The Bar Association's Annual Convention is in town this weekend, and you girls were personally requested." Nausea starts to set in.

"The car will be here in an hour to pick them up. Make sure they're ready," he instructs as I close out the cash registers. He is such a liar. Last week he promised if we worked the last convention, we can have this weekend off.

"Carly and Bre are just getting over the flu and need some time to rest," I add in this defeated voice.

"Raylene, these are friends of mine," he continues.

I wait, for a moment, to see if he will change his mind before I continue. "Besides, Sosa told me last time not to show my face in his town again, remember?" I add.

"I didn't promise shit, and fuck Sosa, he don't run a damn thing around here!" he shouts. "And . . . I told you to get those girls to the doctors! My people pay good money and they don't want no sick-ass, infected-ass hoes!" he bellows. His aggression is building again.

"I did take them to the doctors," I retort in my defense. "And he wanted to admit them but said he would not if I promised him, they would be able to rest. Big Daddy, please, can't we…"

"No!"

I step back and take a deep breath. I'm fighting a losing battle. He isn't going to listen, and all the begging and pleading in the world will fall on deaf ears. "Well, can I at least ride with them?"

"No, you're coming with me."

"I…"

"Shut the hell up, Raylene. I need to talk to you!"

As Big Daddy and I head toward the limo, panic and fear sat in. I have no idea what he wants to talk to me about. I start racking my brain with every conceivable idea of what he may possibly have to say to me. The books are balanced, both sets, there isn't any product missing from the vault, and other than Bre and Carly being sick, he already knows there isn't anything else I can think of. I'm making myself sick with worry and am about to pass out, but I fight to control it. I shove a handful of mixed nuts in my mouth and almost choke because I don't chew them well. I swallow, clear my throat, and say, "Big Daddy, I got—"

"You got what?" he interrupts. "And don't tell me it's your period because you finished that last week," he says. Ain't that a bitch, this motherfucker keeps better track of my period than I do!

By the time we reach Atlantic City, he has changed his mind and agrees to let the girls rest tonight, especially Bre and Carly. The Bar Association is his biggest clientele, and he does not want to take a chance of them passing anything to his lawyers' friends or their wives.

"You know you are staying with me tonight," he tells me as he grabs his crouch, licks his lips, and adjusts his pants and then growls at me like he wants to eat me up in one gulp. I frown and look at the driver. He is watching me through the rearview mirror, and he is just as repulsed as I am. I look at Big Daddy again and see nothing but mounds and mounds of fat flab around his neck and a double chin, which turns my stomach even more—ugh, gross.

We head straight for the crap table as soon as we get to Atlantic City. That is his favorite game to play, and I must admit he is pretty good at it, but like always, I am bored out of my mind. I sit there, smile, and look pretty, which he says always brings him luck.

My mind, however, is on the girls, especially Bre and Carly. I want to go and check on them to see how they are feeling, but Big Daddy will not let me leave his side. Hours pass, and we are still there. I watch him win and lose thousands and thousands of dollars, and before every roll, he will hold the dice to my face and demand that I kiss them. Then he will yell, "Daddy needs a new pair of shoes!" which is just downright humiliating and embarrassing.

It is a little after 2:00 a.m. before we get to the room, and his fat ass is happy because he ends up winning twenty-five hundred dollars, as if he needs more money. He sits at the table, pulls out his winnings, and starts counting, and then out of nowhere he blurts, "Amanda told me it was you who helped Brandy escape." I fall off my seat and drop to the floor. That fucking bitch, why has she told him that? I have to think quickly because if he thinks for one minute that I may have betrayed him, fuck an ass whooping, my ass is dead. All the while he never stops counting his money and he never looks up. "Two hundred and twenty-four, two hundred and twenty-five," he says and then kisses the wade of money and puts it back into his wallet.

Now all his attention is focused on me. "And don't even think of lying to me." He adds, "I hate a liar!"

If there is one positive thing I have learned from Big Daddy over the years, is how to think fast on my feet. I run toward him and start brushing up against him. I immediately go into my little-girl routine to divert his mind from anger or betrayal to sexual healing and satisfaction.

"Amanda is always talking a lot of shit, but let's not talk about her right now," I say as seductively as I can while gyrating my hips and taking off my clothes. In addition to all the alcohol he has gulped down at the crap table and his heavy moaning and breathing, I have just saved my ass. I take my hand and reach for his crouch and tightly grab around the shaft of his cock. He is as hard as a rock, and I have not even done anything. I smile. I am a genius at telling niggas what they want to hear.

"Damn it, Raylene, I love you, girl and would hate to think that you would do anything to where I can no longer trust you," he cries as he pulls me closer to his round frame.

"Shh . . . now just relax. I'm here, and Amanda is just jealous, she always has been. She's just trying to start some shit between you and I. I love you too, Big Daddy," I say in my softest, childlike voice. Tears roll down his cheeks, and then he starts kissing me harder and harder. Within seconds, he picks me up and carries me to the bed. He rips off his pants and extra-large boxers and is about to insert his penis in me when he passes out, which is fine with me. I'm able to wiggle my way from under him, which is difficult enough, and then go into the bathroom and put on the nightgown he bought for me last year for Christmas. It's actually my favorite, but I will never tell him that.

I fall asleep on the love seat around 4:30 a.m. I'm awoken by this heavy object being shoved in me. My pussy is on fire, and I do not like it. I open my eyes and see Big Daddy on top of me. He has this crazy look in his eyes, and he has pinned both of my legs under his arms, which stops me from moving, and I cannot see what he has in his hand. It feels like a stick of some sort, and he jams it repeatedly three or four times deep into my pussy. All I can do is scream at the top of my lungs. He stops shoving the object in me so I will stop screaming and throws it clear across the room. He picks me up and throws me over his shoulder and carries me back across the room onto the bed. He rips off my nightgown and then inserts his uncircumcised penis in me. All his 320 pounds are on top of me, and there isn't a damn thing I can do to get him off me. He is hurting me. It's like he has snapped because there is no life in his eyes.

I'm scared. "No, stop! Stop, you're hurting me!" I yell. I call him every degrading name I can think of, "Fat black bitch, pig motherfucker," anything I can think of to get him off me.

"What the hell did you call me?" he growls and then balls his hand into a fist and once again introduces it to my face. My body begins to tremble, and then I tense up. The pain is unbearable, and I go numb. It is a matter of life and death, mine, and I have to fight back.

"No, stop! Get your stupid ass off me!" I yell again as I manage to push him off me. I slide out from underneath him and stand to my feet. As I start to run, he catches me by my ankle and pulls me back down, and once again I feel this object being forced in me, and this time the pain that fills my body takes me to a whole other level mentally.

Our eyes meet. "You stupid, stupid bitch, I'm going to kill you!" he announces as he picks up my 135-pound frame, holds me high over his head, and then throws me clear across the room like a lightweight bar ball. My body hits the wall near the desk and then bounces off like a tennis ball. Before I can get to my feet, for a second time, he is standing over me kicking, punching, spitting, and hitting me in my face and abdomen.

I guess it's true what they say about adrenaline because I don't know where this uncontrollable rage comes from. My therapist talked about out-of-body experience before, and it sounded like a crock of shit to me at that time, but today I'm experiencing one. I feel different, and I'm not myself. There is something or someone else inside me, and it is taking control. Any self-control or common sense I should have had is gone, but I know one thing: I don't want to die. I stand to my feet and reach for the telephone sitting on the desk and then close my eyes and swing with all my might. The phone strikes the side of his face, which causes him to bleed. He wipes his face with the back of his hand and then looks at his hand. He comes toward me, so I run. Even though I'm dizzy myself, I can't let him catch hold of me. I assume with all the noise coming from our hotel suite, someone will have called the police or security guards.

The ironic part of Big Daddy being overweight ends up working in my favor because the more he chases me around the room, the more it causes him to tire easily. It gives me time to get my switchblade from my purse. I lung toward him kicking and screaming, and then I start stabbing him over and over again, and with every stab, the only thing I think of are the years and years of sexual, physical, emotional, and mental abuse since I was seven years old. I stab him in the stomach, chest, and arms, which must have hit a main artery because there is blood squirting everywhere and he still manages to talk shit.

"You stupid bitch, how dare you do this to me!" he gurgles through his blood and falls to his knees.

As the door flies open, I'm standing there, paralyzed. I've never been so scared in my life. "Drop your weapon!" I hear someone yell, but I can't move. After that, everything goes blank. The last thing I remember is standing in the middle of the room butt naked staring into the eyes of a dead man.

Detective Sosa
World-Famous Boardwalk

For as long as I can remember, my only desire was to become a Detective. I work long, arduous hours, and I dedicate my life to the war on drugs. Operation Crackdown has helped earn me some top recognition from the governor's office, as well as other top officials.

I've spent the last seven and half hours on our world-famous boardwalk because two bodies have been found. After careful identification, they are confirmed to be that of a white male, aged forty-five, William Moorland, and his wife, a white female, aged forty-two, Rita Moorland. They have been shot execution style.

"Jeez, isn't that William Moorland?" the officer says as he covers his nose from the odorous smell escaping from under the sheets.

"Yep, and here's his wife," the other officer confirms as he imitates the same action.

"How much you want to bet they were not here to gamble?" I ask Sullivan, whom I call Sully. Patrick Sullivan is a 265-pound, 6-foot-3-inch Irish bulldog. We were childhood friends as well and boot camp partners. He looks and acts more like my personal bodyguard than my partner. I trust Sully with my life. He hails from a long line of law enforcement agents. His father, grandfather, and uncles all served as CIA agents for Presidents JFK, Gerald Ford, and Bill Clinton.

"The landlord called because of the foul stanch. It's hindering his business," Sully says. He's just as focused, determined, and dedicated to his job as I am.

We close off a section of the boardwalk, which causes all kinds of chaos. I can't let any of the evidences collected get compromised by nosey spectators. I roll up my sleeves and bend down to get a closer look at the bodies. At first glance, it appears to look like a robbery gone bad, but my careful eye and training has taught me better.

"Okay, what the hell is going on?" I yell. "What robber in their right mind would not take something as valuable as this?"

My grandfather was a jeweler. I have been around fine diamonds all my life, so I knew immediately when a 24k gold pendant encrusted with black diamonds and has a retail value of $25,000 or more is left behind, that this is not about a robbery. William and Rita's deaths plaque my conscious, and it bothers me they are even in my town.

It is 2:00 a.m. by the time I get home and into bed. I finally drift into a deep sleep when the phone rings. It's Sully.

"Get up, you'll never believe this." He adds, "Guess who was murdered tonight?" It's late, and the last thing I want to do is play a guessing game.

"Who?" I ask while wiping the sleep out of my eyes.

"Your buddy Cornell," he tells me.

"Oh yeah?" I dryly respond.

"Yeah, and guess who did it."

"Who?" I ask with even less enthusiasm.

"Chambers," he blurts, which changes my whole attitude. I cannot believe it. I have warned her about coming back into my town. This is not my first encounter with her. I have busted Ms. Chambers and her crew several times in the past for solicitation in my town. This girl is fearless. She is either as clever as a fox or as dumb as a duck. Her perseverance always surprised me, but her defiance is pissing me off. I like Ms. Chambers, and I have offered to help her several times in the past. I've never understood why she would allow herself to get mixed up with a scumbag like Cornell in the first place, and now to be charged with his murder does not make any sense to me at all.

Sleep is nonexistence now. "Don't let anyone near her. I'm on my way!" I yell to Sully. I jump out of bed and literally repeat the same clothes I took off three hours earlier and rushed back to the station.

My instincts are always dead on, and I have had a bad feeling about this from the moment I found the Moorlands' bodies. Now with Cornell added into the mix of things, this shit just gets that much more interesting, and now I am more anxious to see Ms. Chambers because I know she is somehow the common denominator in all this.

As I pull into the station, I'm accosted by the media. Television and radio news crews all want firsthand scoop on who killed the FBI's number 1 kingpin, Cornell Watkins.

"Detective, detective, is it true that Cornell was killed by one of his own girls?" one reporter yells as I push my way through the pack of reporters all hoping to get first-hand scoop on Cornell's demise, but I have no time to stop and answer questions, especially questions I don't have answers to. I run straight to the interrogation room.

"Elle," Sully calls me for short. "Wait, a minute!" as he steps in my pathway to slow me down.

"Wait for what?" I yell as I'm slowed by his huge frame, which stands between me and the entrance into the interrogation room. He is Michael Jordan on defense.

I acquiesce because time is ticking and I don't want to do this dance all night. "What, what is it?" My blood is boiling. "And don't tell me someone talked to her already!"

"No, no. No one talked to her, calm down. I just want you to be prepared. She looks like hell, Elle. He beat her up pretty bad this time and she is pissed," he admonishes me.

I pause and take a deep breath before I open the door. He is right. I need to calm down because if I come at her too hard, she's going to shut down, and I won't get any answers. I'm well aware of her temper. We have history.

"Well, you've done it now!" I exclaim in my authoritative voice. I'm going to push her. I need to push her. "And there's isn't anything I can do this time! You do realize this is your third strike? Do you want to go back to jail?"

She is mute. Just sitting there with her arms folded, and her eyes are dark and cold, and no life in her body, but then again, she is a master at the art of manipulation. She may have the others believing she is a victim, but I know better. I go into my bad-cop routine and make a conscious decision to skip the formalities or protocol. "You've been Mirandized," I say more as a statement than a question. I keep my eyes on her and her every move. I know how to handle Ms. Chambers if I want answers. Sully is right about one thing: she does look like hell though. I toss a one-and-a-half-inch folder with her name on it in front of her.

"What happened tonight, Raylene? Why are you here?" I yell and then pound my fist on the table, right in her face. We are eye to eye, and she doesn't even blink or flinch, not one inch. I've never met anyone as obstinate as Ms. Chambers. She has more common sense and street smarts than your common thug, but she still never moves. Her breathing is slow and shallow, and if, I have not been looking directly at her, I will have thought she was dead.

"Are you going to tell me what happened, or are you just going to sit there? Why did you kill Cornell?" I yell for the last time.

Cornell Watkins is Big Daddy's legal name. After what seems like eternity, her eyes widen, and I can see her bloodshot pupils through her blackened and bruised skin that are starting to develop.

She wipes her runny nose with the back of her sleeve. "I was just defending myself. He attacked me first," she utters softly.

"Excuse me," I say to confirm what I think I hear.

Fear paralyzes her, but anger enrages her. "He attacked me!" she repeats. "He attacked me!" she repeats twice. "He fucking attacked me!" she yells at the top of her lungs as the tears fall nonstop from her eyes. Her emotions soon escalate and quickly internalizes on herself. She begins pounding on her chest with her fist. Her blows to her upper torso become harder and harder, and before I know it, she grabs the pen and starts striking herself in the leg.

"Leave me alone, just leave me alone . . . I just want to die," she cries.

I accost her and rip the pen out of her hand and throw it across the room. We fall to the floor simultaneously as she curls into a fetal position. Her body feels like a broken rag doll. I have had myriads of encounters with Ms. Chambers in the past, but I have never seen her like this before. I am worried for her.

Hours later we are at the hospital where the doctors had to sedate her. It is clear I am not going to get any answers from her tonight, and it is evident I am not leaving her side. I speak to Sully on the phone. He tells me that the arresting officers brought her directly to the police station.

"I will deal with their asses later," I tell him. "I'm here. I'm not going anywhere until she wakes up."

"No doubt," he replies. "I will see you in the a.m." are the last words I hear before I place the receiver on its base. I sit by her side the whole night and watch her.

I first arrested Ms. Chambers when she was thirteen years old. I arrested her and another girl for shoplifting. Over the years, I've tried to reach out and help Ms. Chambers, but her resistance and anger overpowered her decision to make good choices.

As the sun rises, I hear a voice say "What the hell are you doing here?" as I open my eyes.

"Good morning to you too," I reply. "How are you feeling?"

"Like a busted can of biscuits. Where am I? And what the hell are you doing here?" she repeats, stronger.

"You're in the hospital."

"The hospital? Why?"

"Raylene, calm down. You were hurting yourself, and I—"

"And you what?" she abruptly asks as her defense mechanism jumps into play. "Look, I need to know what happened, okay?"

"What the fuck do you think happened?"

I'm trying to hold my patience with her. I take a deep breath. "Can you please just tell me what happened?" I repeat.

She rolls her eyes and then exhales. "What the fuck was I supposed to do, let him kill me? One minute, I'm asleep on the love seat, and then the next thing I knew he was all over me, and then I felt something in me! He was sticking something in me, and it hurt! It hurt like hell! I was defending myself, for God's sake! Then he started kicking me . . . punching me . . . hitting me . . . and spitting on me." The tears build again.

"Why?" I ask. "What provoked him?"

"Amanda told him I was the one who helped Brandy escape. She asked me to help her, so I did, but that did not give her the right to tell him that, that bitch!

You know, now that I think about it, she has always been jealous of me." She shakes her head. "He felt betrayed by me," she says and throws her hands high in the air.

"Who is Brandy, Raylene?" I ask.

"She and Lexie were just some stupid young girls who were in the wrong place at the wrong time," she confesses. Her personification is rough, and it is in attempt to get me angry, but I refuse to let her pull me into her trap. Like I said, I know her.

"Where is she now?"

"How the fuck would I know!"

"So you risk your life to help some girl you barely knew. Come on, Raylene, I wasn't born yesterday. There's more to this than what you're telling me," I say to her. I hit a nerve.

"Doctor!" she yells.

"Raylene!"

"Doctor!" she yells again.

"Talk to me, Raylene. I want to help you."

The doctor enters and begins to examine his patient. "How are you feeling?" he asks her.

"I'll feel much better once you get him away from me," she retorts. I voluntarily leave and wait for the doctor outside her room. I talk to the doctor to get a better assessment of her condition.

"Her physical wounds will eventually heal. It's her psychological and mental state of mind which needs addressing. There's years of sexual, mental, and emotional abuse," he tells me. I know what he is implying, but I have a job to do.

"I'm posting a guard at her door for tonight, and she'll be taken into custody in the morning," I tell him before I turn and walk away.

By 11:00 a.m., she is being released, and by 1:00 p.m., she is back in my interrogation room.

"How can someone so good-looking be so stupid?" She offers, "You think I wanted to come back here? You actually think I had a choice in the matter, because I didn't! I told him no! I told him to stop, but he wouldn't, he just wouldn't! Why wouldn't he stop? Why didn't he just stop?" which sounds like a rhetorical question but isn't, in which I have no response for.

"So what brought you back here?"

"It was their annual convention."

"Whose convention?"

"The Bar Association," she replies as she fumbles to find a comfortable position in the chair.

"Raylene, focus!" I yell. "What the hell happened?" I have her repeat her story again and again as I listen for any inconsistencies because the slightest change, I knew she is lying.

"Why were the Moorlands here? Were they meeting with Cornell too?"

"What? No, I don't know . . . Who the hell are the Moorlands?"

"Come on, Raylene, give me something! You can't expect me to believe that there were three major players in my town at once and you know nothing about it! Look, I can either tell the prosecution you were a cooperating witness or you hindered a triple murder investigation, it's up to you!" I say as a last attempt to get some kind of viable information from her.

She jumps to her feet. "Fuck you!" she yells. "And get me a lawyer!" which confirms she is done talking.

I have Sully check out all conventions that are in town this weekend, and the National Bar Association is holding their annual convention at the Marriott Hyatt. Lawyers from across the country come together and jockey for top positions within the association.

"Carl Goldman Sr.'s position as president was available, and Eli Weinberg was next in line to receive it," Sully reports. "You know, for someone to be appointed to such an auspicious position could really open doors for some very special privileges which they're entitled to and some which they are not. Goldman, Goldman, and Weinberg's main headquarters are in Seattle. They also have firms in New Jersey, Chicago, Illinois, and New York, New York. The chairman of the board and CEO, Carl Goldman Sr. is currently in a nursing home suffering with Alzheimer's. His son, Carl Jr. and partner, Eli, have been running the company ever since. And I've also discovered that William and Rita Moorland had a net worth of half of a million dollars last year," he says as he hands me a copy of their latest bank statements.

"How the hell do people with no job accumulate a half a million dollars in savings and holdings?" I say, not expecting an answer as I shake my head in disgust and disbelief.

Raylene

A Girl Like Me

Sosa has posted a security guard at my door for the night, and the moment I'm discharged from the hospital, I'm sitting back in the interrogation room. He has me repeat my story over and over again. I know what he is doing, trying to see if my story will change. I'm no amateur. I'm not falling for his tricks, and he says I'm a master manipulator, but he should be the last to talk. He doesn't like me one bit, and the feeling is mutual.

"I don't understand, Ray, why the hell are you mixed up with a scumbag like Cornell?" he says to me every time he arrests me, as if I have a choice.

Sosa is a man of integrity and he can never understand a girl like me. Although I do respect the fact that he has a job to do, but so do I. Sosa is very pleasing to look at and I love his hazel colored eyes. He has this smooth olive complexion, which I personally think is too pretty for a man. He is so delicious looking you can gain five pounds just looking at him. He stands about five feet eleven or six feet, and he always dresses like he has just finished a fashion show. The men I have slept with over the years has never looked anything like Sosa. He is a smooth operator, and he has this glide in his step when he walks, which can easily be mistaken for conceitedness instead of confidence.

My probation officer, Ms. Martin, arranges for me to be represented by this old-ass, decrepit attorney, which I believe she did on purpose because the girl I beat up at Big Daddy's club that night ends up being her niece. Ain't that a bitch!

"Ms. Chambers, my name is Richard Wright, and I'm your court-appointed attorney." He stretches his right hand in my direction for me to shake, and all I can see are veins popping through his alabaster skin, which makes me sick to my stomach.

"Damn, your ass is old," I utter.

I'm the last one scheduled on the judge's calendar today due to all the media that is bombarding the courthouse. The judge does not like the idea of his courtroom being turned into a celebrity gossip forum. These sleazy tabloid reporters always report their vicious lies and inaccurate truths, and not to mention how I hate all this attention, and if one more reporter shoves another camera in my face, I'm going to take that camera and shove it straight up their ass!

"Bail is set at two hundred fifty thousand dollars with no ten percent, cash or bond," the judge says as he hits the gravel on the desk.

As they escort me from the courtroom, I see Amanda in the back. I ask the judge if I could speak to my sister for one minute.

"Two minutes," he says as he looks at the guards to make sure they enforce his instruction.

"What the hell are you wearing?" she says as a failed attempt of humor. I ignore her.

"You guys didn't have to stay here," I say, pleasantly surprised.

"No, it's just me, Ray-Ray," she quickly replies. "I sent them home." Amanda is acting peculiar. Her demeanor is stiff, and she is showing no kind of emotions, and her eyes are vacuous.

"What happened?" she asks, which I assume she does out of concern for me, but the boldness in her tone is evident of something different.

Before I can get a word out, "I cannot believe he is gone!" she weeps. I am flabbergasted. "What the fuck do you mean you can't believe he is gone!" I yell at her.

"Are you serious? I'm glad he is gone!" I yell at her.

She is on defense. "He was there, Ray-Ray. He took care of us. Unlike your parents or mine, Big Daddy was there! You should have thanked him instead of killed him!"

"Thank him? Bitch, he kidnapped me, he kidnapped you. All of us!" You might as well have put a fork in me because I am done. I cannot believe what I am hearing. Amanda is in some kind of shock or something. She stands there shaking her head no.

"We were kids, Amanda, for God's sake, kids, fucking babies! Big Daddy was a sick-ass, perverted bastard who manipulated and abused us! Amanda, come on, it's me, Ray-Ray! You cannot be serious!" I beg and plead with her, but my words fall on death ears.

"It's time," the officer announces, adhering to the judge's instruction.

"Wait, please, Amanda, I need you to do me a favor!" I start yelling.

"It's time," he enforces again.

"No, wait," I plea. I have to tell her the combination to the safe. "Big Daddy has a safe! It's hidden in the front hall closet! The combination is 15 right, 24 left, and 12 right! There is money in there! Check it out and come and bail me out, please!" I scream as they force me along as one officer grabs one arm as the other officer grabs the other. "Amanda, did you hear me, 15R, 24L, 12R?" I shout at the top of my lungs.

As they escort me back to my cell, one guard states to the other, "This one is going to be trouble," as they practically throw me in headfirst. I trip over my own feet. My every thought while sitting in that cold-ass place is about Amanda. Am I wrong about her? Our lives are torn up from the floor up, and she is acting like we are the fucking Huxtables. Incessant thoughts take journeys through my mind nonstop, and not one of them is of anything pleasant or happy. There isn't anything I don't think about.

Why didn't Big Daddy stop?
What would my life been like if Big Daddy hadn't taken me?
Where did I come from?
Why didn't my parents want me?
Am I going to spend the rest of my life in jail?
Why did Big Daddy do all those things to me, to us?
Why wasn't I ever adopted?
Do I have any brothers or sisters, and where are they?
Why wasn't I rich like Ms. Martin?
Why didn't she like me?
Why didn't Detective Sosa like me?
Why is my life so fucked up?

I feel like my head is going to explode, and the fact that this is such a high-profile case, which has my face plastered all over the media, has these bitches tripping, and letting my guard down is not an option. The only thing left for me to do is go to sleep because all this worrying gives me a headache.

Leslie is this big-ass dike bitch who has been pushing up on me from my first day here. Every opportunity she gets to fuck with me, she takes. She tips the scale at two hundred and twenty pounds, and most of that is muscle. She towers over me. I weigh one hundred thirty pounds soaking wet, and I'm only five-six, which is intimidating to some people. I'm not afraid of Leslie. It's just that I do not want anything to do with a female; strictly dickly.

She corners me the other day in the shower, and she has that bitch-ass partner of hers keep watch so no other inmates or officers comes in.

"If you just relax, Chambers, you might actually like the touch of a woman than some stupid-ass man," she says to me as she licks her lips and walks in my direction. My back is against the wall. There is no place for me to run. I warn her as a final attempt not to come any closer.

I ball my fist, and as she takes one more step in my direction, I say, "Stop, I mean it! Don't come any closer!" I don't know where the energy or the strength comes from, but by the time Leslie is within three feet in front of me, I'm all over her. I start biting, kicking, and punching the shit out of her. I'm doing all these specialized maneuvers I did not think I knew how to do. You would have thought I was trained by Bruce Lee himself because by the time I am done with her ass, she is lying in her own blood.

Her partner runs in and sees her lying on the floor. "What the hell did you do to Leslie?" she screams and then yells for the guards. This bitch fabricates some piss, poor-ass story, which they believe. I start screaming at the top of my lungs and then feel a blunt blow from the guard's nightstick across my back. The last thing I remember is falling to the floor, and the next time I open my eyes, I'm in solitary confinement, ain't that a bitch.

I spend three days in the hole for nothing, and by the time they let me out, I'm seething with rage. I don't give two shits about any of these bitches in here or the horses they ride in on. I refuse to let anyone play me ever again.

I'm advised that Mr. Wright has died while I'm in lockup and new counsel will be coming to see me in a few days, which is fine by me. I'm determined to see these bitches again because if I'm going to spend time in solitary confinement, it should be for something I have done.

The next morning, I'm summoned to the visitors' lounge. When I walk in, I see this regal-looking white man sitting there.

"Ms. Chambers, my name is Eli Weinberg, and I'm here to represent you," he tells me. He is dressed in a dark-blue double-breasted Armani suit, and his teeth are perfectly aligned and white. I've always trusted a person who takes good care of their teeth.

"I know who you are," I reply. "You don't remember me?" I ask him, which surprises me because all through Big Daddy's trail last year, I was right there.

"I'm sorry," he says.

"You represented Big Daddy last year in that big drug bust," I remind him.

"Big Daddy, oh, you mean Cornell."

"Yeah, Cornell." I guess we are the only ones who calls him by that name. "What are you doing here?" I ask him.

"Amanda Adams hired me to represent you," he says with confusion in his voice. He looks at his paperwork. "You are Raylene Chambers, correct?"

My mouth falls wide open because I have not heard from Amanda since that day in the courtroom. I tried calling a couple of times, and the phone just rings. I smile. "Yeah, I mean yes. I'm Raylene Chambers, and Amanda hired you to represent me," I say while nodding my head in agreement.

"Good then," he sighs and sits down, unbuttons his jacket, and crosses his legs. "It says here you killed him, may I ask why?"

"I was defending myself. He was going to kill me," I tell him, feeling like I'm already on the witness stand.

"How do you know that?"

"Know what?"

"You said he was going to kill you. How do you know that?"

"He told me that?"

"He did," he asks surprisingly.

"Yeah, and this time he meant it."

"And how do you know that?"

"The look in his eyes," I say. I wait for some type of response from him. He smiles, and within seconds I see his pearly whites.

"Then I guess he got what he deserved," he adds.

There's relief, and I smile back. I nod my head in agreement. "Yeah, I guess he did. Look, Mr. Weinberg—"

"Eli, please, I insist. Mr. Weinberg was my father. Look, why don't you just tell me everything that happened? Start from the beginning and don't leave out anything," he says.

"Okay, well, Big Daddy—"

He holds up his hand. "Excuse me, but why do you call him Big Daddy?"

I shrugged my shoulders. "I don't know. That's what we've always called him ever since we were kids."

"We?" he asks.

"Amanda, Brittany, Bre, Carly, Nikki, and I," I tell him.

"The other girls he prostituted?" he says as he begins to write on the yellow notepad that he pulls from his briefcase and places it on his lap.

I cringe. I never thought of myself as a prostitute before, but hearing him say it makes it sound dirty, and I'm embarrassed. It makes me uncomfortable.

"Is something wrong?" he asks.

"No." I inhale and slowly exhale as I begin to speak, "Um . . . well . . . yeah . . . we worked for Big Daddy, I mean Cornell."

"Okay," he says as he loosens his silk necktie. I like him and want him to like me. I don't want him to think I'm just another stupid-ass hooker who doesn't know her right from her left. He continues, "I wasn't sure what to expect when I first read your file. I must admit I was a bit concerned," he adds.

"And now?" I ask.

"Now, now I'm impressed. Continue please." He smiles. I know what he's doing, and it helps. It feels like two hundred pounds of worry are lifted off my shoulders, and I'm relieved that he believes me.

"Anyway, he told me to get the girls ready because we were going to Atlantic City. The Bar Association was in town that weekend."

"Oh yeah, I was—" he starts to say and then pauses. He has this far-off, distant stare in his eyes as if he's in deep thought.

"Were you there?" I ask, which brings him back to reality.

He smiles graciously and then says, "I made an appearance."

I continue, "Anyway, as soon as we arrive, we head straight towards the craps table while the other girls went to their room and…"

"And how long were you there?" he interrupts.

"Three and half to four hours at the crap table alone."

"So why didn't you go with the other girls?"

"He would not let me."

He looks at me. "Okay, continue. So you and Cornell went to roll dice."

"No, he was playing. I was just there." I can feel the tension and anxiety starting to build again. I fight hard not to lose my composure in front of Eli. My therapist has taught me an exercise to do whenever I start to feel like I am losing control.

"Raylene, close your eyes and take three quick deep breaths and then immediately exhale slowly. Repeat as needed."

"Are you okay? Just try to calm down and don't be dismayed. I'm here for you, and it's my job to give you my best defense possible, but in order for me to do that, I have to fully understand what happened that fateful night. I wasn't there, and the only other person that was there is dead. Now please, just take your time and just tell me everything that happened," he assures me, which helps greatly.

I'm in control again. "Okay," I say, "by the time we left the casino and got to the room, it was around 2:00 a.m. I was exhausted. He was excited though because he was up twenty-five hundred dollars. He sat at the table and started counting his winnings when he blurts, 'Amanda told me what you did.' I didn't know what he was talking about at first, but then it hit me."

"What was he talking about?"

"He was referring to Brandy."

"And who is Brandy?"

"She was a girl I help to leave one night." I pause and wait for him to say something; he does not, so I continue. "Anyway, she and this other girl named Alexis frequent the club using fake IDs, and one night they got caught. Well, needless to say, Big Daddy found out, and he wasn't pleased."

"What did he do?'"

"What he always do with young girls: use them for his glory. You see, Big Daddy figured with them being so young and innocent looking, he could use them to pick up and drop off his product, and they did it for a while because they were runaways and they did not have a place to eat or sleep. But those girls did not belong there. They were just two naive, young girls who made a stupid mistake and were in over their heads trying to grow up to fast. The one girl, Alexis, would cry night and day for her dad. That shit really started to get on my last nerve."

"So are they home now?"

"I assume Brandy is. I hope she made it home! Alexis was murdered," I tell him.

He stops writing and looks at me. "What happened?" he asks.

"I'm not sure . . . I heard asphyxiation, suffocation, strangulation, one of those ations. Anyway, like I told the police, the last time I seen her alive she was with Big Daddy," I add. He starts writing again. I do not know what he's writing, but whatever it is, I hope it is helping. I stop talking again to give him chance to catch up. After a few moments, he looks up at me.

"Is that all?" he asks.

"No," I say.

"Then continue and don't stop. You have my attention," he instructs without ever looking up again.

"Anyway, the next morning, Big Daddy asked me where was Brandy, and I lied. I told him that she was turning her first trick, and when I went back, she was gone. He never said anything else, and I thought that was the end of it, until he asked me about it that night," I tell him.

"So you think Amanda set you up?"

"At first I did not, but it all makes sense now. Amanda was the only one who knew I even helped her."

"That was very brave and admirable of you. You took a real risk by helping her."

I shrug my shoulders because I'm not looking for any kind of praise for doing a good deed. "I'm no hero or anything. They just did not belong there. They were not like us," I add.

"What do you mean?"

The realization sets in. "These girls had families, someone who wanted them, who cared about them. Their family did not throw them away like our families did."

There it is. I finally say it out loud. Something I've felt all my life but refused to believe. He looks at me, clears his throat, and utters, "You are not trash, Raylene. Okay then, it would be safe to say that Cornell had a reason. A motive to want to kill you, and with the knowledge of your betrayal, you feared for your life?" he states.

I'm speechless as I nod my head yes.

"So it seems you had the right even a duty to defend yourself," he continues, which just makes my fucking day.

"Yes, exactly!" I yell out in relief and excitement because he understands. He smiles.

"It hurts because she is like a sister to me, all the girls are. They are all the family I have."

"It does not make sense, to me, for her to set you up and then turn around and retain me," he states when his phone rings. He looks at his watch, stands up, and places the writing pad on his seat faced down. "Excuse me for a moment, I really need to take this call." And then he walks out. I tell the security guard I need to go to the bathroom while my attorney has stepped out, and as I pass by, I hear him yelling at the top of lungs.

"Look, I worked too dam hard and sacrificed too damn much for this shit to happen. Just handle it, damn it, and make sure I'm left out of it!" Whoever that is really pissed him off as I double-time to the bathroom.

He returns. "My apologies, now where were we?" he says calmly. "So let's continue. What happened next?"

"No problem. Okay, so once it dawned on me what he was talking about, I quickly improvised and went into my little-girl routine to get his mind off betrayal and on to sexual gratification." As the words leave my mouth, I want to die, but I forge forward. "When he gambles, he drinks a lot, so I knew he would be easy to manipulate and distract and before I knew it, he passed out. I fell asleep on the love seat until I was awoken by this unbearable pain. He was on top of me, and I could barely breathe, and plus the fact he started jamming something in me, and that's when, that's when . . . I lost it."

"What was it?" he prods for more information. "Was it his penis?" he asks as sensitively as he could.

"No, I don't think so, at least it didn't feel like a penis," I tell him. "It was harder and extremely painful." The thought of it makes my body cringe all over again.

"You do not have any idea what it could have been?"

"I could not see anything."

"Is that when you told him to stop?" he asks.

"That's when I started calling him every degrading name I could think of," I respond.

"Did you tell him to stop?" he asks again, demanding an answer.

"Yes!" I yell. "I told him no, I told him to stop, and he wouldn't. He wouldn't stop . . . Why didn't he just stop?" I cry.

"Has he ever done anything like that before?"

"No," I say. "But as soon as I seen that look in his eyes, I knew."

"You knew what?"

"That he believed I betrayed him and he was going to kill me. Everything about him was different. He was more sinister, and all his anger was focused on me. I knew it . . . I just knew it," I repeat over and over.

"Okay, what happened after that?" Eli asks. He is focused, and he is determined to keep me that way.

"What happened after that? After that, I was being thrown around the room like a tennis ball, that's what happened!"

"So that's how you obtained your bruises," he says as he points to my arms, neck, and back.

"Um, yeah, I guess, some details are fuzzy. They come and go," I add.

"Do you remember striking Cornell? Do you remember stabbing him? He pulls pictures from his briefcase, which I've never seen before. I look at them and then pushed them away. "That's disgusting!" I shout. There is blood everywhere, and the sight of those pictures makes my stomach turn, and I want to throw up. "I didn't do that!" I protest.

He slides the pictures back in my direction. "Raylene, look at the picture. Did you do this?"

I turn my head away. "No! No, I did not do this! I mean, everything happened so fast."

He continues, "You were found at the scene with the switchblade still in your hand. Your fingerprints are the only prints found on the phone and the switchblade, and you expect me to believe that you don't recall any of this?"

I'm speechless. My muscle tenses up, and my breathing becomes shallow. "Where did you get the switchblade from?" he asks.

"Big Daddy," I mumble after a few seconds.

"Cornell gave you a switchblade to stab him?"

"No, for protection, he gave all of us one, a while back." I feel depleted and defeated, but he keeps firing question after question.

"And prior to that night, have you ever used it before?"

"No."

"Okay. Go on."

"That's it," I say.

"That's it? Where did you get the switchblade from?" he asks me again.

"I just told you that Big Daddy gave it to me."

"No, Cornell gave it to you for protection. Where did you obtain the switchblade from that night?" he clarifies his question.

"My bag, my purse," I answer.

"So you carried it with you?"

"Yeah, all the time. Why the attitude?" I ask.

"Ms. Chambers, the prosecution is going to try to prove that you knowingly and willfully, with malice aforethought, brought a concealed weapon with you in order to do bodily harm to Mr. Watkins, and the last thing they are going to be is cordial with you."

"But he attacked me, and I was defending myself!"

"The prosecution is going to say that this was all carefully planned in retaliation for all the years of abuse he has put you though. They're going to try and discredit you any way they can."

"Look, I may not have been a fan of Big Daddy, but I was scared because he believed I betrayed him. Look, I'm sorry things ended up this way, and if he would have just stopped—" I start to explain when he stops me.

"Raylene, relax, I know. I'm not the bad guy here. I've read your statement and the police report. I just needed a little clarity from you because there is no room for error," he stresses. "Every little detail, no matter how trivial or annoying you might think it is, it's important. Understand?"

"Understand," I respond, nodding my head.

"So to reiterate, you arrived to the room around two, he confronted you about information he received from Amanda. He passed out, and then sometime later you were abruptly awakened by him. He began inserting some type of foreign object in you." I nod my head. "You remember being thrown around the room but you don't remember striking him and stabbing him," he adds.

"Yeah," I say.

He opens his briefcase and puts the notepad in. "Okay, Ms. Chambers, that's enough for today. I've submitted my application for a new hearing for bail reduction."

I'm happy that he is here. "Thank you," I say as graciously as I know how and not caring how desperate it may sound.

"Well, don't thank me just yet. Besides, there's something about you that seems very familiar to me," he says as he stares deep in my eyes. "Don't worry," he continues, "and the five thousand dollars' retainer fee is fine."

"Five thousand, that's all Amanda gave you?"

"Yes, why?" he asks.

"Oh, nothing, I just thought there were more in there than that."

As he stands up and puts his overcoat on, he chuckles. "The money is not important right now. We will deal with all that later. In the meantime, I do not want you to talk to anyone, and it is imperative that you stay out of trouble! No more solitary confinement!" he orders.

"But that wasn't . . ." I start saying. "Okay," I just concede. "Thank you so much, Eli, and I promise you, I'll do whatever it takes to get you the rest of your money. You can even have my firstborn child, if I ever have any," I tell him.

"That's all right, Ms. Chambers, I'm here, and I'm not going anywhere. Oh, and by the way, all of my children are already grown, so I won't need yours." He smiles and then grabs his belongings and walks out.

Being in solitary confinement for the past three days was pure hell, but knowing that Eli is on my case now brings me such joy and relief and knowing that I have a chance at freedom again has made the three days' worth it. He is such a cool guy for being an attorney, Jewish, and white.

I have been staying out of trouble like he suggested, but it isn't easy because these bitches act like they do not have anything better to do than to fuck with a sista. To keep myself occupied, I enroll in their GED program and start taking writing classes.

After several months, finally, my trial is due to start, and over these past few days, Eli and I have spent a lot of time together prepping me. At times, I will catch him staring at me.

"I'm sorry, it's just that you remind of someone I used to know. It's amazing, your resemblance to her."

I smile. "Who is it, an old girlfriend or something?"

"Oh, heavens, no, she was my goddaughter."

"Was?" I ask.

"I'm afraid so. She was murdered close to twenty years ago," he informs.

"Wow, I'm so sorry to hear that. What happened?" I reply.

"Oh, it's a long story, but the resemblance between the two of you is astonishing. You know, you even have that same dent on your left cheek like she had, so uncanny."

"I'm probably her daughter," I say in jest because at this point I want to be anyone else but me.

"It's funny that you say that. Do you have any sisters, identical?" he asks, which strikes a nerve in me as well.

"Me? No, I doubt it. I was put up for adoption from day one. I do not have any siblings that I know of."

"You know what, never mind. It was silly of me to even mention something that so far-fetched," he says and then diverts all his attention back to the subject at hand—my trial. The news media is all over this story from day 1. Cameras flash nonstop in my face, and people I don't know and have never seen before are calling my name repeatedly. "Ms. Chambers, Ms. Chambers, why did you do it?"

Eli does his best to shield me from all the press, but they are relentless. "Raylene, are you glad he's dead, and would you do it again?" one reporter shouts from the crowd, which makes me stop in my tracks. The words resonate through my entire body, and the thought never entered my mind about being happy about someone getting killed. I'm just trying to survive.

Eli looks me in my eyes. "You are going to have to learn to ignore some things, all right?" he states as an order than a question as we continue into the courtroom.

"All rise. The Honorable Harry J. Mullnick presides. Docket number 2C456-7, the State of New Jersey versus Raylene Chambers, charged with first-degree murder," the court clerk announces.

"Counsel for the state, are you ready for your opening statement?" the judge asks.

"Yes, Your Honor," the prosecutor says as he gets up from his chair and walks toward the jury. He isn't your average-looking attorney, and he speaks more like a fast-talking salesman rather than someone who has a law degree. The prosecution tends to prove that on the night in question, Ms. Chambers knowingly and willingly brought a concealed weapon with her to deliberately and maliciously kill her pimp, Cornell Watkins, in retaliation for all the years of sexual, physical, mental, and emotional abuse he inflictive on her," he announces as struts in front the jury. "As well as," his voice rises, "we also tend to prove that Ms. Chambers had ample opportunities to leave at will, but she chose to stay and ultimately took the law into her own hands." This guy is good, and I have no choice but to sit there and listen to all the bullshit he is spewing, and it is making me sick to my stomach.

After a few minutes, my attorney, Eli, stands up, buttons his jacket, and then starts to speak. "The prosecution would have you to believe that Ms. Chambers isn't the victim here. The prosecution wants you to believe that Ms. Chambers had a choice and she chose to stay, with the only person that represented the only kind of an authority figure she has ever known her entire life. When the reality is Ms. Chambers is the real victim here, a victim of bad circumstances which were beyond her control from her birth until the tender ripe age of seven, where she was subsequently kidnapped and then forced into a life of prostitution and fear. Her formative years were spent under the strict ruling of a madman who for years constantly and consecutively abuse her in every degrading and despicable way you could imagine. Ms. Chambers's failure is our failure because you, you, and you," he says as he points to each jury member, "let her slip through the system like a junkie on crack and on more than one occasion. On the night of October twentieth, at the Merritt Hyatt here in Atlantic County, Ms. Chambers was in the biggest fight ever, the fight for her life, and not one of you can look at her and say that you would not have done the same thing!" Eli speaks with such integrity and authority that I'm starting to feel better. I just may get out of here after all. I've never seen an attorney that has so much presence. He demands and commands respect, and he gets it. He is a thousand times better than the prosecutor, and he has the jurors eating out of his hands. "Let the games begin." He winks at me and then sit down.

The prosecution presents a list of witnesses that is bogus as hell. I do not know any of those people they plan on calling to testify.

"What the hell could they testify to? They don't know me!" I say to him.

The first person they call is the dealer at the crap table where we sat. He gives some bullshit testimony on how I was acting while I was there. "She seemed fine to me. I mean, she was kissing the dice before each roll, and she looked like she was having a good time," he testifies, but Eli quickly shuts his ass down.

"Objection, Your Honor, not an expert on human behavior!" Eli yells. He doesn't even bother to stand.

"Sustained," the judge says.

He leans in my direction. "They're trying to establish your state of mind earlier on. Clever," he whispers in my ear.

The prosecutor continues, "Rephrase, Your Honor. Mr. Raymond, did you have an opportunity to observe the defendant at any time within the four hours while she sat at your crap table?"

"Yes, she was doing a lot of laughing and drinking, and at one point she would kiss the dice for good luck or something. I overheard the victim ask her if she was having a good time," he volunteers.

"Objection to the use of the word victim. It's misleading and prejudicial," Eli jumps in. He is commanding attention in the courtroom, and the jury is following his every lead.

"Overruled, I'll allow it," the judge says.

"Your Honor!"

"Overruled, I'll allow it," he sternly repeats.

"And what was her reply?" The prosecution continues.

"She said, 'There's no other place I'd rather be.'" Before the prosecution could take his seat, Eli is on his feet and starts firing question after question at him.

"And what do you think she meant by that?"

"Um, not sure, didn't ask."

"You're not sure? Was this your first encounter with my client, Mr. Raymond?" Eli asks him.

"No, but I've seen her around before."

"Around where?" Eli fires back.

"At the casino. She and the other girls came down frequently and stink up the place."

"Fuck you, bitch!" I yell toward him.

"Order!" the judge yells.

"Permission to treat as hostile, Your Honor." Eli asks, "Mr. Raymond, you yourself has on more than one occasion used their services, haven't you?"

"No, that's absurd!" he shouts.

"Careful, you're under oath."

"Look, okay, okay, Cornell and I were friends, and he may have sent one or two of his girls my way every once in a while, but that doesn't mean that—"

"Oh, it most certainly does," Eli interrupts. "That's exactly what it means." By the time Eli finishes with his ass, he is going to regret even getting on that witness stand.

The prosecutor looks desperate as he springs from his seat. "I have a surprise witness, Your Honor," he announces and turns in Eli's direction for any kind of objection. Eli looks toward me for my approval. I'm not concerned, so I agree. There is a brief moment of silence while I sit there with my eyes glued on the rear door wondering who it may be. Within seconds, the rear doors open, and Amanda struts into the courtroom like she is on the catwalk. She looks like a fake-ass Tyra Banks. I nearly fall off my seat. I can't take my eyes off her. She looks good, damn good, and she has the nerve to have on my new black mini skirt and my black silhouette pumps I just bought. There isn't anything about this girl that resembles the old Amanda I know.

Eli looks at me. "What the hell is going on?" As if I fucking know, I jump out of my seat and yell at the top of my lungs, "What the hell could you possibly testify to, bitch? Your black ass wasn't even there!"

"Quiet in the court, I will not have my courtroom turned into a three-ring circus!" the judge instructs as he bangs his gravel on the desk. "Is there a problem, Counselor?"

"No," the prosecution ensures him as the ruckus starts to die down before the prosecutor begins with his line of questioning. "State your name for the courts."

"Amanda Adams," she replies in an accent that I've never heard before. I could not believe what I'm seeing or hearing. The commotion starts again.

"Quiet, quiet in the courtroom, or I will clear the entire room," the judge says again as a last warning.

"And how do you know the defendant, Raylene Chambers?"

"We're friends."

"No, the hell we aren't!" I quickly retort.

"Last time, Counselor!" the judge admonishes.

"Yes, Your Honor, it won't happen again," Eli says as he leans in my direction. I'm hot, and it's hard for me to be quiet while the prosecution lets her spew her lies. Amanda looks in my direction as she clears her throat. "Please continue, Ms. Adams," he instructs her.

"Well, like I said, we're friends and coworkers."

"Coworkers? Where at?" the prosecutions asks.

"The Do Drop Inn in Philly."

"Coworkers my ass!" I shout. I try to contain my anger but can't as the guards head in my direction. Eli waves his hands in their direction and pleas with the judge. He then leans within an inch of my face, and through his pearly-white tightly clinched teeth, he says, "One more word and I will leave!" he threatens.

"Ms. Adams, what's the Do Drop Inn?" The prosecution continues as the judge waves off the guards.

"It's a nightclub."

"I see, and what's this nightclub primary operations?"

I can't believe it. My skin is starting to curl and boil at the same time. I want to—no, I need to—get my hands around her neck. I can't believe she has the audacity to come into this courtroom, put her right hand on the Bible, and swear to tell the truth and nothing but the truth, so help me God, and lie, because by the time I get finished with her, not even God will be able to help her.

"Primary operations?" she repeats. "It's a nightclub, gentlemen's club. We provide entertainment, relaxation for our clients, you know, we entertain them," she says in this seductive tone, which was just downright embarrassing.

"And do you know where the other monies that the club derived came from and who ran those operations?" he asks.

"Big Daddy and Raylene, I mean, Ms. Chambers ran most of the daily operations together," she testifies.

I throw my hands up in the air as my head drops to the table. "Un-fucking-believable!" I mumble to myself.

"Ms. Adams, the victim, Cornell Watkins—" he stresses.

"Objection!" Eli yells again. "Leading and prejudicial!"

"Overruled," the judge says again as the prosecutor smugly smile in our direction as he graciously takes his seat. "No further questions for this witness at this time."

Eli gets up from his seat and slowly walks toward Amanda without taking his eyes off her. "I'm curious to know, Ms. Chambers, why are you here?"

"Excuse me, I'm here because I want to tell the truth."

"The truth?" Eli states. "And what exactly is the truth?"

"The truth is, Big Daddy was in love with me, and she was jealous of me and that's why she killed him!" she says from the witness stand as she jumps from her seat and starts yelling in my direction. Amanda is having one of those out-of-body experiences I have. She is extremely hysterical, and she isn't making any sense. I've known her for seven years and for the first time in my life, I don't know who the hell she is.

Eli is able to have her entire testimony stricken from the record due to the fact that she is the one who retained him as my counsel. They say something about conflict of interest.

Amanda stands up from the witness stand and yells all types of disparaging remarks at me, and that is the straw that breaks the camel's back. Before I knew it, I was out of my seat. I jump across the table, and I am heading for any part of her body I can get my hands on, but before I can reach her, I am detained by two uniformed court officers. I want to choke the shit out of her. Eli does some fast-talking and pleading with the judge not to have me removed from the courtroom. All I can do is watch Amanda as she sashays her black ass out the door.

And once again order has to be restored in the courtroom as two uniformed officers and Detective Sosa walk in. What the hell is he doing here? I watch as he speaks with one of the officers and then hands him some papers. The officer heads toward the bench and hands the papers to the judge. After looking through the papers, the judge summons both counselors to the bench and covers the mic with one hand. I'm not exactly sure what happened, but the next thing I hear is Eli screaming.

"What!" Eli yells at the top of his lungs as the judge motions the guards to come forward. "Take him into custody," he orders the guards.

Now any kind of equanimity or professionalism for the law, the courtroom, or himself that he should have exhibited is gone. "You have got to be kidding me! This is a mistake and heads are going to roll for this shit!" he yells, which echoes throughout the courtroom.

The judge bangs his gravel on his desk as he yells, "Order, order in the courtroom!"

Eli is yelling all kinds of colorful and disparaging remarks at the officers and at Detective Sosa. He is extremely irate, rude, and out of control that the officers literally use excessive force to subdue him.

I am speechless as I sit there with my mouth wide open. This cannot be happening to me, especially now. I'm scared shitless. My only hope of freedom, my saving grace, is being fucking arrested himself. The courtroom is in total chaos, and more officers come in with their guns drawn and start escorting people out. The courtroom is practically empty before order is restored. The judge explains to the jury and me as to what is going to happen next.

Two days later, I'm sitting back in court with new counsel, and all my hopes and dreams of freedom are gone. I think about the time Big Daddy broke my nose; did not hurt as much. The time Amanda, Carly, and I got into that barroom fight with these girls from the south side of Philly did not hurt as much. Not even the time I lost my virginity at nine did not hurt as much as the words that came from the juror's mouth: "We find the defendant guilty!"

This has got to be one of the worst days of my life, and to make matters worse, today is my twentieth birthday.

Robyn
Niggas and Flies

It shocks the hell out of me as I walk in our bedroom and see Hakeem and Amber in bed together. "Niggas and flies, both of you are a pain in my ass!" I shout at them. Amber jumps out of bed so fast that she nearly breaks her neck trying to get dressed and follows me at the same time. She scrambles to find her shorts and shirt that have been ripped off her in their heat of passion I can only imagine. She follows me into the hallway begging and pleading for me to stop and listen to her.

"Robyn wait, it's not what you think!"

Is she serious? My temper is at its boiling point. I look at her. Her clothes are on inside out. What the fuck am I supposed to think? I cannot do it! I cannot listen to another one of her lies!

Two things for sure and one thing for certain, I have $3,700 in my savings account, and it's time for me to go because, for certain, if I don't, someone is getting hurt!

"Robyn, wait, it's not what it looks like!" she still protests.

"Oh yeah? Because it looks like you're in bed with my boyfriend!" I yell as I lunge toward her and grab her neck in a failed attempt to punch her in her face. Amber is about her looks. Yeah, she is that shallow. With all the yelling, cussing, and fussing going on, Hakeem decides this is a good time for his black ass to sneak out. He knows how unpredictable I am when I am pissed. Anything can happen.

"Get off me, you bitch!" Amber yells at me as she continues to defend herself from my hitting her. "I'm telling Mommy!"

"Tell Mommy, tell anyone you want to, because by the time I get finished with you, you better hope you can talk!" I scream as I'm picking up items to hurl at her, which she manages to avoid getting hit by.

"You know what, Robyn, your stupid ass walks around here for months not caring about Hakeem, and now that he starts to pay some attention to me, you're jealous!"

At that moment, it's confirmed she is crazy. I can't believe she has the audacity to say some off-the-wall shit like that to me. "Hakeem and I have been seeing each other for two whole months!" she says boldly and then proceeds to confess all types of shit to me.

I scream, "That did it!" I'm at the point of no return. I turn around and head back toward her. Hell, I should be awarded a gold medal because I leap so high in the air and so far that I land on her back. I ball my fist and commence to punching her uncontrollably. If it isn't for the cries of our baby sister, I will not have stopped. I'm pissed! I hate getting this angry because I have problems controlling my temper. I've felt at a very young age that I'm different from anyone in my family and I look different too.

I want to kill Amber. I can't believe that they are trying to play me of all people. "Neither one of you motherfuckers are worth my time!" I tell her as I get off her and adjust my clothes. Damn, I just bought this shirt!

"Robyn," Autumn cries. She's our baby sister, and she hates it when Amber and I fight. She should be immune to it by now because it's something we've done all our lives, and I honestly do not know why. She always is in competition with me and constantly comes at me for no apparent reason.

"Robyn," Autumn cries again.

"What?" I snap and then soon regret.

"Are you all right?" she whimpers.

"Hell no . . . but I will be," I say as I stand over Amber's semilifeless body as she looks up at me from the floor. I notice some blood, and I'm not sure if it is hers or mine, and it really doesn't matter.

"You want Hakeem? Take him. In a month, he'll be cheating on you too."

"Hakeem loves me," she tells me while trying to keep her dignity and pride in tact from the floor. I do not know if she is trying to convince herself or me of that.

Hakeem and I have been dating each other since our junior year of high school. He moved to LA in his freshman year of high school after his parents' divorce. When I first met Hakeem, I did not like him. He was not like any of us around here. He had this B-boy, wannabe-gangster attitude that I could see right through. However, his persistence in trying to talk to me and his corny-ass jokes finally won me over. Besides, I just figured he was just another punk who was insecure about the size of his dick, which probably made all his decisions.

Amber is no joke. She truly is stunning. Her caramel complexion and her athlete ass and thighs are very desirable to the opposite sex. She has always acted as if she's better than me. I am the darkest member of my family, and my cheekbones sit higher, and my eyes are set farther apart. I've always felt like an outsider growing up in my own family. My body isn't anything like Amber's I'm eleven months older than her, and all I've ever heard growing up was, Amber is so smart. Amber is so pretty.

"Amber can kiss my ass," I wanted to say to my parents because for years they made me feel like grade A shit, and one night I found out why.

I overheard them arguing, and they were drunk as usual. "Sterile, my ass, they couldn't figure that shit out before we adopted Robyn?" my father slurred. No wonder, I'm not even their fucking daughter!

I can't put up with Amber's shit any longer, so the next morning I'm at the bank closing my account. I withdraw every penny I've ever saved, $3,700.43, my life savings.

While there, I run into a very special friend of mine, Alex Taylor, a trucker who came into LA every so often.

"On the move again, baby girl?" he asks as he brushes up behind me as I'm leaving. I was around thirteen or fourteen when I first met him because I was always running away from home. He would look out for me and let me stay with him when he was in town. We became fast friends, but before he left, we would convince me to go back home.

"These streets will eat you alive, baby girl, and that would kill me if anything ever happened to you," he would say.

I like Alex a lot, and I trusted him from the moment we first met. For a mature man, he can relate to me, and I can talk to him about anything. He is attentive, understanding, and nonjudgmental, and it doesn't hurt that he is fine as hell either. I love his salt-and-pepper sideburns, which blends well into his beard, which he keeps closely shaven. What first made me notice him is his light-brown eyes and his broad smile with his perfectly aligned pearly white teeth. It drives me crazy the way his smile is slightly crooked.

I jump. "Alex, you scared me. When did you get into town?" I ask as I give him a huge hug.

"Last night. I was coming to see you. What are you doing here?"

"Closing out my account," I tell him.

"Why? What happened?" His concern is genuine.

"Amber and Hakeem in bed, together," I say as the thought triggers another nicotine reaction. I reach in my bag and grab my Newports. Alex hates when I smoke and constantly pleas with me to stop. I continue, "I can't believe it!" as I light the cigarette, inhale, and nearly choke all in the same breath.

He takes the cigarette from my hand and throws it on the parking lot ground while not offering any assistance. So what if he is right? The thought of not smoking is foreign to me, and nothing can ever make me stop.

"Where're you going to go now?" he asks.

"I don't know, Alex. I haven't thought that far," I respond as I finally caught my breath.

"Baby girl, you can't keep running away from your problems," he says as he looks at me and shakes his head from side to side. "Unbelievable!" he mumbles.

"And why not? What other choice do I have?" I ask, determined to show him I'm not going to let the cigarette defeat me. I reach for another cigarette as I clear my throat. "It just went down the wrong pipe," I mumble.

"Because you'll be running for the rest of your life," he says and repeats his previous actions. It is clear. I can't smoke around him.

I turn toward the highway and watch as the cars and trucks fly by at top speed. I've always wondered where all these people are going. "What's it like?" I ask him.

"What's what like?"

"Out there," I say, looking at the open horizon as far as my eyes can see.

"Robyn, you've never been outside of California before?" Why he sounds so surprised is beyond me.

"Alex, I've never been outside of LA," I tell him. "Being a trucker, I'm sure you've been all over the place."

"Yes, I have."

"So what's it like?" I ask again, hoping to get some type of response.

"Baby girl, that's something you'll just have to experience for yourself. It's not too late, you know."

"Where the hell would I go, Alex?"

"Quitters never win and winners never quit, baby girl."

"First off, I'm not quitting, I'm being realistic," I rebut. "Unlike you, my options are far and few," I say, which makes me sad.

"Stay with me," he blurts without hesitation. "I mean, with my sister. My mother is sick," he adds as pain fills his eyes. "Look, you coming or not?" he continues, trying to mask his pain from me. Alex talks about his mother, a lot. He has told me many stories about his family and all the crazy shit he and his childhood friend turned business partner Cornell used to do.

"What's wrong with her?" I ask without giving him an answer to his last question.

He turns in my direction. "Robyn, I'm pulling out at 6:00 a.m. Are you coming or not?"

"And do what, Alex?" I explode. "I'm not like you!"

"Robyn, you're a beautiful, smart, and very sexy African American queen, and don't you ever let anyone ever make you feel inferior or less than the shining star you are. Do you know what I thought the first time I laid eyes on you? You were this firecracker thirteen-year-old, you kind of reminded me of my daughter, and I knew you were special then. Robyn, I watched you grow into this amazing woman over the years. I see you. I see your essence, your soul, and your determination. You're a fighter Robyn and stop listening and letting these dumb-ass mother-fuckers that don't give two shits about you or the horse you rode in on, your energy. Because when you let someone change your attitude, you give them power over you, and when you let someone's opinion dictates your actions, they win."

Alex always knows what to say, and I can't stop smiling from ear to ear. "Are you sure your sister won't mind me staying with her?"

"She's been looking for someone to look after her condo when she's out of town," he says, which piques my curiosity.

"Out of town? Where does she go?"

"She's a pilot in the Marines. I'll tell her you're a friend of mine. Everything will be fine, okay?"

"But I only have—"

He stops me again. "Everything will be fine!" he stresses again. "Trust me. You do trust me, don't you?" he pause for a moment and then pulls me closer to him and brushes my hair off my face. His touch is soothing and reassuring.

I was seventeen when Alex first introduced me to the art of making love. He was the first man I'd been with, and he took me to levels of excitement and ecstasy I never knew existed. Alex brought me into womanhood that night, and he made sure I was pleased and satisfied. Hakeem did nothing like that. Alex is eighteen years my senior.

I make sure I'm there on time to meet Alex at 6:00 a.m. sharp because I don't want to take a chance on him leaving me.

"Thanks for being on time, baby girl," he says as he helps me into the passenger side of the cabin, but I'm just as anxious to start my new life as he is. I pack a small backpack and leave before anyone wakes up to avoid all the bullshit questions. Besides, the only person I'm going to miss is Autumn, and I leave her note apologizing.

The inside of his cabin smells like chlorine bleach. "You sleep in this thing?" I ask as I buckle up and place my backpack on my lap. He grabs it. "That's all you have?" he asks as he places it in the back.

"Yeah, well, I was kind of in a rush," I tell him. "I'll just pick up a few things when I need them."

He looks at me and smile, "I'm sure we can do better than a few things. Just relax and make yourself comfortable. This is my home away from home," he says as he honks the horn and then pulls out.

"Thank you, Alex."

"Baby girl, stop thanking me, it's time," he demands.

"You left home when you were my age?" I ask. His pearly whites and crooked smile isn't the only thing I love about Alex. I also admire his straightforwardness and the fact that he isn't afraid to hurt my feelings when I'm fucking up.

"Naw, I was fifteen when I left home. Anne wasn't putting up with any shit in her house. There were six of us, and my father was a trucker as well, so he was barely home. The strongest woman I know, she's my best friend." He talks about his mother with such passion as the tears fall from his eyes and roll down his cheeks. I'm envious of him because he knows who his mother is and he has a relationship with her. That's a relationship I will never get to experience.

I often think of my biological mother and wonder what she is like and why she didn't keep me. I like to believe that she was a teen mom and really wanted me but couldn't because she could not afford me or her parents force her to give me up for adoption. I like to believe that she put me up for adoption so I would have a better chance at a better life a life she couldn't provide. I like to believe that she came looking for me but I was gone after they adopted me and never told her where I went. Thousands of scenarios run through my mind. My mind is on overdrive.

"Why did you leave? What were you doing?" I ask Alex to help with the ongoing confusion running rampant through my mind.

"What wasn't I doing is a better question. Cornell, Black, and I were into everything. We came in hard and heavy, and we took no prisoners." He snickers as if he is reminiscing.

"So what happened?" I ask because that snicker piques my curiosity. As Alex talks and drives, I listen and absorb all the beautiful scenery I've never seen before. There is a whole new world outside the city limits of Los Angeles, and I'm in total awe of it all. Alex tells me everything about all the shit he and his friends did and how they practically controlled the whole east and south side of Philadelphia.

"We had it all," he glimmers.

"What made you stop?"

"The look in my mother's eyes," he says as his head lowers. It's hard for me to believe Alex used to be a drug kingpin, but that doesn't change my opinion of him. He is still a hero in my book.

"Damn, that's fucked up," I say. "What was your poison?"

"Pure heroin and pure coke, grade A shit," he says with pride and then falls silent. I stop with the questions because there is a familiarity in his voice that I don't want to explore any further.

"Can we please talk about something else?" he asks, which is fine with me. It seems like he is starting to have some regret about his past life or maybe he is starting to miss it, but whatever it is, I know it is time to leave it alone.

My first time out of LA and my first road trip, and Alex makes my first experience the best time I've ever had. We've been on the road for four days now. I have no idea how long of a drive it is going to be, and I'm dying for a cigarette, but I don't dare smoke. I like being with Alex, and at times, on open highways, he'll let me drive. He teaches me all about trucks and shows me how to drive them. I love the confidence he has in me.

We stop in Chicago because the truck needs to be fixed, plus the fact we both were tired, not to mention in need of a nice hot bath. The mechanic tells Alex it will be a day or two before the truck will be ready, and Alex knows anyone who is someone. The owner of the Chicago Bulls' basketball team gives him complimentary tickets for tonight's games, which I really, really enjoy. That is my first time ever at a professional sporting event. After the game, Alex shows me the beautiful city of Chicago. "Let me take you on a magical ride," he says, and a magical ride it is. Alex takes me on a whirlwind shopping spree and in one trip replenishes my entire wardrobe and then some. He takes me on a romantic horse and carriage ride through the park, and we eat dinner and go dancing. This is my first time Step dancing. Alex spares no expense, and all his attention is focused on me.

Our hotel is a beautiful, five-star, grade A hotel. Alex treats me like an African queen the whole night.

"I reserved two rooms. I do not want you to feel pressured," he tells me.

"I don't feel pressured," I tell him. "As a matter of fact, I've never been happier." And I want to be with Alex again. He cancels the second room. Our room is awesome. I've never seen anything like it before. It is adorned with ancient Roman busts, which are beautifully handcrafted. There are ceremonial weapons and two-foot-tall Egyptian statues on each side. After we get into the room, we drink some wine and talk, which builds suspense. He makes me a nice hot bubble bathroom with jasmine and lavender bath oils and places scented candles all around the tub, which I've only thought happened in movies. Once the bath is ready, Alex slowly picks me up and carries me into the bathroom as he slowly starts to undressed me. My internal pleasure-seeking organs are on fire, and I'm paralyzed with anticipation and excitement. Each time he takes off a piece of clothing, he kisses that body part. He guides me in the tub. He grabs the soap and begins lathering my body. After a few minutes, he stands up and begins to undress while never taking his eyes off me. I watch him as he takes off his clothes and drops them to the floor. For a man of a certain age, his rock-hard abs and six-pack make me quiver.

He slowly eases his way behind me, and once he is situated, he continues to lather my body with the soap in his hands. His grip is strong and firm, just how I like it.

"You are so beautiful," he whispers in my ear and then blows in it. Heat is building in my body, and I'm at my boiling point. I want Alex right then and there.

"Patience, baby girl, I'm right here, not going anywhere," he whispers. My nipples react to the sound of his voice. We exit the bathtub as he wraps the towel around me and then carries me to the bed, which has rose petals sprinkled across it.

He dries my naked body and then starts massaging me with hot baby oil. He caresses every part of my body. This man has me in such a state of ecstasy I'm losing my mind. I start to cover myself. "No, let me look at you for a minute," he says as he stops me. I'm not as comfortable with my body as Amber is with hers.

"I want to see all of you," he demands as he moves my hands and with his free hand. He begins to stroke the shaft of his cock as I watch with excitement as his nature begins to rise.

"Now," I ask.

"No, not now," he responds. Why does he insist on teasing me? There is a full-length mirror mounted on the wall. He turns me around so I can see myself in the mirror as he curls up behind me and our bodies lie in a perfect S formation. He licks his two fingers and then reaches around my waist area and inserts his two fingers into my moist pussy without warning. "Tell me you like that," he orders. I like a man that takes control and knows what he wants to do and does it while blowing and licking my ear.

All I can do is moan, and I'm extremely vocal about it. This man has me so out of control I feel like I'm having an out-of-body experience. I want him in me now! "Yes, yes . . . I like that! I want you!" I moan even louder.

"No, not yet," he says again. Why does he insist on teasing me?

He turns me on my back and spread my legs and looks me dead in my eyes and begins to kiss me passionately. He is an excellent kisser. He begins working his way from my mouth to my neck and back to my lips. He leaves my mouth and begins a mad assault on my titties, which keeps my nipples standing at attention. Then he proceeds south and starts kissing my inner thighs. He approaches my pussy and then pauses. He looks up at me. "Do you want me to continue?" he asks.

"Are you fucking kidding me?" I scream. I can barely breathe, and he stops to ask me some dumb shit. "Yes, continue!" I exclaim. He then proceeds to spread my legs as wide as they'll go. He inhales every part of my essence and then goes headfirst with his tongue straight into my pussy. Alex kisses it, blows on it, and softly nibbles and sucks on the labia, which causes my eyes to roll to the back of my head until I explode in pure ecstasy. I scream and moan so hard that my whole body shakes uncontrollably with passion.

"Oh shit!" I scream at the top of my lungs. "Damn it, Alex, fuck the shit out of me!" I insist.

Alex eats my pussy for what seems like an eternity. He heads back north. "Damn, baby, you taste good," he tells me. Finally, he is ready to enter me. I feel every stroke that he pushes deep into me. Our bodies are in complete harmony with each other. We move from the bed, to the floor, to the couch, to the table, and back to the bed again.

I rode him hard, and he fucks me harder. He licks on me, and I suck on him. Alex has great control because ten minutes has passed and he still hasn't cum. "Cum with me, baby," he pleads. "Can you do that for me?"

I nod my head yes because I'm not able to speak. He begins to thrust his unit harder and harder into me.

"Are you cumming, baby girl?"

"Uh-huh."

"Are you cumming?" he asks again. Alex begins shaking uncontrollably and exhales a loud moan and groan. I grab him as I hold him as tight as I can. As warm cum fills my body, I look into Alex's eyes and see peace and happiness take over his body as we fall asleep in each other's arms.

We are on the road early the next morning. Alex tells me he has come to a decision about his marriage.

"Things haven't been the same since Lexie died." I know he can't still love her, especially not after the way he made love to me last night.

"What's going to happen when we get to Philly, Alex?" I ask.

"Relax, baby girl, you have nothing to worry about. You do trust me, don't you?"

"Of course I do. What kind of question is that?"

"I know you're just going to love Philly. We have about fifteen hundred miles, and I want to drive straight through," he tells me as I climb in the back cabin to get some rest.

He smiles. "That's right, you just relax, and we will be in Philly before you know it," and those were the last words I heard uttered before I fall asleep.

Alex

Robyn Can't Have a Twin

With Robyn resting comfortably, I'm able to do these last fifteen hundred miles in no time. Being with Robyn makes me feel alive again, and I need that. My intention is to drop her off at my sister's first, but there isn't enough time. I call home, and Russell tells me that Mommy has taken a turn for the worst. It is imperative that I get home ASAP. I pull my truck in front of the house and barely has it in park before jumping out. I run right in the house, passing my wife and stepdaughter, who are sitting on the front porch. I take the steps two at a time straight to my mother's room. "Mama!" I yell. My sisters and brothers are already there surrounding her bed. "Mama, I'm here," I say as I kneel by her bedside.

"Son, I've been waiting for you," she struggles to say as she reaches out and touches my face. I've been gone a week, and I can't believe the amount of weight she has lost in such a short period of time.

"Mama, I'm so sorry. I should have never left," I try to explain. "And then the truck broke down, and I had to . . ." I stop as she places her hand on my mouth.

"Shh, there's no need to explain," she says. "Alex, baby, who's that man standing over there?" she asks as she drifts in and out of a consciousness.

I look to my left and to my right, and the only men I see are my brothers. "It's Ronnie and Russell," I tell her as I redirect her attention back toward me.

"Not them, the other guy? Can't you see him, Alex? He's standing right there," she says again, pointing to an empty corner in the room. "He's waiting for me." She is hallucinating, and there isn't anything I can do about it.

"Mama, listen to me." I grab her hand and hold it tightly. A cold chill passes from her body into mine.

"No, Alex, baby, you listen to me. I'm going home now, and when I get there, I'll find Lexie for you. I'll let her know that her daddy loves her and misses her dearly," my mother says to me as she becomes lucid again.

"Mama, please don't go," I weep as a floodgate of tears rolls down my face. I want to be strong for her, but my heart is crumbling and I want this pain to stop.

"Stop it, stop that crying right now! I'm going home to be with my Father, my Lord and my Savior! There are no tears where I'm going, just joy and no pain!"

My mother is literally slipping away from me, and she's trying to ease my pain. "I love you," she says as she takes her last breath and closes her eyes. My best friend is gone forever. I can feel a gentle peace and a sweet spirit, which fills the room. I'm numb, and an hour later, I'm still sitting on the floor by her bedside. As long as her body is there, so am I. Second later the medical examiner come and officially announces her deceased. After the pain starts to subside a little, I remember I've left Robyn in the truck sleeping. I jump up and run downstairs. Robyn is sitting on the front porch with my wife and stepdaughter.

"I'm so sorry. It's just that—" I start to say when baby girl stops me.

"Alex, you don't have to apologize. I understand. Are you all right?" she asks, which is one of the things I love about Robyn. Her affectionate and caring nature is something that Jacqueline has lost somewhere in our marriage.

"I'm fine," I tell her. She gets up from her chair and walks toward me as she wipes the tears from my eyes.

"I don't' know what I would do if you weren't here," I say to her, and after the words left my mouth and a couple of seconds of awkwardness, I realize that Jacqueline is there. I clear my throat and turn in my wife's direction. "Robyn, this is my wife, Jacqueline. Jacqueline, this is Robyn, and she'll be staying with us for a while," I say to my wife before turning back around and walking back into my mother's house. A few seconds later, Robyn follows. I introduce Robyn to the rest of my family.

"I feel like I know you all already," she says.

I advise them that she'll be staying with me. "Robyn, these are my sisters, Verdine, Barbara, Debra, and my brothers, Ronnie and Russell."

"Nice to meet you all," she says cordially and without getting any response. I'm annoyed by their frigid reaction towards her, but I cannot deal with this now. I have too much to do, and do not have time for their childish behavior.

I do, however, feel bad for just springing this on Jacqueline like this, but things are happening so fast.

My mother made me executor of her estate after Daddy died. I consult with my siblings out of respect, but I know her wishes, and I'm going to make sure they are followed.

I need some time to collect my thoughts. My feelings and emotions are running ramped, and I can't control them. Her body was gone but I needed to feel close to her, I sit in her room on the floor. I need some peace and quiet, but Russell comes in behind me and is determined not to let that happen.

"You know Mama would like to wear that red diamond suit you bought her for New Year's Eve last year," he says.

"Yeah, I know" is all I could say. For the second time in my life, I'm plagued with this unbearable pain that no one can take away. First, with the death of my only daughter, Alexis, and now my mother, the two people I love the most in the world are now dead. I feel useless as hell. Russell keeps demanding that we talk. I can't comprehend what the hell is so important that he has to talk to me now. I feel useless as hell. Russell keeps demanding that we talk. I can't comprehend what the hell is so important that he has to talk to me now.

"Have you lost your mind? What the hell are you doing?" he says.

I have no intentions on giving into his pleasure-seeking ways. "Not now, Russell. I'm not in the mood for you or your nonsense."

"Nonsense my ass, why did you bring that girl here especially after what she did!" he yells as he closes the door. "And you bailed her out of jail too!" he exclaims.

"Robyn? What the hell did she do, and who did I bail out of jail?" I ask him.

"Robyn?" He laughs. "That's the name she's going by now? Okay, whatever, I'll go with that, but did you have to bail her out and bring her here! What the fuck, she kills Cornell, and Mama just died. Damn, man, what kind of shit are you trying to pull?"

Russell has always been an asshole most of his life, but after he says that, he has my undivided attention. "Russell, what the hell are talking about? Cornell is dead?"

"Yeah he's dead. Where the hell you've been? It's all over the news." Russell throws last week's edition of the New York Times Magazine at me. On the front cover is a picture of Cornell with Robyn's image next to it. I'm already in shock, and seeing Robyn's image on the cover doesn't make it easier.

"What kind of sick joke is this?" I ask him. "What happened?"

"What happened?" he repeats my question. "Your girl whacked the hell out of your boy, that's what happened. Damn, man, its right here in black and white. Last Saturday in Atlantic City, your girl stabbed the shit out of him," Russell says as he feels the need to demonstrate on me. I push him away.

"But—"

"But what? According to this, she is claiming it was self-defense, and your soft ass bailed her out."

Nothing is making sense. I knew there isn't any way that Robyn could have killed Cornell because she was not there. "Russell, that is not Robyn," I insist.

"Who the fuck is Robyn? Her name is Raylene," he says, waving the magazine in my face. "Look at it! Read it for yourself!" he shouts. Russell isn't listening to me. His only concern is to prove me wrong. He has this sinister laugh whenever he thinks I've gotten into some shit I can't get myself out of, which just aggravates the hell out of me.

"Man, you got your nose so far up this girl's ass you can't think straight. Jackie never had you this whipped," he says.

"Fuck you, Russell, and now is not the time for this! Besides, there's no way Robyn killed Cornell."

"And how do you know that?"

"Because she was with me in LA!" I retort.

"Well then, she has a twin!" he says laughingly. He jests, but that is the only logical answer, especially since she told me she was adopted and never knew her birth mother.

"Russell, I know this girl, and I know that she didn't kill Cornell, but what I didn't know was she has a twin." I wipe my forehead and take a deep breath.

"What the fuck are you doing, bro? She's young enough to be your daughter! I mean, grant it, she is fine as hell, and I bet that shit is tight as hell," he adds. Russell is one for always taking shit too far, and his candor comment pisses me off, and I punch him square in the jaw. Ronnie runs in and breaks up the fight, while Verdine chastises us to acting like niggas on the day our mother died.

My blood is at its boiling point. I cannot take it anymore. I storm out the house and a few minutes later return. He never was much of a role model for an older brother and his incessant questions about Robyn and this girl invades my every thought.

"You're not upset about Cornell?" he asks after a short cooling-down period.

At first, I have no intentions on going round 2 with his ass or justifying that question with a response, but then I change my mind. "Was Cornell upset about what happened to my daughter?" I retort.

"You can't still believe he had anything to do with Lexie's death, do you?" I cut my eyes in his direction. "Well, what about her?" he asks as he points to the image on the magazine. "You think she knows what happened?"

"I don't know!" I scream out of pure frustration. "Look, Russell, stop, just stop," I say. "I can't deal with this right now! Mommy just died, and now this. It's just too much too soon! Just leave me alone, please!" And if all this is a dream, I really like to wake up now. I can't believe any of this is really happening. My mother shouldn't be dead, and Robyn can't have a twin.

"Well, you better start dealing with it, all of it, and very soon!" he says and then looks at me with the same look I've seen on his face my entire life, jealousy and envy. He leaves the room, and I lock the door behind him so he cannot return. I fall to my knees and begin to cry and scream at the top of my lungs from pure anguish and pain. If there is a God in Heaven, he needs to appear right now!

Robyn

I Don't Know This Chick!

The moment we arrive all hell breaks loose. His mother dies minutes after we arrive, and Alex loses it, and it kills me not to just hold him tightly in my arms. After they remove her body, Alex introduces me to his brothers and sisters. "Robyn, this is my oldest sister, Verdine, and that's Barbara and Debra, and over there is Ronnie and Russell." Then he takes me to his wife, Jacqueline, and stepdaughter, Sharon. "This is Robyn. She will be staying with us for a while," he says, which surprises the hell out of me, but I'm glad he has changed his mind.

His wife is a giant compared to me. She stands nearly six feet tall with ice-thick thighs. I won't call her fat, just big boned. She has this stern outward appearance about her; unsociable, or maybe she just does not like me. Alex has told me that she is two years older than he is, and even with all their problems, she is determined to keep her marriage together.

I'm waiting for Alex on the porch while he is upstairs talking to his brother, Russell, and it appears they have some kind of disagreement because Ronnie has to break them up.

I go to the funeral home with Alex so he can make all the arrangements and then we go to his home.

"I cannot believe you had the audacity to bring that little bitch into my home, Alex!" she slurs, which reminds me of my parents. She looks and smells like hell, and I can smell the aroma of alcohol, which is oozing through her pores, and it is making me sick to my stomach. Alex seems embarrassed by her appearance. "We'll talk later!" he tells her as he takes me upstairs so I can get settled.

She follows closely behinds us. Alex stops in front of a door with the words "Lexie's room" hanging on it.

Jackie quickly pushes by me and throws her body in front of the doorway. "Damn it, you're not putting her in there!" she screams hysterically. Alex physically lifts her up and moves her to one side so I can get by. I pass quickly. "Make yourself comfortable. I will be right back," he says while closing the door behind me.

I press my ear against the door as hard as I can so I can hear what they were saying.

"You're making a spectacle of yourself! You're drunk, and I'm not going to talk to you as long as you're like this!" I hear Alex yell.

"You're damn right I'm drunk and mad as hell! Do I look stupid to you, Alex?" She continues, "I wasn't born yesterday, you know, unlike your bitch-ass girlfriend in there!" She called me a bitch earlier. Now that's twice in one day she has disrespected me. I want to open the door and punch that drunken hag right in her face.

"Jackie, you are making more out of this than what it is," he tells her.

"And what is it, Alex? She is not Lexie! I am your wife! And I will not allow you to treat me like this!" she hollers.

"I know she is not Lexie, damn it!" he hollers back. "Look, can we please just talk about this later!" he pleads with her again.

"No, we are going to talk right here and right now!" she insists. "What? You are afraid she will hear us? Well, I do not care, Alex, and as far as I am concerned—" she yells.

He interrupts, "Well, I do! Jackie . . ." he yells back.

"Don't touch me!" I hear her say. "Why did you marry me, Alex? Was it because I told you I was pregnant?"

"Come on, don't be ridiculous," he responds to her. It is quiet for a few minutes. Finally, Alex says, "Look, you're right, I'm sorry. I should have talked with you first, but can we please talk about this later?"

After a few seconds, I hear a knock on the door and see the knob turning. I run and jump onto the bed. He pushes the door open and walks in. "Robyn, I need to talk to you." He sits at the foot of the bed. He has this look on his face that I've never seen before, and he is stumbling over his words.

"I did not mean to cause any problems between you and your wife, Alex," I apologize to him. I feel bad for bring all this chaos on him at a time like this.

"That's on me, baby girl. I should have asked her first, but that's not what I want to talk to you about," he says as he stammers over his words.

I look at him. "Alex, you're scaring me. What's wrong? What is it?"

"Look, I'm just going to come out and say it because there's no other way to . . . Why didn't you tell me you had a twin sister?"

"Because I don't. What are you talking about?"

"Well, then you're the most ubiquitous person I know."

"Alex, English. What the hell are you talking about?"

He pulls a copy of a magazine from his back pocket and hands it to me. On the cover are two images, one of the faces I recognize because it looks just like mine, but it wasn't me. I don't recognize that other face at all. I start stammering myself. Finally I'm able to speak. "What kind of sick joke is this?" I ask him.

"Joke, this looks like a joke to you? You really don't know who this is?" he asks me as if I'm lying to him.

"I said I don't know this chick," I adamantly repeat.

"Robyn, she's a carbon copy of you!" he shouts, which surprises me. Alex has never raised his voice at me before.

"Do not yell at me, Alex! I am telling you the truth! I do not know her!" I say as I throw the magazine on the floor.

He picks up the magazine. "It says here her name is Raylene Chambers. That name does not sound familiar to you?"

"Kiss my ass, Alex," I say as I get off the bed and walk toward the other side of the room.

"Where are you going?" he asks. "Come back and sit down. It's just hard for me to believe that you and this girl look exactly alike and you don't have the slightest idea who she is. How is that possible?" he says.

"Well, believe it, because it's true. I don't know her, and I've never seen her before in my life!"

"Robyn, you have to go and see this girl," he suggests.

"What, no . . . I can't! Why?"

He walks towards me. "Robyn, you have a sister out there! Family, which you know nothing about, maybe she can tell you something about your birth mother. I know you have always wondered about her, and she might be able to help you."

A cold chill ran through me. Anxiety sets in. My palms start sweating, and I start shaking. My voice dries up, but this time it isn't from the cigarettes. He wraps his arms around me. "Robyn, relax, didn't I tell you I'm here for you? You're not alone," he says to me. We hear a bump outside the bedroom door. Alex runs and opens the door. It is Jacqueline. She is standing there with suitcases in her hands and shaking her head in disgust.

With Alex's mother dying, his wife leaving, and me finding out about a twin sister that I've never known existed had to have happen on all days, my twentieth birthday.

Alex convinces me to go and see this girl, and the following day we are on our way, but I have major reservations about this, and every three miles or so I tell Alex to turn back, "I've changed my mind. Just take me back," but he is unwavering and forges forward.

"Robyn, it's going to be all right," he reassures me just like the thousands of times before. So many thoughts run through my mind. It is on overdrive.

Who is this girl?

Where did she come from?

Where the hell has she been for all these years?

Why hasn't she ever come and look for me before?

Why did my parents keep her and not me?"

"Robyn, breathe. Are you okay?" Alex instructs as we approach the parking lot. We are met by the warden himself, who is another close personal friend of Alex's. "Is there anyone you don't know?" I say. He escorts us upstairs and into the visitors' center as he stands off to the side, and a few seconds later she walks in. I'm standing slightly behind Alex, so she doesn't see me right away. I'm stuck on stupid and immobile. Her hair is cornrowed going straight back, and she has on this bright-orange one-piece jumpsuit, which is unflattering as hell.

"Who the hell are you?" she says to Alex. She looks pissed as hell. Shit, I'll probably be pissed too if I'm forced to wear that jumpsuit and locked up in here.

"Take a seat," the guard orders as she stands there with her arms folded and a frown glued to her face.

"My name is Alex Taylor," he utters one word at a time as the look of astonishment invades his face.

"Is that supposed to mean something to me, and what the fuck are you staring at?"

"Is that supposed to mean something to me, and what the fuck are you staring at?" she barks at him. I'm still standing frozen behind Alex. I'm paralyzed with fear. Suddenly he steps to the side, and our eyes meet for the first time. She abruptly jumps out of her seat, which causes one of the female guards to quickly tackle her.

"Get the fuck off me, bitch!" she yells uncontrollably as the guard strikes her with her baton.

Alex looks toward his warden buddy for type of assistance. "Is this really necessary!" Alex asks hypothetically.

The warden is calm but demure in his response. "Enough!" he says, which causes the guard to stop. I'm near tears, but the anger in her eyes is filled with rage. They escort her back into her seat as Alex escorts me in the one across from her.

I'm speechless but manage to formulate some words after I clear my throat. "My name is Robyn, Robyn Richards."

She is still frowning. "What kind of sick joke is this?" she mumbles as she quickly becomes belligerent and combative. Her emotions are all over the place.

"I can assure you I'm no joke and I'm just as confused as you are," I tell her. She snickers and rolls her eyes still in disbelief. I'm sitting right here in front of her, and she's acting like I'm not real.

"What's so funny?" I ask her because now I'm beginning to feel disrespected and I'm getting pissed.

She rolls her eyes. "You are and this whole charade is some type of bad joke that's not funny at all," she keeps insisting. "Can someone tell me what's going on?" she yells toward the ceiling into thin air and then begins to cry. "I'm just so sick and tired of motherfuckers playing mind games with me and I'm tired of always fighting . . . I-I just can't do it anymore. I won't do it anymore." She weeps.

Alex slowly walks toward her and gently places his hand on her shoulder. "Baby girl," he calls her, "I can only imagine how you're feeling and how confusing this all must be for you as well as Robyn. I mean, after all these years, living and believing one thing and then to find out something different can be a bit overwhelming, and believe me, we were just as shocked and surprised as you are when we first saw the article, but the fact is, you and Robyn are sisters, identical sisters, and she was given up for adoption, and she's hoping you can help shed some light on who her birth mother is," he tells her.

"Who her birth mother is? And how the hell would I know that?" she says sarcastically. "I lived in an orphanage most of my life until I was seven, after that, I've been living with Big Daddy up until the day, well…. you know, I killed him. So, no, there isn't anything I can tell her about our birth mother because I don't know a damn thing myself!"

All the oxygen in the room evaporated because no one says a word, much less takes a breath. After a few minutes, Alex says, "You mentioned that Cornell took you from an orphanage?"

"Yeah, that's right. You knew Cornell?" she asks surprisingly.

Alex lowers his head, "Yeah, we used to be business partners…and friends," Alex adds reluctantly. "I heard he gotten into other things. I had no idea that it had escalated to all this."

"Or you didn't want to know," she adds.

He drops and nods his head. "Did you happen to know Alexis?" he continues.

"Who…oh, her…yeah, I knew her. What of it?"

"She was my daughter, you know and I was wondering if you can tell me what happened…" Alex pleas with her before she abruptly stops him.

"Look, I'm really sorry but I've already answered questions about a girl I barely knew. I've told the police everything and now, if you don't mind…I really just want to go back to my cell." She slowly rises from her seat and looks at me and says, "Well, for all it's worth, it was good meeting you, and I wished we could have met under different circumstances, but we didn't and at this point, there's really no need for you to come back or for us to try to get to know one another," she utters and then turns and walks away.

Jessica

It's My Life!

He has orchestrated every part of my life. I walk like he walks, I talk like he talks, I eat what he eats, and I read what he reads. Although I have lived a privileged and comfortable life, I've always felt there is something missing. I love my parents very much, but my father's massive hold is suffocating me. I'm trying to find a way to tell him that I've dropped out of college and joined the police academy. It isn't an easy decision for me to make, but it's my life.

"Well, I think you fell and bumped your head, Jessica," Tamara says to me. "Not to mention your father is going to literally kill you when he finds out what you've done. Are you crazy?"

Normally Tamara is at my house on the weekends, but her parents are going out of town and they've asked her to stay home. Tamara is the oldest of her brothers and sisters, and she is the only one with a valid driver's license. Her brother Tony failed his test because he listened to his best friend and leaned to the side while taking the road test.

"That's really going to impress 'em, dog!" Tony told us his friend told him.

"My father loves me, and he will not kill me. He'll just have to understand," I tell her as I'm determined to believe that myself.

"Jessica, who are you trying to convince, me or yourself? Going to Princeton was all you've ever talked about. Why are you doing this?" she asks. I can hear frustration in her voice.

"Thanks for your support," I say. Tamara is my best friend, and she of all people should know how important this is to me.

"Jessica, I know how important this is to you, but I would like to admonish you that your father will not. Finally!" she yells.

"What are you doing?" I say because all I can hear is her struggling with something.

"Don't worry about what I am doing and figure out how you are going to stop your father from killing your ass," as she stresses the word kill.

"Shut up, Tamara, and stop saying that!" I yell into the receiver.

"Face it, Jessica, I beat you up when we were kids. What makes you believe that you can be a police officer, but more importantly, why?"

"First of all, I let you win!" I retort. "And secondly, when do I get to do what I want with my life?"

Tamara and I met at my seventh birthday party. Her father has worked for my father for the past fifteen years. We attended Williams Academy together. It is a private institution, where we both met and liked the same boy, Joseph Wallace. Since he could not decide which one of us he liked best, we decided to fight, and I let her win because I realized he wasn't worth it. Ironically, Joseph still picked me and then shortly after that dumped me for Myra Perkins, and after that fight, we were inseparable. Tamara and I spend so much time together that my father has contemplated filing her on his yearly tax returns.

I know my decision to quit college and join the police academy will not sit well with my parents, especially my father.

"Jessica, your altruism is sickening," Tamara says as a final attempt to discourage me. I love Tamara dearly. She is like a sister to me, but for her to be so negative and nonsupporting of my dream is beginning to piss me off.

My father, Matthew Lovejoy, is the founder and owner of Hip-Hop Record and Designs. He literally built his company from the ground up. He first opened and operated his studio out of his father's garage. Today he is responsible for discovering some of today's rap and R&B recording artists. The design division is a division which was created by him for my mom. She gave up her career of becoming an interior designer to help support my dad and his dream.

"Dad, can we talk?" I say as we head toward the dinner table. I have to take two steps to his one because the sweet smell of Rose's cooking is his sole focus.

"Rose, everything looks and smells delicious," my mother adds with her pristine and gracious smile.

"Yes, pumpkin?" That is his nickname for me. Rose has to have had her own agenda because she's made all of Daddy's favorites tonight: mashed potatoes with homemade gravy, black eyes peas, corn bread, baked salmon, BBQ and baked chicken, collard greens and string beans both with smoked turkey parts, baked beans, mac 'n' cheese, and his favorite dessert, pineapple upside-down cake.

I look into his eyes and know it's now or never. When you're dealing with Matthew Lovejoy, it's best to be straightforward, respectful but straightforward. I pause for another thirty seconds. "Say what you mean and mean what you say" is the motto he lives by.

"Daddy, I quit college and joined the police academy," I say with my head held high, shoulders back, and with confidence and authority in my voice. My father is a very obstinate man. He stands about six feet three inches tall. He has a very strong outward appearance and a solid stocky frame, which can be very intimidating. He has a serious expression that is constantly glued to his face. My father is a tacit person. He does not like to repeat himself, and those who know him know this.

"Excuse me?" he says, believing he hasn't heard me clearly.

I clear my throat and repeat myself. "I said I quit college and joined the police academy," I repeat while my eyes lock on the mashed potatoes and gravy.

The kind of man that my father is, he is well refined and always in control. After all, he has negotiated million-dollar contracts and put together some unbelievable deals in the past. There are times when he puts his company and his reputation on the line and still keeps his cool.

He clears his throat while his eyes lock on his favorite dessert as he utters. "If you think I'm going to allow this kind of disrespectful behavior in my house, you've lost your mind," he says to me in this poignant but surreal tone.

"Disrespect, Daddy, how am I disrespecting you?"

"Jessica, please," he says, which really means "Drop it." Never in my life have I questioned or debated with my father or his decisions. I have attended every etiquette class or charm school you can think of. My father has spared no expense when it comes to me or my education. By the time I was seven years old, I'd attended more social events than Queen Elizabeth and I speak two different languages. I grew up in the rich hills of Northern Jersey. Although my father has made his millions in the hip-hop, rap, and R&B sector, he has made sure I have exposure to all types of music ranging from classical to opera. I was a skilled violin player in my formative years, and it was my ambition to one day play at the Met with the Philharmonic Symphony.

"Daddy, I'm not trying to disrespect you or your household, and this isn't about you. It's about me and what I want to do with the rest of my life," I say with vim and vigor in my tone.

"Jessica, you can't be serious. You've always been a bit impetuous, plus do you have any idea the kind of unsavory people that are out there? Why would you even want to put yourself in those types of situations?"

"Because it's my life," I say as his stare pierces through me, but I'm not going to back down.

"I see," he says.

I hit a nerve, which isn't my intention. "Dad, it was never my dream or desire to get into the entertainment industry," I try to explain. "You've followed your dream. Now please let me follow mine. I love you, and I need and want your support on this."

"You call this a dream, it sounds more like suicide," he retorts. Cynicism is one of our family traits that's best served cold. "Besides, do you really believe you have what it takes to become a police officer?" he continues in his tongue-in-cheek expression. My father has never acted this way toward me before, and it's hurting me to my core, but I'm not going to let his callous tone deter me. As I've said before, Matthew Lovejoy can be very intimidating.

"And yes, I do believe I have what it takes to be a police officer. You have sheltered me my entire life, but I'm not as weak as you think I am."

"Well, I just assumed—" he starts to say before I interrupt him and then blurt, "Well, you assumed wrong! Daddy, listen—"

"No, Jessica, you listen!" he explodes as his fist hits the table, which makes me and my mother jump. "I've work too hard and too long for this family. I will not have this type of disobedience in my house! Get your ass back in college and forget about the Charlie's Angels shit or . . . ," he bellows and then extends his hand to retrieve his plate that Rose fixed for him.

"Or what?" I inquire because it sounds like an ultimatum. Rose hands him his plate and exits quickly.

"Or get out of my house!" There isn't a flinch or pause in his voice or his words. My father utters those words to me like I'm not even his daughter, as if he doesn't love me anymore.

"Matthew, no!" my mother interjects. Vivian Lovejoy is a paragon. Her picture-perfect five-foot-ten-inch slender frame complements her body perfectly. She is compassionate and soft natured, and she has always supported her husband in all his decisions, but this time she believes he's being unfair and unreasonable. Her belief in God and her faith has carried her through some very trying times when she and my father first met and married. She had two sisters. Her oldest sister died about two year ago shortly after her son, Brandon, was murdered, and she and her other sister haven't spoken in years because of a disagreement they had concerning my father, which she never speaks about.

"Matthew, you can't be serious!" she shouts. "She's our daughter! I'm sure if you two sit down, you can talk this out," she pleads with him.

"The only thing is for Jessica to come to her senses and stop with all of this bullshit about becoming a police officer," he demands. He has to be in control of everyone and everything. He's suffocating me, and I'm not going to take it anymore.

"Damn it, Daddy!" I stand up and yell at the top of my lungs. "It's time for me to start taking control over my own life. It's time for me to start making my own decisions!" I protest. My father is the only man in my life, and I've never been this mad or defiant before. "You can't keep telling me what I can and cannot do!"

"Yes, I can!" he yells.

"You're being unreasonable, you know!"

"Yeah, I know!"

"Go to hell!" I retort.

"Jessica!" My mother yells in disbelief of my insubordination. No one eats dinner that night.

It's been two whole days, and my father has yet to utter one word to me. We've always been close, but his flippant manner toward me and this whole situation is extremely irritating. He spends most of his time in his study with the door closed. Even my mother has contemplated going in there.

"This is ridiculous," I say as we pace back and forth outside his study door.

She agrees, "I can't believe he's being so obdurate. We usually discuss things together before making any decisions." My mother explains, "But this is . . . well, you know, you know how he gets when it comes to you. He just loves you so much, Jess. You do realize that, don't you?"

"Yes, Mother, I do," I say. I pause for a moment. I want, no, I need to know how she feels about my decision. I ask her, "You know, you never told me how you feel about my decision?"

I can see my question makes her uncomfortable but she never says a word. Growing up, I watched my mother closely, and she has always been genteel and refined, but after the death of her sister, she has become more abrupt and outspoken. I was groomed to be just like her. I completely understand her role in this family, and I love and respect her for the sacrifice that she has made for this family, but that's her life, not mine.

"Enough is enough!" I announce as I knock on the solid oak door. I don't dare wait for an invitation to come in because I will not get one. I push open the door and walk in. As the door closes, I turn and look at my mother and see worry in her eyes.

My dad is sitting in the dark at his desk. He is staring at an old picture of him and me when I was seven at one of our company cookouts. The sparkle in his eyes is dim, which concerns me. "Are you okay?"

I get no response. "This is ridiculous," I continue. He won't even look in my direction. "Will you please look at me? I'm not leaving until you talk to me! This is not some flyby night decision that I've made. I've thought long and hard about this." He starts turning his chair in my direction, which leads me to believe I'm making progress. He opens his mouth and then closes it without saying a word.

I continue, "Fine then, I'll talk, you listen. My entire life, you and Mommy have always provided the best for me, and I appreciate it. Daddy, I love you, but I need to do this for me, and I really need your support. It's important to me that you understand that. I'm just trying to find out who I am because I've always felt different and I don't know why. I've always done what you wanted me to do, and I'm searching for something else."

"What do you mean who you are? You're my daughter, for God's sake," he says.

My careful and tactful plan to present my case to my father is failing drastically. He sits in his chair and looks at me as if he has never seen me before. My patience is wearing thin. This is the first time in my life that I don't do what my father wants me to do, and he is making me feel like a criminal. I'm scared, but something deep inside me says not to give in. The more I try talking to him, the more he blatantly ignores me, which infuriates me more and more.

"Oh, I see, the great Matthew Lovejoy has spoken. What's wrong, Daddy? No one has ever stood up to you before? I'm not one of your employees who fear you because I don't want to lose my job!" I say. I have no idea where that comes from. I'm pushing my luck and his temper. He completes the turn in his chair and looks me straight in my eyes. We are now in direct eye-to-eye contact with each other.

"You want me to look at you," his baritone voice booms toward me as he stands up. "You're right, you are not an employee of mine. You are my daughter, which holds you to a higher standard! Yes, I expect you to do as I say. Your mother and I have worked our asses off to give you the things we never had!"

"Daddy, I know you have, and I appreciate it, but—"

"But nothing!" he says as he stops me. "You haven't the slightest notion about the shit that goes on out there, Jessica, because I've protected you your entire life! Because that's what parents do, protect their kids, keep them safe."

"Protecting me? From what, Daddy? What is it you're not telling me? When can I start making my own decisions?"

"You mean mistakes!"

"Oh, so if it's not your way, it's a mistake?"

"Damn it, Jessica, it's not the same, and you know it! Everything you need is right here!"

"Yeah, for you and Mommy…" I stop, "Daddy, have a little faith in me, please." I beg and plead. "Trust me," I say, believing I'm starting to get through to him, "You and Mommy have instilled in me morals, values, strength, understanding, acceptance, everything. So now it is time for you to start trusting me."

"I do trust you, pumpkin. I just don't agree with your decision wanting to play cops and robbers, Jessica. It's suicide, plain and simple," he says. It's clear that he is never going to accept my decision. His frivolous treatment toward me and my decision speaks volumes, and it clarifies what my current relationship is with him. My first time standing up to my father, and I'm losing.

"Maybe and maybe not, but it's a good thing that the final decision isn't yours," I tell him.

He stands up. "I see. Then there isn't anything left for me to say," he says and adjusts his necktie. The look in his eyes is something I will never forget. He walks toward me, kisses my forehead, and walks toward the door. Before exiting, he turns around one last time and looks me dead in my eyes before dropping his head and walks out of his own study. It takes everything I have in me not to run after him. I want to tell him I've changed my mind, but my feet are frozen to the floor. I sit in the dark for an hour before I pick up the receiver and dial my best friend's phone number.

"Hello," the voice on the other end say.

"I'm moving out," I blurt into the receiver.

"Jessica, calm down. You told him, didn't you?"

"Yes, can I stay with you?" I cry.

"Stay with me? Jessica, don't be ridiculous. Why do you think I'm at your house all of the time?" she says. For the first time in my life, I feel alone.

"You didn't see the look in his eyes, Tamara. He hates me," I say to her through the worst case of hiccups I've ever encountered, which further complicates things.

"Jessica, your father doesn't hate you. He's worried about you, and I don't blame him. Why don't you think about this a little longer before you make such a rash decision?" she says to me.

"You're my friend, you're supposed to be on my side," I remind her.

"I am your friend, Jessica, and this ain't about sides. I'm worried about you too, but I happen to agree with your father on this," she says.

I feel betrayed, and I'm at a loss for words. After a few minutes, I collect my thoughts. "So you agree with my father?" I say while still trying to get control of these hiccups that insist on taking control of my body.

"Yes, I do, and frankly, I'm trying to understand why you're trying so hard to be someone you're not?" she has the audacity to add.

"Who do you think you see when you see me?" I ask her. My curiosity is piqued as my hiccups miraculously stop.

"I see someone trying to be someone they are not," she says in this Valley girl accent. Never in a million years will I have thought my best friend will ever say something so insensitive and insulting to me. My mouth drops wide open. "Wow, I can't believe you just said that." My feelings are hurt because we share and do everything together. I have confided in her many of times about my feeling different, and she knows how sensitive and personal of a subject this is for me but for her to throw it all back into my face makes me rethink our whole friendship. I'm quiet after that

"Jessica," she calls. "Are you still there?" her raspy voice says into the receiver.

After a few minutes, I say to her, "You and my father seem to have some ass-backwards misguided misconception about me as if I can't take care of myself," I say to her as I'm now seated in my father's chair in his study.

After a few minutes she calmly says, "Let me ask you something, Jessica."

"What is it, Tamara?"

"What are you searching for? For as long as I've known you, you've been on this journey to find answers. What is it your looking for? You ever heard the old adage 'Be careful what you're looking for because you just might find it'?" she rebuffs.

Tamara has summoned up my feelings and insecurities about myself, which I've never shared with anyone, and this feeling of déjà vu is never going away. It is unnerving, but for her to feel so indifferent about something that means so much to me is unacceptable. By the end of our conversation, I'm emotionally drained and mentally depleted I can't argue with anyone else, even if I wanted to. Our very first and last physical fight didn't hurt as much as the words she has uttered to me. It is quiet for a minute longer before I hear the receiver being slammed onto its base.

My parents are my parents without a doubt, but at times growing up they even seem like strangers to me. In a single day, I've managed to alienate my father and my best friend. "Ugh!" I yell into the air plus the fact that no one has wished me a happy birthday.

It's been several days since Tamara and I last spoke. I hate the tension between us. My mother has told me that her father had a stroke the other day and was rushed to the hospital. I start to call her, many times, I pick up the receiver and dial the number. I manage to hit 973-555-42 and then hang up. The tension between my father and I isn't any better either, and if I want him to take me seriously, I have to get out his house. I talk with my mother, and she tells me he put a freeze on my trust account. I plan on using that money to live on until I found a job.

"Why is he doing this?" I ask her.

By noontime, my mother has found and paid the first year's lease in a gated-community, two-bedroom condo in Montclair, which surprises me because she has never gone against my father's wishes before.

"Thank you," I say. "I know this wasn't an easy thing for you to do. As soon as I get a job, I'll pay you back," I tell her.

"Jessie, baby, I don't want your money," she tells me. "What I want is for you to make amends with your father. I'm trying to understand your decision too. Yes, your father can be unreasonable at times, but he's my husband and I love him dearly, and you are my child, but my duty and concern for you is that you have a safe place to lay your head while you are trying to figure things out. That's one thing I will not compromise!" she says in her matriarch voice.

I know how important family is to my mother. When my cousin Brandon was murdered nearly two years ago and shortly after my aunt passed away, I watched this matriarch of a woman crumble and fall. My dad sat by her bedside for months until she was ready, willing, and able. My mom told me when they first married they lived in a run-down, one-room apartment where the hot water worked every so often.

"Believe it or not, those were some of our happiest times," she told me on one of our mother-daughter days we used to go on. It was a day of pampering—hair, nails, foot, full-body massages, and a massive shopping spree—but needless to say with support, determination, and love, they made it through some very trying times.

Since my mother is gracious enough to pay the first year's rent, I know I can take my time decorating. I ask if I can keep my bedroom set, but she has other plans. "Charge it!" she yells as she waves my father's platinum American Express card high in the air. In the next two days, we spend over twenty-five thousand dollars on utilities, living room, bathroom, kitchen, cookware, accessories, clothing, electronics, and food. By the time we are done, my condo looks like a miniature model of my parent's house. My mother has excellent taste, which is no surprise. After all, she did give up a promising career as interior designer for my father.

As we stand in the middle of the living room admiring our accomplishment while sweat drips down our brows, we give each other a well-deserved compliment. "Not bad," we say simultaneously and then laugh as we give each other a high five.

"Let's celebrate," I announce as I make a huge pitcher of my world-famous pineapple tea. I hand her a glass. "Salude. I love you so much."

"I love you too, sweetie," she replies. "Besides, what's the use of having a rich husband if I can't spend the money?" she says as we finish the rest our pineapple tea. She looks at her watch. "Oh my, look at the time," she says as she jumps to her feet. "Your father is going to be so worried about me."

I assist her with her coat and add a big bear hug just like I used to give her when I was little. She holds my face in the palm of her hands and looks deep into my eyes. "I pray that you find what you're searching for, Jessica. I just pray that you are prepared for the answers you might receive," she says and kisses my forehead and walks out.

I am ready to spend my first night in my new condo, and I'm excited and exhausted at the same time. I'm ready to embrace my newfound freedom, and I would have loved it if my best friend is here, but she isn't. It's been a week since we last spoke, and I forget to ask my mother how her dad is doing.

As I'm preparing myself for bed, there's a hearty knock on my door. I check my watch. It's 10:00 p.m. Who the hell can that be? At first, I think it's that cute neighbor I've been seeing the last couple of days, but to my surprise, when I open the door, Tamara is standing there.

"What are you doing here?" I say in my I-don't-give-a-damn voice while trying to contain my excitement.

"You don't know how to return phone calls?" she says as she barrages her way in without a formal invitation.

"You called? When?" I ask. "I thought you were mad at me."

"Jessica."

"No, Tamara, you really hurt my feelings."

"I've been calling you these past several days. Rose didn't tell you? As a matter of fact, I wanted to—" she starts to say and then stops and looks around. "Not bad," she says, nodding her head in approval. Tamara is never good at apologizing. Even after our fight, she never once uttered the words, "I'm sorry."

"What are you doing here?" I ask again as she practically throws the latest issue of Time Magazine in my face, and on the cover are two images and one of the images looks exactly like me.

"What's this?" I ask her. She gives me this crazy-ass look as if I'm lying to her.

I laugh. "What . . . you think this is me? I think I would remember taking a mug shot, Tamara." I throw the magazine back at her. "What's this about?"

She picks it back up and practically waves the magazine in my face, again. "What's this about?" she repeats. "It's about you having a twin sister."

"Tamara, don't be ridiculous, I don't have a twin sister. I'm sure my parents would remember having twins," I say as I continue to laugh it off because this is a notion too insane to think about.

She is still determined to push the magazine in my face. "Jess, look at her . . . really look at her. This girl looks just like you! It says her name is Raylene Chambers and she is currently being held in Atlantic City's county jail on murder charges! Aren't you the least bit curious about her?" she asks as she keeps trying to put it next to my face, but I keep pushing her hand away. I'm speechless and confused and don't know what to say. Plus the fact that a stranger can look exactly like me is extremely unsettling and nerve wrecking to me.

In our thirteen years of friendship, that was the worst it has ever been between us, and I tell Tamara I never want to fight like that again. My best friend is back, and I'm not going to let anything come between us again. I just want to get back to the way things used to be between Tamara and me, but all she wants to do is talk about is this girl.

"I heard from the police academy, and I'm scheduled to take my written exam and physical by the end of the week," I say.

"Jess, her name is Raylene Chambers. Does that name sound familiar to you?"

"No," I reply and continue with my news. "Anyway, as I was saying, I'm excited to—"

"Damn it, Jessica, look at the article! What is wrong with you?" she interrupts, determined to keep me focus on the issue at hand.

"What's wrong with me? You wanna know what's wrong with me? It's because for years and years I had questions and I had doubts. It's because there were things that just didn't seem right to me. I had this feeling, this gut feeling that something isn't right, and I always just dismissed it or justified it, but the moment I do decide to speak on it, I lose my father and my best friend in one day and on my birthday, of all days, which by the way neither one of you wished me a happy birthday. And now you're back, you're here, and I just want things back to normal, and now you want me to read some damn article about a girl I don't even know." I pick up the magazine, and I look into these sad eyes. "And you want me to believe that my parents had twins girls and give one away? That does not make any sense to me, and they would not have done anything like that. My parents would not lie to me," after I utter the words there is a bad taste left in my mouth as I fall to my knees onto the floor.

"Lie to you about what?"

A few months ago, I asked my mother for a copy of my birth certificate, and she kept giving me a lot of excuse, as if she lost it or something. After a while, I just stopped asking her, and I go to city hall myself. The lady there tells me that there is no record of a Jessica Lovejoy being born here. "What, that does not make any sense whatsoever. Are you sure? Maybe she just started working there or something," Tamara adds as an alternative solution.

"She wasn't new, Tamara, but you are right, it did not make sense to me either. She told me there were several Jessica's born around that same time frame, but none with the last name of Lovejoy."

"Then the only other explanation is…they are not your real parents," Tamara says; she could not shut-up and she kept asking question after question that I did not have any answers for.

"Of course, they are my real parents, don't be ridiculous," I interject so she would shut the hell up. Her silence was short-lived; Tamara yells out of anguish, "OMG, you are adopted!" Her words echo and bounces off every wall in the room.

"Tamara, shut the fuck up, please!" I just need her to be quiet long enough so I can think. The idea of me being adopted is too absurd for me to believe. What is bothering me though is why they only kept me and not my twin sister too. Why would they do something like that? It was not my intention to yell at Tamara, but all her incessant comments were making me uneasy and driving me completely crazy.

"Don't get mad at me!" Tamara retorts. "I'm not the one who gave your sister up for adoption!" and then slowly strut to the chair and sits down.

It's clear Tamara has everything figured out; I wish I did. It does explain why my father was overly protected of me, and why he carefully crafted, orchestrated, and controlled every part of my life, maybe he did not want me to find out. I am utterly dumbfounded and knocked off my feet. I do not want to believe it, but there is no other logical explanation I can think of. I feel completely depleted, and for the first time in my life, I do not know what to say or what to do. Tamara Mitchell has managed to interject so much doubt and speculation into my life, and I don't know if I should be mad at her or thank her.

"So this is what's behind all this wanting-to-be-a-cop crap is about. You wanna do some background investing into your parents," she offers as the final piece to this mysterious puzzle, called my life.

"Of course not, and don't be so silly. I've always had a burning desire to be in position where I can help people," I remind her again, "What's wrong with that?"

She smiles. "Nothing, absolutely nothing is wrong with that. It just sounds like a lot of bullshit to me," she adds jokingly as we solidify our sister friendship with a hug and lots of laughter. Tamara can be aggravating at times, and then there are times when she can be so silly which I think is one of her best qualities.

The two musketeers are together again, and this time we're in my own place which made this reunion sweeter than before. Since my father still has my trust account on lock down, Tamara was able to get me a part-time position where she works.

Claudia, another coworker of ours, is always telling us stories about the fun she has at this nightclub in Philly called the Do Drop Inn. I believe she tends to overexaggerate a bit.

"You think that's something? You two should have been there the time this one girl was beating the hell out of this other girl," she starts telling us and then feels the need to demonstrate. She starts flinging her arms and legs all over the place like a crazy person. I step back so I won't get hit, accidentally or intentionally.

"I'm telling you, you'll have a good time . . . and niggas galore!" she says enthusiastically as she fans herself with her hand to imply she's getting hot.

Even Tamara is getting hyped about the idea of going. "Let's go!" she turns and says to me.

"Great!" Claudia shouts, "Tomorrow night—"

"Tomorrow night? Tomorrow is Thursday," I remind her. Does she forget we have to work Friday morning?

I know, but that that is all the partying starts," she adds excitedly. "Thursday, Friday, Saturday, and Sunday nights are the best times to go. What's the problem? I do it all the time. We'll come to work straight from the club," she says like it's nothing. She pauses and waits for a response. "So you coming or not?"

Tamara and I stutter in unison, "Um, yeah, sure, I guess, I mean . . ." She laughs and then walks back toward her desk while dancing and singing.

We arrive at the club around 9:00 p.m., and it is already crowded. Claudia is right. Everywhere we look, there are wall-to-wall men. Tamara nearly breaks her neck turning her head so fast trying to see them all. From the moment we arrive, people are staring, whispering, and pointing at us as if we are world famous.

"Why is everyone staring at us?" Tamara asks Claudia.

"You're just a new face around here. I would not worry about it," Claudia says, trying to appease us. "Keith!" she yells across the room, and that is the last time we see her for the rest of the night.

Tamara and I are on our own, and the attention we are receiving is overwhelming. I try to relax and have a good time, but everyone is focus on me, and it is making me uncomfortable. An hour pass, and I can no longer take all this attention. "Let's go," I say to Tamara. "You want to leave?"

"Yeah, I do, but what about Claudia? We cannot leave her here," she says. We look around and spot Claudia sandwiched between two guys, one front and the other in the back.

"Oh hell, she's good, let's go," Tamara says as we head toward the front door. But before we can reach the exit, a group of girls surround us like SWAT, which makes me more nervous as I feel a light tap on my shoulder. I turn around to see who is touching me. This girl, whom I've never seen before, stands there, looking at me with this look of astonishment on her face. I focus on the words coming out of her mouth because the loud music drowns out any audible words.

"Oh shit," she mouths one syllable at a time. "Follow me."

I look at Tamara. She shrugs her shoulders because we both have reservations about following girls we don't know, but since we are outnumbered, we decide to go without any resistances. Tamara and I follow these strangers upstairs into a penthouse apartment. Once upstairs, another girl walks within three inches of my face and looks at me from head to toe.

I'm not intimidated by her. "What the hell are you staring at?" I ask with a touch of boldness in my voice. I resent the fact that I'm being examined.

"Who the hell are you?" she asks snobbishly.

"Who the hell are you?" I retort in the same tone and manner.

She does not respond. "Why do you look like my home-girl Ray-Ray?" she asks me with one hand on her hip and then rolls her head around her neck in three different directions which I've never understood why some black girls did that.

Tamara breathes a sigh of relief. "Jessica, the article!" she says, "Remember? We thought you wanted to fight us," Tamara adds laughingly.

"Shut up, Tamara. Look, I do not know who this girl is, and I do not know who you are and why we look a little alike—"

"A little!" everyone yells in unison, including Tamara. Another girl holds up the same copy of the Times Magazine that Tamara shoved in my face earlier. Tamara grabs it out of her hand and repeats her same action, which is ignoring the hell of me. "Jessica, you can't honestly think that you and this girl only look a little alike!"

Here we go again, "Tamara, stop it! You know me! You know I don't have any siblings! This girl is not my sister!" I protest. I'm frustrated, tired, and ready to go, and this good time Claudia talked about isn't happening.

"Can we just go?" I turn and demand to Tamara.

"Why is this so hard for you to believe?" Tamara asks me while the other girls listen to us debate back and forth. I'm fighting a losing battle.

"Because I know my parents and so do you! My mother would not have had twin girls and not kept both! There has to be another explanation."

"What other explanation could there be? Your parents had twin girls and gave one up for adoption!" Tamara insists, and she's beginning to aggravate me again to no end.

"Tamara, stop it!" I cannot bear to listen to this anymore. My stomach starts turning. I'm getting warm, and my head is spinning.

"Your name is Jessica?" asks the same girl who's been interrogating me from the moment we got here.

I've already decided I'm not going to answer any more of her questions until I get some answers of my own. "Who are you?" I ask her with just as much attitude as she has been giving me.

"Amanda Adams, HBIC," she states.

The look of confusion is all she needed before she clarifies. "Head bitch in charge," she replies as if it is a badge of honor.

"How colorful," I respond. "So what's her story?" I continue, determined to keep the attention off me.

"Home-girl and I are from Seattle, and we all live here with Big Daddy and in all my years of knowing her, not once has she ever mentioned that she has a twin, so I am going to ask you one more time, who the hell are you?"

It's quiet, and you can hear everyone's heartbeat. After several minutes, Tamara shouts, "I'm telling you, Jess, this girl is your sister!"

Tamara is more excited than I am as she starts to speculate every inconceivable and outlandish scenario she can think of. She's making me physically sick to my stomach.

"Remember all of the stories your father used to tell us about how difficult it was for them financially because he just started Hip-Hop Records from his father's garage and a year later they got married," she blurts.

"Your father owns Hip-Hop Records?" they all say in three-part harmony, which surprises me because they sound really good.

I really need her to stop talking now. I hold up my hand. "Tamara, please!" But she continues. "Your mom must have gotten pregnant shortly after that and couldn't afford to keep two babies and they just never told you, you had a twin because they were too embarrassed or ashamed," she volunteers, which is the most absurd thing I've ever heard in my life.

"Tamara!" I yell again, but nothing is stopping her.

"And then by the time you were old enough to know the truth . . . it was too late and—"

"Tamara, shut up!" I scream at the top of my lungs. "Stop it, just stop it! None of that happened! My parents would not have lied to me, especially about something like this!" I sit down and hold my head in my hands.

"But earlier you said—"

"Yeah, well, earlier I was wrong. And so are you." I turn toward the HBIC. "Can I have something to drink, please?"

"Bre, get her some water, or would you like something stronger?" Amanda speculates. She acts like their drill sergeant than their friend. she gives a lot of orders, and they follow her instructions, no questions asked.

"Water is fine," I assure her. She hands me a glass of iced water, which I gulp down in one sip. I don't think I take a breath. "Thank you . . ." I manage to say as I hand my empty glass to Amanda. She looks at me and then at the glass she snaps her fingers and calls for another girl to collect it. I watch as she barks all kinds of orders at them. I do not like Amanda Adams, and I am not impressed by her one bit.

"Bre!" she yells.

"Thank you, Bre," no one utters a word afterwards. I just need time to think. Thousands of feelings and emotions start running rampant through my mind: betrayal, confusion, tricky, deception, lies, lies, and more lies. Finally, "I want to meet her," I blurt into the atmosphere and stand up.

"What!" Tamara yells. "Are you sure?"

"Yes, I'm sure!"

"Fine, I'll have Carly take you there in the morning," Amanda says and then walks out the room. I don't trust her, and I usually get along with everyone, but she gives off this weird vibe that I don't trust. Her claim to fame is HBIC, but the other girls seem to fear her more than respect her. After it's clear she's gone, the other girls become more relaxed and introduce themselves to me.

"Hi, I'm Brittany."

"I'm Nikki."

"And I'm Carly."

"And you've met Bre," Brittany says. "You have to excuse Amanda. She's just, well . . . she's just going through some things, that's all," Brittany tries to justify, which I think is admirable of her.

"No, I don't have to excuse her, and I don't care about that, but I am concerned about her," as I point to the picture on the cover of *Time Magazine*. "What can you tell me about her?"

"What would you like to know?" Carly asks.

"Everything," I reply.

"Well, that could take all night." Carly laughs.

Moments later Amanda comes back into the room. "It's late. You two might as well stay here tonight." I can't sleep, but I'm glad Tamara is finally quiet. I stay up half the night talking to Carly and the other girls and asking a myriad of questions. By 6:00 a.m., we are on our way to Atlantic City. Tamara calls into work for us and tells them some outrageous story. I never knew she could lie so well. I'm able to find a semisecluded area where I can sit and be alone. I appreciate Tamara's efforts on trying to comfort me, but I'm just not in the mood to talk. I need quiet time, and I need to be focus on what I'm going to say to this girl. How do I even begin to explain that our parents only wanted one of their children and not the other? I've always wanted a sibling, and when I asked my mother why she never had any more children, she would just say, "Why mess with perfection?"

I consider Tamara more of a sister than a best friend, but she isn't blood, and now after twenty years to find out that I do have a blood relative, it's scaring the hell out of me. It's a long train ride, and my mind is on overdrive: Who is this girl? Where does she come from? Why hasn't she ever come and look for us before? Why did my parents give her away? Why did she kill that man?

Tamara walks over and sits next to me after a while. "How are you going to be a police officer if you're not strong enough to deal with this?" she says. I know what she's trying to do, but I'm not in the mood.

"Just leave me alone," I say to her and then get up and move to the next empty seat I find. We're approaching our station, and I still haven't the slightest idea of what I'm going to say to this girl.

"We'll be pulling into the station soon," Carly tells us as she gets up and walks toward the doors. Tamara follows, and a few minutes later I slowly make my way over. Tamara is indifferent toward me now because I pushed her away, but I can't worry about her feelings right now.

"Why didn't Amanda come?" I ask Carly.

"I don't know. I stopped trying to figure out Amanda a long time ago," she says.

My nerves are shot. The moment of truth is here. I'm about to meet my long-lost sister, and I haven't a clue on what to expect. I've never visited anybody in jail before, and this is my first introduction into the criminal justice field. I take notice of the guards and how they interact with the public, which is a bittersweet feeling. I feel violated when they ask for every kind of identification under the sun and then search me like I'm the criminal.

"Do you want me to come upstairs with you?" Tamara offers.

"No," I say and turn and walk away. I know she feels slighted, but I don't care.

After passing through the metal detectors, Carly and I head toward the elevators. "Just try not to excite her too much," she says as the doors open and we step onto the elevator.

"And what does that mean?" I desperately reply.

"It just means she's been under a lot of pressure and I don't want to excite her any further."

The elevator comes to a stop, but it takes a few seconds before the doors open.

"Well, it's a little too late for that, don't you think?" I retort as we step off the elevator. I'm already nervous, and Carly isn't making it easier. A red flag goes up. I follow Carly down this long corridor until we reach another guard who is sitting at a desk. He tells us to go in and take a seat. He rattles off two or three more rules and regulations we need to adhere to, but I'm oblivious to what he's saying. Finally, the door opens from the opposite side of the glass partition, which separates inmates and visitors. I'm sitting to the side of Carly, and I can see her, but she can't see me. My mouth drops wide open, and she is dressed in a bright-orange jumpsuit and her hair cornrowed going straight back. I'm flabbergasted. She is an exact carbon copy of me.

"Carly, what are you doing here, and why is the number changed?" I hear her say. I can't take my eyes off her.

"Amanda changed it," Carly informs her.

"What the fuck!" she yells, "Did you know she was going to testify against me too?" It's evident that she's upset and maybe this isn't such a good idea.

"What? No," Carly quickly defends herself. "But, Ray-Ray, listen, there's someone here you need to meet."

"The only person I need to meet is a fucking legitimate lawyer! Someone who can get my black ass out of here," she protests.

"She's not a lawyer, but she is your—" Carly starts to say when I step alongside her and finish her statement.

"Sister," I announce. "I'm your sister."

After a few minutes, she says, "What the hell are you doing back here?" There's no look of shock or excitement on her face at all. When she looks into my eyes, there's no spark or connection whatsoever, and it isn't the reaction I expected at all, which makes me curious.

I look at Carly. "Excuse me," I say to her. "I'm back from where?"

"Look, Robyn, I don't have time for these games, okay! Carly, what's going on?" she yells. Her demeanor is changing, and more frustration is setting in her voice, and her actions are becoming erratic. She jumps out of her seat and starts pacing back and forth in that small room she's confined to.

"Jessica!" I yell toward her. "My name is Jessica Lovejoy. Who is Robyn?" I keep asking without any response.

She stops pacing back and forth and moves closer to the window for a better examination. We are eye to eye, and she repeats the same actions from head to toe, just like Amanda did. I hold my ground. No backing down, but I'm glad that glass partition is between us, and I refuse to let her see me sweat. Then without notice, she starts screaming uncontrollably. Three guards come rushing in and uses what looks like excessive force to subdue her. She is so hysterical she passes out.

Our visit is immediately cut short, and we are told we had to vacate.

"Leave? No! What's going on? How is she doing? I'm not done yet," I protest, which falls on death ears. I refuse to leave things the way they are.

A guard comes in and tells me that she has been checked out by the doctor and he has heavily sedated her. "Listen, she's out for the night, but if you come back tomorrow, I'll let you back in, all right?"

I don't want to leave, but Carly and Tamara convince me that there's nothing more I can do and it will be best to come back. I finally agree.

Twelve hours later, we are once again sitting face-to-face, and she is more calm and relaxed. Personally I think she looks like hell. "How are you feeling?" I ask while trying not to make it so obvious that I'm staring at her.

"Where's Carly?" she practically slurs.

"I came alone. I don't need any more chaperones," I say to her.

"Well, that's unfortunate for you because I have nothing to say to you," she advises me.

"And why not? You're not curious?" I ask her.

"Curious about what, Robyn?" she says in this tranquil-like voice. If it's easier for her to believe I'm Robyn, then I'm going to go along with that because the last thing I want is a repeat of yesterday. I just want to talk with her for a while.

"Where are you from?" I start as a foundation.

"I was born in Seattle, Washington, but been living in Philly since age seven," she tells me.

"Oh, so you moved to Philly with your parents?" I ask with skepticism in my voice.

"No, Big Daddy brought me and Amanda here. It's a long, ugly story," she adds.

I look towards my right and then my left. "I have nowhere to go," I say as I make myself comfortable in my seat. I'm trying to make her comfortable so she will open up. There are so many pieces missing from this puzzle. She sits quiet for a minute longer, then she releases a big sigh. "Look, Robyn I really don't know what you want me to say or what it is you want to hear. Like I told you last time, I'm being charged with murder, and unless by some God-given miracle, she pauses for a moment and drops her head, I don't think it's worth us trying to create some sisterly bond that obviously been destroyed from day one."

I refuse to let her words discourage me, and I'm not buying into this I-don't-give-a-shit attitude she is putting forward. I know she's scared and feels alone, but I need her to let her guard down and work with me. Again, I let her know my name is Jessica, not Robyn, and proceed to speak slowly with conviction in my tone. "I'm not going to bullshit you and act like I understand all the hell you've been through your entire life! I won't insult yours or my intelligence like that! I'm not going to sit here and try to explain or apologize for the actions of my parents because I don't know why they made the choices they made! The only thing I can offer is my truth and my reality, which is my name, my parents name, and where I'm from," I tell her and then stop talking. She is quiet and calm, as if she is surrendering to the notion of the situation. Moments later, her eyes start twitching, and she begins to take long, deep breathes ands exhales slowly to maintain control. I continue with caution, "When Tamara first showed me the article, I was taken aback as well."

"What article?" she slowly speaks.

"The feature article that Times Magazine did on you and that man you killed, Cornell Watkins." I stutter to say the words. "You haven't seen it?"

She shakes her head from side to side. "You mean to tell me your friend's name isn't Alex?" she inquires.

"No," I say as I shake my head from side to side. "I don't know anyone named Alex," I advise her. I watch her closely, and I can see it was finally sinking in as she looks around and clinches her teeth.

"I can send you a copy of the article if you like," I say as gently as possible. I'm preparing myself for another outburst, but she flips the script.

"Well, if what you're saying is true and your name isn't Robyn, then that means there are three of us," she says as she sits back in her seat with amazement. Now I'm speechless.

She opens up. "Last week I receive a visit from this guy named Alex and he's with this girl that looks just like you . . . me . . . us . . . Anyway, he introduced her and said her name is Robyn."

"No way," I say.

"Yes way." She continues, "So my only question is, why you two and not me? Why was I given away?" It's a poignant question that I have no answer for. The vacuous look in her eyes is heartbreaking as she mumbles the words over and over again, "Why?" She becomes serene and tranquil, like she's been heavily sedated once again, but this time it isn't from the effects from any medical drugs. It's from the reality that she has been discarded like a piece of trash twice in her life. I can feel her pain. I sit quietly and watch her for a few minutes. I watch her mannerism and her actions. I notice several scratches and scars all over her face, neck, and forearms, and the more I look at her, the more bumps and bruises I notice. We may look exactly alike, but we are as different as night and day.

"Are you all right?" I ask after a few seconds.

She starts to laugh uncontrollably. "No, no, hell no!" she says, "Boy, you're good. You almost had me fooled," she retorts.

"I'm sorry." I would like to laugh too.

She is an enigma. Her mood swing goes from one extreme to the next within seconds, which makes me apprehensive about saying another word to her.

"What are you staring at?" she asks abruptly. "Oh, I see you're curious about these bumps and bruises, aren't you?" she says. Damn, am I that obvious? "Have you ever been hit?" she asks.

"God no."

"So no man has ever on occasion introduced the back of hand or his fist to your face?" she continues. I frown. "How about being kicked, punched, spit on, and made to feel like grade A shit?" she continues. I'm horrified, and I want her to stop asking me such horrifying questions, but she's relentless in her pursuit.

"Are you a virgin?"

I smirk. "What kind of question is that? That's personal and it's nobody's business," I tell her.

"So it's safe to assume that at the tender age of seven, you were still playing with Barbie Dolls and shit, not being forced to have sex with men who were three times your age?" she says.

"Okay, stop it," I tell her. "What are you doing?"

"Proving a point," she says. "Because the only thing I've ever been good at is telling niggas what they want to hear, and now here you come trying to play some mind games on me, of all people!"

Her demeanor is rapidly changing, and the more she talks, the angrier she becomes. I sit quietly as she goes on with her tirade. I have no idea where all this is coming from or what I've done to provoke her personal attack on me, and from now on I'm going to scrutinize every word that comes out my mouth.

"Are you done?" I finally ask after she finishes spewing her venom toward me. She doesn't respond. She sits back in her chair and folds her arms.

"I came here to meet you because it's obvious that we're related, and unlike you, I would like to know what happened to us, and how and why we were separated at birth. And just because you refuse to believe that my name is Jessica, you think you've proven a point. Well, FYI, my life has been turned inside out as well," I tell her as she starts to open her mouth, but I stop her and stand to my feet and start to leave.

"Robyn, wait!" she yells. "I need your help. My bail is two hundred and fifty thousand, cash or bond. Can you post that?" Her boldness shocks me.

I shake my head. "My name is not Robyn, and no, I cannot post a two-hundred-and-fifty-thousand bail."

"Then leave me alone and don't bother coming back, whoever the hell you are!" she says as she knocks on the rear door so the guard can open it.

Two days later I start my training at the police academy.

Detective Sosa

Intriguing, Unbelievable, and Disturbing

I'm consumed by this case, which is intriguing at times, unbelievable most of the time, and completely disturbing all the time. With Eli being arrested in the middle of her trial, it only takes the jury less than three hours to come back with a guilty verdict. Ms. Chambers has played her last wild card, and it doesn't help her one bit.

All leads from our investigation has one common denominator: Seattle, Washington. I contact the authorities in Seattle and speak with a Captain Joe Morris, and I'm on the red eye the same night. Seattle is a beautiful city, and I've been out west several times before, but never there. I am mostly greeted by hookers, homosexuals, and homeless people, which is aggravating enough, but their attraction usually turns when they find out I'm a cop and not a model.

I check into my hotel, order something to eat from the kitchen, and call Morris.

"I'm eager to speak with you too. I'll see you in the morning," he says.

"The sun is up in some parts of the country. I can be there in a thirty minutes," I tell him because time is of the essence. As I arrive at the station, I'm met by two uniformed policemen and piles and piles of folders marked Unsolved, which haven't been touched in years.

"I was the first one to stumble across the illegal practices at Goldman, Goldman, and Weinberg. I can't believe after all these years Jade and Jonathan are going to get some justice," he announces with a sigh of relief as he approaches me from behind. As I turn in his direction, I finish the last bite of my sandwich and shake his hand.

"Excuse me," I say, "who are Jade and Jonathan?"

He looks at me as if I'm speaking Spanish. "You are here about the Armstrong case, right?" he asks with concern in his voice. I take a deep breath and collect my thoughts. I have no idea what he is talking about. I'm under the impression I'm here to find the connection between Eli, Cornell, and the Moorlands, not add two more homicides into an already disturbing case.

"Excuse me for my ignorance, but what the hell are you talking about?"

He pulls out his seat and tells me to make myself comfortable. He clears his throat and then begins to speak very slowly. From the moment he opens his mouth, I'm drawn to his every word. He speaks with such passion I get the feeling he's talking from personal experiences.

"Jonathan Armstrong was the local hero around here. You know a celebrity. He went from being high school quarterback, to colleges' number one draft pick, until his shoulder injury ended his career. He went to law school, graduated top in his class, and married his high school sweetheart, Jade Lambert."

"Jade Lambert," I repeated. "Of Lambert and Associates?" I asked.

"The one and only. Charles was her father."

"Impressive," I say, shaking my head. "Please continue," I encourage him because he has my undivided attention.

"Anyway, Jonathan started making strong moves in the community and caught the eyes of some movers and shakers and went straight into a senate seat. They were the perfect couple. Everyone was in such awe of them. I've never seen two people so much in love." He digresses, "They remind me of my relationship with my wife." He then smiles. "Anyway, Jade had problems conceiving. She and her best friend, Paula, were participants in the Southside Clinic's study, and within two months, Jade was pregnant."

"Who's Paula?"

He throws an eight-by-ten colored photo in front of me. "Paula Green now, then Paula Manchester," he says like I should have known what he is talking about. The gray hairs sitting on the top of his head is evidence of a diminishing mind.

"Oh, I forgot, you're not from around here."

"No, I'm not." I confirm even though I'm held captivated by his story.

"Anyway," he says as his eyes began to water, "Paula Manchester is first cousin to the Brewster family . . . the beer people." I become more intrigued. "You're familiar?" he asks.

"If only I had stock," I reply.

He smiles. "Anyway, Paula and her husband were less fortunate, and they were never able to conceive."

"And . . ."

"And that ended up causing major strife between these best friends. Jade gave birth to three of the most perfect babies you could ever lay your eyes on," Morris tells me. "I overheard the call on the radio, and I rushed there, but by the time I had arrived, her water had broken and those babies were coming and I had to delivered those girls right there, myself! You and your wife have any kids, Detective?"

"No," I reply abruptly, which I don't mean to, but his diversion from the story is driving me crazy. "So what happened after that, Captain?" I have to keep him focused.

"After the girls were born, they were on top of the world. I mean, there wasn't anyone or anything that could stop them now. They had it all, and that's what makes this case so disturbing because to be brutally murdered one week later just didn't make much sense."

"Murdered!" I yell. "What happened?"

Captain Morris gives me play-by-play horrifying accounts of the murder scene. It takes a lot to make me sick, but the photos that Captain has placed in front of me turns my stomach. I don't know them personally, but a cold chill runs up my spin the moment I look at those photos. My face frowns.

"My sentiments exactly," Captain adds.

"Why so brutal?" I ask as I close the folder.

"Don't know. No motive was ever established, but Paula and her husband became our number one suspects because of the threats that were overheard after the girls were born."

"What were the threats?"

"Paula claimed that Jade did something to the test, which caused Paula's eggs to be invalid, and Paula literally said that Jade would die before she allows them to be implanted, but they were, and they took successfully. One week after Jade gave birth to triplets, she and Jonathan were dead."

"Did she have an alibi?"

"They were never questioned."

"Why not?" I asked.

"Because the triplets and the Greens were never found after the murders occurred."

Seconds turned into minutes, and minutes turned into hours after he uttered those words. Morris and I sit there and examine and reexamine every piece of evidence that was collected at the crime scene. "This case is twenty years old and I still remember it like it was yesterday," he says.

I told Lita I will call her once I arrive, but from the moment I arrive, I am consumed by every little detail. Lita never was a fan of my job or the long hours I dedicate to my cases. Thanksgiving is less than a month away, and there are only eight weeks left until our December 31 wedding.

"How the hell are you going to marry me when you're already married to that damn job?" she says to me all the time.

Night and day are the same to me, and by the time I leave Morris's office, I'm completely jaded by the images that keep repeating themselves over and over in my mind like a bad dream. William and Rita Moorland, Cornell Watkins, and Jade and Jonathan Armstrong are all connected in one way or another, and I'm determined to find out how.

I'm back at the station bright and earlier that I beat Captain Morris. I tossed and turned all night long because one image plagued my mind.

"You're here awful early," the captain says to me.

"I was wondering if I could take another look at the photographs."

"You didn't have enough yesterday?" he says jokingly, but I'm not in a joking mood. "You know, Detective, I too have since learned to follow my first instincts," he says as he hands me the folder. "It must be pretty important," he implies as he waits for me to say something.

Is it the look of desperation sprawled across my face that he notices, or is his intuition the same as mine? This feeling is overwhelming, and I can't let it go. I know I've seen it before, but where? I scramble through picture after picture. I know I'm not losing my mind. I've just seen it. "Got it!" I scream out in relief and to no one in particular.

Paula is wearing the same 24k gold pendant encrusted with black diamonds like Rita Moorland had on. I've never seen anything so uniquely designed. I grab my cell and call Sully immediately. "Put a trace on where, when and how many of these were in circulation."

"She is wearing the exact same pendant I found at my crime scene in New Jersey a few months ago," I finally tell him.

"It was part of their consultation gifts for their participation in the study," he informs me. "All participants received one."

Within seconds, Sully calls back. "Elle, twelve pendants were made and distributed to a small group of women who participated in this lucrative study held at the Southside Clinic in Seattle in the mid-nineties, but only half of them were successful in conceiving," Sully explains.

"And Rita Moorland was part of that study, which means she had to have known Paula and Jade."

"Who's Paula and Jade? Elle, what's going on?" Sully asks.

"I'm not sure, but I could use your help in finding out. How soon can you be here?" I ask.

"I'm on the next thing flying," he says and then hangs up the phone.

I turn toward Captain Morris. "My vic Rita Moorland has the same pendant, and she was murdered a few months ago," I reiterate to Captain Morris. "What can you tell me about the Southside Fertility Clinic?"

He looks at me and proceeds to make a pot of coffee. "Aw, the Southside Clinic," he repeats and then becomes very silent and still. After several minutes, he speaks and offers me a cup of coffee. "They were anxious to get this new drug approved by the FDA called RENU, and there were a selective group of people who were chosen to participate in this lucrative study."

"RENU?"

"Yeah, it was developed by a group of local doctors, but problems developed between some of the participating parties."

"Like what?"

"Severe abdominal pain, cramping and heavy, uncontrollable bleeding."

"Why didn't they stop the study then?"

"Because only half of the participants complained and ones who were successful in conceiving didn't. It was chalked up to an allergic reaction. You're talking millions and billions of dollars in research governmental aid. Who's going to forfeit that kind of aid?"

"But the potential harm to the body. Then why participate?"

"Do you have any kids, Detective?"

"No."

"Then you can never understand what desperate people do to have a child. Those pendants were given out as part of their consultation gifts, you know, a small way of saying thanks for their time and participation. Thousands of couples applied, but only twelve qualified and were chosen. The deciding factors were race, family's history, paternal and maternal, as well as physical and mental genealogy and education. Look, Detective, it's a known fact that healthy, blue-eyed, blond-haired Caucasian babies are a dime a dozen, but to find a well-bred African American or Hispanic baby today is damn near impossible, and there are people out there who will pay to have one of those babies. Look, Detective, I'm not saying that it's right or fair, but it is what it is."

"And Goldman, Goldman, and Weinberg were more than happy to help assist desperate people who were willing to pay damn near anything for a healthy minority baby?"

"Yes, they were." Morris confirms as he stares at the picture that he pulls from the bottom of the pile and then hands it to me. This is personal for him. He begins to reminisce, "You know, not a day goes by that I don't think about those triplets, and I remember every detail of that day like it was yesterday. It was a cold rainy January night on Chess Mar Street," he says as he places his right hand over his heart, sits down and starts to speak as delicately as he can. He details horrific scenes that he witnessed first-hand. I'm jaded, and after a while, all his words sound like a run- on sentence. "Find those girls, Detective and bring them home," are the only audible words I hear.

Sully is in Seattle that very afternoon, and I introduce the two men. Morris turns over to me all original documents: birth certificates, Social Security cards, foot- and handprints, as well as photos of Jonathan and Jade holding their newborns. There are stocks, bonds, bank accounts, and mutual funds, which are established in the names of Jordan, Jasmine, and Jessica Armstrong, the sole heirs to the Lamberts' dynasty. Today, it's the number 1 company on the NYSE, as well as *Wall Street Journal's* top five companies producing a billion dollars or more in the twenty-first century.

As his phone rings, he places his hand over the receiver. "Detective, this case is twenty years old. Find these girls and give them their rightful inheritance, please," Morris pleas. Sully and I exit as he calls again. I turn and walk back towards his office. "And any questions they have, they can call me," he adds as he hands me his business card.

Sully and I start at the only solid lead we have, but by the time we locate Carl Goldman Sr., he is living in a senior citizens' home suffering from Alzheimer's, he barely remembers his name, much less anything that happened twenty years ago.

As Sully and I enter the room, we see an elderly woman and another gentleman about my age sitting at his bedside. I push on the half-open door. "Excuse me, I'm looking for Carl Goldman Sr."

"I'm Carl Goldman Jr.," he introduces. "And what do you want with my father?" he says abruptly as he briskly walks in our direction. He is short in stature, but his personality is tall. "Who are you?"

I flash my badge. "What do you want?" he repeats again. Sully and I know he is going to be a problem.

I clear my throat. "I was hoping to speak with your dad about some of his dealings with the Southside Fertility Clinic," I advise him.

"Well, as you can see, he's in no condition to answer any questions, especially questions pertaining to something that hasn't existed for nearly twenty years. Now if you don't mind, Detectives, my mother needs me." He is defensive and dismissive in his tone and manner.

"Is everything all right?" the meekly woman asks as she approaches us. "Do you know my husband? Carl, don't be rude. Invite your father's visitors in," she says, but Carl refuses.

"No, Mama, and they were just leaving," he strongly suggests as he escorts her back into the room. Sully isn't a fan of Junior's rude behavior towards us, and it's a matter of time before Sully gets fed up with his disrespectful attitude and starts to heads in his direction. I step between the two men.

"We're looking for Eli Weinberg?" I quickly explain to the junior Weinberg. His arrogance and contentious manner, is a defense mechanism to help make up for his small stature and small size, I assumed.

He snickers and shakes his head. He has no intentions on answering any of our questions. "Did he say something funny?" Sully asks him as he takes another step toward him.

"Detective, I know what you're trying to do, and I can assure you, you're wasting your time," he adds. "Now if you don't mind, I need to get back to my mother," this five-foot-nothing smugly-ass man says to me.

We begin to leave as Sully turns towards Carl Jr. and says, "Yeah, besides we'll have better luck at their headquarters."

"My sentiments exactly," I say.

"If he's any indication of what we're dealing with, you do realize we're going to be stepping into a pile of shit."

I look at our footwear. "We better get some boots," I add sarcastically.

Thanksgiving is in two days, and it looks like Sully and I are going to be stuck in Seattle, and to make matters worse, Lita leaves a message on my cell. She's calling off the wedding, again. Whenever she gets upset, she gives ultimatums and makes irrational decisions.

"Hey, man, I'm so sorry. You know, if you need to leave, I can handle things here," Sully offers but knows once I start something, I'm going to finish it.

The next day we were advised that Carl Goldman Sr. has succumb to his disease. We show up at the Synagogue, uninvited, of course. The list of moaners' read like a who's who. Senators, doctors, lawyers, congressmen, business executives, and entertainers all come to bid farewell to their confidant and friend. His funeral is one of the most highly publicized events in Seattle's history. The atmosphere seems convivial and jovial, so Sully and I decide to talk to as many guests as possible. Sully goes to the right while I take a sharp left.

"I understand you've reopened the Armstrong's case," this unidentified woman walks up behind me and whispers in my ear.

I turn around. "Excuse me?" I say to this weary, drab-looking, uninspired female.

"Meet me at the café on the corner of Spruce and Pine in thirty minutes," she whispers in my ear. "If you're one minute late, I won't be there."

Before I can look for Sully to let him know I'm leaving, "I'll see you when you get back," he announces as I turn in his direction.

"When you're fifteen minutes early, you're on time. When you're on time, you're late. And if you're late, it's unacceptable." That was my college motto, which I still live by to this very day. I look around for the mysterious woman and don't see anyone that remotely resembles her. I check my watch, more out of habit than anything. After several more minutes, I decide to leave. I hate being sent on wild-goose chases.

"Hey, good-looking, can I buy you cup of coffee?" I hear someone say, which makes me smile. She removes her Foster Grants as her salient blue eyes jump out at me and commands my undivided attention, but as flattered as I am, I'm not here to pick up women.

"No, thank you. I'm waiting for someone," I tell her as I glance around the diner one last time and then proceed toward the front door.

"Whoever she is, she's a fool to let you go," she says, following closely behind.

"Look, miss, I'm really not—"

"Me either," she says, cutting me off. "I needed to make sure you weren't being followed. Don't look so surprised. It's me," she says.

Her look and her wardrobe is the complete opposite from what she look like and was wearing at the Synagogue. "And you are?" I ask as I firmly grab her right elbow. "Because I'm getting sick and tired of this cat-and-mouse game you insist on playing."

"No games," she replies as she jerks freely from my grip. "I had to be sure you weren't being followed and I could trust you. Is this your car?" she asks as she tries to pull on the door handle but is denied access because the doors are locked.

"Who are you? What do you want?" I demand to know.

"My name is Lisa, and that's all I'm saying until we get the hell out of here," she says as she continues to yank harder and harder on the door handle. I click the remote to unlock the car's door before she breaks it. She jumps in and slouches down. She is extremely jumpy and nervous, which doesn't sit well with me.

"It's not safe here! Go, drive!" she demands. I drive for twenty minutes before she begins to relax. I need her calm so she can talk to me.

"You want to tell me what this is all about?"

She is frantic and keeps looking around as if she is being followed.

"Shut up and just keep driving."

"Enough!" I yell as I slam on the brakes and pull off to the side of the road. "What the hell are you doing?"

She yells back, "Keep driving!"

"I'm not going any further until you tell me who you are and what's this is all about, because if you want my help, you're going to start answering some of my questions now!" I threaten. "Now who the hell are you?" I scream.

"I told you my name is Lisa!"

"Lisa who?"

"Lisa Moorland!" she finally says as she sits up and wipes her hair from her face. "You found two bodies about a month ago in Atlantic City, right?"

"Your parents?" I confirm. She nods her head while trying to speak. "Okay," I say. "So what else do you know?"

"I know who killed them," she responds with conviction.

"Who?" I ask inquisitively.

"Eli Weinberg and Carl Goldman," she says without a stammer or a stutter in her voice. Through her tears, her frustration elevates.

"And how do you know that?"

"Because I know the family and I know how they operate. They think they're above the law. This is a small town, Detective, and they have always been major players through their contributions and political connections," she says with vigor and vim in her voice. She is hysterical, and revenge fills her eyes, which is a dangerous combination. She's scared. Her voice cracks when she speaks, and her skin turns a pale, pasty white. Her rambling is incoherent and slurred. She is becoming unglued in front of my eyes and the only thing I can do is drive faster.

"I got proof and I'm going to make those bastards pay!" she continue through her slurs and hysterics. I'm not going to get any useful information from her tonight. I stop with the questions and decide to get her to a safe place.

"Are you hungry?" I ask in an attempt to change the subject until her emotions are calm.

"I haven't eaten in three days," she tells me. "I'm too upset to eat."

We check into a hotel 150 miles south of city limits. After dinner, I thought we would talk, but her body has other plans. I look over toward the couch, and she's fast asleep. I walk over and watch her. Lisa oozes with sexuality from head to toe, but I do not let that distract me. I carry her and place her on the bed and call Sully to update him on everything that has transpired.

In my fifteen years as beat cop and my five years as a detective, no case has affected me as much as this one has. Even with Lita calling off our two-year-planned wedding for a second time isn't affecting me the way this case is.

The alarm on my cell phone wakes us both up from a sound sleep. When I open my eyes, Lisa is cuddled in my arms. We jump frantically. We both begin to apologize to each other. I look at my phone, five missed calls, all from Lita. I can't deal with her now. I need to talk with Lisa while she is calm.

She begins. "A week before they left for Jersey, my parents came to me. They told me they had important information about the law firm of Goldman, Goldman, and Weinberg which could cripple their whole organization," she says as she fixes her hair and adjusts her disheveled clothing.

"Information? Like what?" I ask.

She pulls a letter from her bag and hands it to me. "My mother gave me this the morning before they left." It reads as follows:

My dearest daughter,

First and foremost, please know how much we love you. You have always been the driving force in your father's and my lives. There are some things that we have done in our past, and looking back on it now, we regret. I pray that God, as well as you, will someday find it in your heart to forgive us for our past sins.

Just know that Goldman, Goldman, and Weinberg have committed some heinous crimes against humanity and must be stopped. We will explain everything to you when we return on Saturday.

Love,

Mom and Dad

PS: Please understand that I'd rather be carried by six than judged by twelve.

"What is this?"

"It's proof that that bastard had something to do with my parents' death."

"No, Lisa, it's a note or a semi confession about their and the law's firm past involvement on some crimes against humanity. What crimes is she talking about? What does she mean?"

"Read it again! It's says right there that Carl Goldman and Eli Weinberg are responsible for everything," she says, becoming irate and hysterical, which is the last thing I need again.

"Okay, okay, we'll figure it out later," I tell her. I'm dumbfounded and at a complete loss. I hope Sully is having better luck than I am.

"My parents were some of the most loving, caring people you could ever meet. Whatever illegal activities they are talking about was done strictly under duress," she adds defensively.

"What do you know about the Southside Fertility Clinic?"

"Nothing. Why?" she asks.

I pull out the picture of Paula Manchester. "Have you ever seen this before?" I ask, pointing to the pendant.

She looks at the picture. "Who this?" she asks.

"Lisa, focus on the pendant," I redirect.

"Of course I have. My mother has one just like this. She loved that pendant. Where is it? Can I have it?"

"Lisa, only twelve of these pendants were made, and they were distributed to a select group of women who participated in this fertility study at the Southside Clinic."

"So what does any of that have to do with my parents?"

"I'm saying that if your parents were part of this lucrative fertility study and—"

"Okay, so what? Lots of women have problems conceiving. What's the big deal?"

"It just puts them in a time and place were babies were being brought and sold into this black market baby trafficking ring."

She snickers. "Yeah, right." Her voice is in complete denial. "You are definitely barking up the wrong tree if you think my parents would have ever been involved into something so heinous, ludicrous, just so downright underhanded and dirty. I just told you, my parents were some of the most loving and caring people you could ever meet. Baby trafficking, I don't even know what that is."

"It's—"

"I know what it is! I was just being facetious!" she yells as the tears begin to flow.

My Achilles' heel, a woman's tears. I grab some Kleenex and walk closer to her. She wipes her eyes and then falls into my arms. The early morning light hits her face just at the right spot, and her eyes glistens. I'm mesmerized and completely paralyzed by her beauty. I'm no longer in control over my actions. I lean closer toward her lips and grab her tightly. I'm at the point of no return. I brush her hair back and kiss her as passionately as I can. I hold her tightly, and she holds on tighter. What seems like eternity lasts only a few seconds as she pulls away.

"What are you doing?" she says, which surprises me because she was reciprocating with the same feelings. "You know, last night was the first night I really got a good night's sleep ever since their deaths."

"I can imagine." I listen.

"And I'm really vulnerable and clarity is not my strongest asset at the present moment either," she continues.

I stand there watching her with my hands on my hips. I hear the words coming out of her mouth, but her actions are different. I agree with everything she is saying and she is right, until our eyes meet and never break connection with each other. She is quiet. You can hear our heavy panting and breathing as we slowly walk toward each other. Three seconds feels like three hours as we stare at each other down without saying one word. Before I know it, she leaps into my arms, and we are kissing passionately. She is such a chameleon. Her words say one thing, but her body does another.

She initiates by taking off her shirt first, and I assist her with mine. Stopping is no longer an option for me because I have already crossed the line, which is forbidden and against all the rules and regulations both professionally and personally. When she touches me, all the pain I'm masquerading fills my body, and I react the only way I know how, and the only thing that matters at this point and time is self-satisfaction and sexual gratification.

I meet Sully at Morris's office early the next morning, and from the look on his face, he isn't too happy with me.

"Don't," I say as I hold my hand in front of his face and walk pass him. While Sully is working, I'm fucking around, which makes me feel like grade A shit even more.

Sully also determines that Jonathan and Jade's triplets were brought and sold into this black market ring and at least two of the girls have been adopted.

"The adoption records are sealed, but from what I gathered through Goldman's records are extremely large payments made to the law firm from a Matthew Lovejoy as well as other names," Sully informs me. "And with all their original records from the hospital, it's enough for a search warrant, and this here is a picture of the infamous, Charles Lambert, their grandfather. I found entire portfolios that he has set up in the names of Jordan Armstrong, Jasmine Armstrong, and Jessica Armstrong."

Sully is on a roll nonstop, and though he is a man of very few words, he doesn't hold his tongue when you fuck up. "I told you before, if you need time to deal with this Lita situation, then take it. Otherwise, I need your head back into this," he states and then walks away.

I call in a favor from an old friend of mine, Monica. She is able to get Lisa into protective custody until it's time for the trial. "Thanks, Monica, I owe you one."

"And I will collect," she says seductively.

The Seattle judge issues arrest warrants for Carl Goldman Jr., Eli Weinberg, and all their associates, and knowing Lisa is safe now, Sully and I catch the red eye back to New Jersey. Our plane ends up being delayed, and there is no time for me to go home to shit, shower, and shave with the extradition papers in my hand.

"You know, Chamber's trial starts today," Sully informs me.

"I heard her public defender died. Who's representing her now?"

"Eli is," the Irish bulldog tells me, which makes my mouth fall wide open.

"Step on it," I say to Sully because nothing is going to make me feel better than to personally hand deliver these papers.

The courtroom is like a media circus. Raylene's trial is making news headlines across the country, and I feel bad for her. We stand in the back of the room and observe Eli for a few minutes as he deposes a witness. That is very entertaining to watch. His charismatic ways and the way he struts around the courtroom is a class act. I hand the papers to the court officer, and he brings them to the judge. He looks through the papers and then summons Eli toward his bench.

Raylene's and my eyes meet, and the look of confusion engulfs her entire face. I have no way of preparing her for what is about to transpire. The next sound I hear is Eli yelling and screaming profanity throughout the courtroom. He is quickly subdued by court officers, and the entire room erupts into chaos. Cameras flash at the speed of light, and the jurors are immediately escorted out.

Ten minutes later, they reconvene. "In light of what just occurred, I'm sorry to say that this trial is postponed for forty-eight hours in order to give the defendant time to acquire new counsel," he announces. "Court adjourned," he says as he hits the gravel and bolts through the rear door.

I come back two days later. I feel obligated to be there for Ms. Chambers after her attorney is arrested. With all the evidence the new counsel has, it should have been an open and shut case. Her statement, the doctor's report, and the photos taken on the night in question are presented as evidences and motive, which all end up working against her. She is getting railroaded, and it takes the jury less than forty-five minutes to return with their guilty verdict. She is escorted out in her bright-orange jumpsuit and chains. The entire time sitting there, she has this vacuous expression on her face, and the tears just pour nonstop. I can't believe it myself, and for the first time in my entire career, I feel helpless.

After Raylene's trial, I personally escort Eli back to Seattle. I'm not taking any chances that he will scheme his way out of this one. The day before Christmas Eve, the grand jury hands down their indictments. Eli Weinberg is being charged with twenty-two counts of kidnapping, conspiracy to commit fraud, extortion, and human trafficking and co-conspirator in connection with William and Rita Moorlands' deaths. At his arraignment, the judge orders that he be remanded. Eli surrenders his passport, and bail is denied. Sully and I follow every lead in this case, and it has proven to be one of most bizarre cases I've ever come across.

I'm back in Jersey by New Year's Day, and Raylene's trial is still the topic of conversation on every news channel and water cooler. She is charged with second-degree murder without the possibility of parole. After the verdict, I was worried about her, and I have to see her. I need to see her mental state of mind. I remember what she did to herself the night she was arrested, and how she started hurting herself. This verdict could really push her over the edge, again. I request she is placed on suicide watch. I'm back two days later, and the correction officer on her unit tells me that she has been very withdrawn, and she has isolated herself from the general population. It disturb me greatly to hear that about Ms. Chambers, but nevertheless, I need to talk to her about all the things I recently discovered.

"She mainly stays in her room doing some reading and writing, except for mandatory recreation," he adds.

I know Raylene, and that is not part of her character to be so isolated and intro-verted. She is not that type to suppress her feelings and I recognize she has been to hell and back and that pressure bust pipes, but I have to confront her with my findings and suspicions about who she maybe. "I can only imagine how you must be feeling," I start as an icebreaker.

"You can't imagine shit" is her quick-witted response. "What are you doing here? Haven't you done enough already?" She is surly and salty and it's not my intention to bring her any more hardship, but I need to speak with her, now.

"Raylene, there's been some new discoveries in your case which you should know about." She looks at me but remains quiet. I tell her about Eli's involvement in a black market baby ring, as well as Cornell's and William and Rita Moorlands' connection. She listens and is unresponsive. I continue, "I believe you are one of those missing babies," I finally say. "But I need your help in confirming that."

She laughs at first after listening to such a bazaar story of conspiracy, human-trafficking, and murder after a few more minutes she asks, "And what help do you think I have or can help you with?" she asks while still smiling from ear to ear.

"I would like you to consent to a DNA test so we can determine if you are one of the missing triplets," I say as the smile on her face slowly fades away.

"You are kidding me, right?"

"Look, we just need a sample so we can compare it to the other evidence we have, to see if it's a match," within seconds, she acquiesce and consent to whatever needs to be done.

"I'm tired. I am so tired, and I don't have the energy, time, nor do I care to fight anymore. Can you appreciate what I'm saying, Detective? I don't care! My entire life has been fucked up from the floor up, and now, after all the shit I've been through after twenty years, you're coming here and telling me that I, maybe, part of some elaborate black-market human-trafficking baby ring. Okay, Detective, you do what you feel you need to do or must do," she says before she leaves.

I am determined to help Ms. Chambers find the peace she needs and my heart goes out to her. I've misjudged her all these years, and it never dawned on me that she was in the biggest fight of her life, and before I leave, she provides me with a sample of her DNA, which I immediately send for testing.

Two days later, I'm the keynote speaker for this year's academy graduates. I remember the day I graduated from the academy and how proud I felt. It's a beautiful sunny day, and everything is going well until I see her, which is another piece to the missing puzzle.

She cannot be anyone else but Raylene's missing twin. After the ceremony, I bolt in her direction, pushing, yelling, and screaming at people to move out of the way. "Sorry, sorry, I'm so sorry, excuse me," I yell frantically. "Miss, miss, can I speak to you for a minute. I am completely flabbergasted, and in a million years, I would have never thought something like this would happen to me, of all people."

She finally stops and turns around. I'm up close and personal, and the moment she turns around, our eyes meet. "Oh my god!" I say out loud but unintentionally.

"Detective Sosa, it's a pleasure to meet you, and I really enjoyed your speech. You know, I heard a lot of your success stories at the academy, and your stories gave me such inspiration and hope. It confirmed that I'm doing the right thing." She talks and talks, but all I hear is blah, blah, blah, because I'm mesmerized. It's unbelievable enough that this twenty-year-old case has fell into my lap, but to have her twin sister sitting in a graduation class, which I happened to be the key-note speaker to, this is downright intriguing all the way around. Her resemblance to Ms. Chambers completely blows my mind. She's an exact duplicate, and to have her sitting right here in a police academy graduation class is nothing but a God-given blessing.

"And I hope I can have a career as successful as yours," is the last audible thing I hear with clarity.

"Thank you," I say abruptly, hoping that I wasn't being rude. "And please forgive my boldness but, do you have a twin sister?" I ask. She seems a bit taken aback by my question but I continue. "Is there a place where we can sit and talk?

Maybe I can buy you a cup of coffee or something to drink. It's all arbitrary anyway," I add and then realizes I'm rambling, which is something Lita says I do when I get excited. "Anyway, it's imperative that we talk," I say as I continue to stare.

"Is everything all right, and why are you looking at me like that?"

I need to get a grip of myself. "Yes, yes, please forgive me. I'm so sorry, Ms. . . ."

"Jessica, Jessica Lovejoy," she says.

"Lovejoy?" I repeat.

"Yes."

I hold up my hand. "Excuse me for a moment," I say as I turn and dial Sully's number. "What were the names of the three payments made to Goldman, Goldman, and Weinberg?" I ask my partner.

"Lovejoy. Matthew and Vivian Lovejoy," he confirms.

I can't stop smiling because the odds of finding two thirds of a trio twenty years later is astronomical. I impress upon her the severity of getting together, soon.

"Detective, you're really beginning to scare me. What is this all about?"

I sigh and then escort her over to a more secluded area. "Ms. Lovejoy, are your parents' names Matthew and Vivian?" I ask as delicately as I know how. Pure confusion fills her eyes.

"Yeah, how did you know that?"

"Are they here?"

"Unfortunately no, they are not exactly a fan of my decision to pursue law enforcement," she tells me. There was sorrow in her eyes and tone.

"No worries. My mom wasn't a fan of my decision either. She wanted me to become a lawyer, of all things, can you believe that? Do you mind if I ask you one more question?"

She slowly moves her head up and down. I look toward my left and then toward my right. I pull out my cell phone from my breast pocket and scroll to the picture of Raylene. Her reaction to seeing the picture was unusual to me. She looks at the photo, rolls her eyes, and hands my phone back to me.

"We've met," she says reluctantly. "Not the most affable person I've ever met."

"So you two met?" I say more as a statement than a question. She did not seem too surprised by the fact she had a-look-a-like. Now my curiosity was piqued.

"So how long have you known about her?" I ask her.

"Not long, I did not know anything about her until I'd seen the article about her killing that man. I mean, yes, of course I was surprised to see someone with the same face as mine. That's why I went to see her, but things did not go well. She was, she was just so angry, and she refused to believe me when I told her my name was Jessica. Then she had the audacity to ask me if I had two hundred and fifty thousand dollars to bail her out of jail," she snickers. "Can you believe that?

Finally, she tells me, if I did not have any money to bail her out, then I should leave and don't come back."

"I've known Ms. Chambers for a long time, and I'm awfully familiar with her anger issues you are referring to, and I can assure you, it's not personal," I tell her, which I hope help to ease her discomfort. "Are you aware of another sister?" I ask her.

"Another sister? God, no, I've just learned about this sister," she replies, and before I can ask another question, I hear my name being called. I turn around and see Lita running towards me. I quickly turn back towards Ms. Lovejoy. "It is imperative that we speak," I say as I hand her my business card and ask her to call me ASAP.

"Lawrence!" Lita calls. "Why haven't you returned any of my calls?" she says as she tries to fix her hair and clothing which became disarray from running towards me.

"What the hell are you doing here?"

"I've been calling you! Why haven't you returned any of my calls?" she repeats.

"Lita, what are you doing here?" I repeat the question. I'm not pleased, impressed, or smiling, and I'm not going to just let it go like I've done so many times in the past.

"How have you been?" she asks seductively. "I know, I know, but . . . it's just that . . . you know . . . I was mad, and you know when I get mad, I tend to say things I don't mean, and it wasn't my intention to call off the wedding, and you never called me back and, and I still want to marry you. You know that, right? Look, I can see you're busy right now, and I didn't mean to interrupt, but I'm asking you, please, if you can call me when you're done so we can talk, just talk like we use to. Okay? Do you think that's something you might be open to doing?" she says as she stutters over her words.

I walk closer toward her and gently place my arm around her waist. I know this is a hard thing for her to do because Lita never admits when she has made a mistake, but if she seriously thinks I'm going to trust her again, she's sadly mistaken. It isn't my intention to hurt her, but it's not my intention to give her false hope.

"Lita, stop," I whisper in her ear. "I care about you too much to see you like this, but I'm done, and the only thing I want from you is my engagement ring back," I tell her as I remove my hand from her waist and turn and walk away.

Jessica

My Name Is Jessica

I'm excited because Detective Lawrence Sosa is this year's guest speaker at our graduation ceremony. He speaks so eloquently about his love and passion for law enforcement that it brings solace for my parents not being there. I'll never forget his poignant words of encouragement: "Let all men and women lead with valor and dignity. Let every new brave soul be the driving force for generations to come in both their professional and personal lives, and finally, let every new cadet that chooses a life/career in law enforcement lead with compassion, understanding, and patience, and let's not be quick to prejudge individuals who are different from us."

I feel so renewed and inspired, and I haven't felt this good in a long time. As I'm leaving, I hear someone yelling in my direction, "Excuse me, excuse me . . ." As I turn around, I see Detective Sosa running toward me. I can't understand his urgency, but my curiosity is piqued, and come to find out that he wants to know if I know Raylene. I tell him that I've met her but it hasn't gone so well.

"Please, please, it's imperative that we speak more," he tells me as he hands me his business card. "Please call me," he says as he turns and walks away with this lady.

Two days later, I'm sitting back in front of her and we are divided by a two-inches of plexie glass. Ten minutes has passed and she still hasn't come. I go to see what the delay is. "Just take a seat. She's on her way," the guard abruptly advises. Sharp pains start shooting through my side and into my stomach. I have this unsettling feeling like I want to throw up, and the last time I felt this way, I was confronting my father. I take deep breaths and look around. God, I can never be locked up. I wonder what her cell is like. Thought after thought run through my mind, but before another thought can enter, the rear door flows wide open, and she walks in.

"What the hell do you want now? I thought I told you not to come back," she yells in an attempt to intimidate me, but my defenses are up, and I'm not going to let her verbally attack me again.

She is different today, a little more subdued, not as hostile like before. "What do you want?" she humbly says again.

"I met Detective Sosa the other day," I tell her.

"And what do you want from me, a medal?" she replies.

"Some respect would be nice, but I'll settle for some answers," I say to her. She is silent, which gives me the green light to continue.

"He asked me if I know anything about another sister," I tell her.

"Robyn," she says and then pauses. "So you're really not Robyn," she says as revelation sets in.

Shaking my head, I repeat, "No, I'm really not Robyn." She slouches back in her seat in total amazement and forms no words. She closes her eyes and takes a couple of deep breaths.

"Do you know where I can find her?" I ask reluctantly.

She slowly opens her eyes. "Sorry, no, I don't know where she is. She came here with some man named Alex."

"Does she know about me?" I ask.

"Hell, if I know! I didn't know anything about you so I can't speak on what she does or does not know," she adds as she sits there with her arms folded.

I scream into the air out of pure frustration. I feel defeated and alone, and I don't know what I should do next. After a few seconds, I jump to my feet. "Who is Alex?" I ask.

"He's a friend of Big Daddy. Alex something. I can't remember his last name. Look, go talk to Amanda. She stays in contact with their friend Black. Maybe he can tell where to find Alex."

I turn and walk back to my seat. Our eyes stay lock to each other until I am completely seated. The notion of going back to Philly was bad enough, but to have to go back and ask Amanda for any kind of help was downright dreadful.

"What's the matter?" Raylene asks as she looks at my face.

"Damn, am I that conspicuous?" I ask.

"You don't like Amanda, do you?" she blurts.

"Is it that obvious?"

"It's written all over your face," she replies as we start to laugh.

"Trust and believe Amanda's bark is bigger than her bite, and the best way to deal with her is not to back down. You have to let her know that she puts no fear in your heart," she tells me. Raylene starts spilling all the "T" about Amanda Adams and the other girls. It's the breakthrough needed in our relationship. I was beginning to understand her, and she was beginning to accept me. We found our sisterly bond. Hours passed before the guard comes in and announces that visiting hours are now over.

"Can I come back and see you again?" I ask Raylene.

"I'll be mad at you if you don't," she responds.

I'm feeling renewed after my visit with her. I know what I have to do now. I'm going to find this girl, and if that means dealing with Amanda's ass again, then that's what I'm going to do. The things Raylene has told me about her has my mouth on the floor, but like Detective Sosa said in his speech, let's not be quick to prejudge individuals who are different from us.

I arrive at the Do Drop Inn around 5:00 p.m., and it is desolate, I see the DJ coming from the back room.

"Excuse me but do you know where I can find Amanda or Carly or Bre?" I ask.

"Did you try upstairs in the penthouse?" he says as he points toward the elevator.

I graciously smile and walk towards the elevator when he says, "It's crazy how life goes sometimes, isn't it?"

"Excuse me?" I respond.

"I'm just saying you lived your entire life thinking you're this person just to find out you're someone totally different," he says and then walks away laughing, but I don't find anything funny. When I get to the top floor, I'm looking around, and no one is home. My frustration builds, I'm tired, and I'm a long way from home. I decide to leave.

While I'm waiting for my Lyft to arrive, I retrieve Detective Sosa's business card from my purse. As I'm dialing the number, this man walks up to me.

"Boo," he says as he snatches my cell from my hands and begins to laugh. "Who are you calling and where is Alex?" he says out of the blue. I haven't got a clue who he is, but evidently he thinks he knows who I am. "Robyn, what the hell are you doing down here, and where's Alex?" he says again.

"Umm, I not sure . . ."

"You do realize my brother is married?" he continues and begins to laugh harder. I can't imagine what the hell is so funny. He takes one step closer to me. I take one step away from him. He insists on being up close and personal, which makes me uncomfortable, and he talks so much and so fast, I can't get a word in edgewise. I try several times to tell him I'm not Robyn.

"Listen, I came here for dinner. Care to join me?" he insists as he opens the door and I reenter through the same door I just exited from.

"Hey, Russell, baby," I hear this female voice say as she sashays herself between us. "You said you would call me." I step back to give them plenty of room and all the privacy she wants. I get the feeling she's trying to make me jealous or something, and for the life of me, I don't know why.

"Hey, Tammy, baby," he says as he grabs her and squeezes her butt. "You know I'm going to call your fine ass real soon. I still got your number," he tells her as he embraces her and winks at me. I frown.

"You better," she says and then looks back at me and walks away.

He's obnoxious, arrogant, and supercilious. A real practical joker, but I don't think he is funny at all.

"Look, Russell, I'm not—" I try to say again, but he interjects.

"Hungry! Nonsense, you have to eat! Besides, Alex will not mind," he adamantly insists, "Look, as soon as we are finished, I will personally take you home, excuse me, to my brother's house. Besides Alex will not mind," he adamantly insists, "Look, as soon as we are finished, I will take you home, excuse me, to my brother's house." Boy, this could not have worked out any better if I planned it.

"So what's the real deal with you and Alex?" he asks me as we're waiting to be seated.

"Real deal," I repeat as the waiter approaches us.

"Table for two, Mr. Taylor?" he asks as he escorts us to a very secluded table in the corner of the room. I watch his hands, because I don't trust him, as he pulls my seat out for me and then flashes me a devilish grin.

"What, you don't trust me? Alex is my baby brother, and we talk all the time," he stresses. I'm resolute on saying as little as possible. "And I'm sure someone as young and fine as you knows how to show a brother a real good time," he says to me as he licks his lips, which repulses me even more. He starts telling me his whole life story. "I'm forty-two. I do carpentry on the side. You know, more as a hobby than a living. I have five sons, but I don't think that last one is mine. Time will tell," he says and then laughs again.

The waiter brings a bottle of wine to our table. "Excellent," he says to him. "Give us a moment." The waiter looks at him and then at me and then walks away. "I'm nothing like Alex, you know. Anne didn't spare the rod when it came to my black ass, not like she did with Alex," he continues, which sounds like pure jealousy to me. "You know, I actually met Jacqueline first." He then goes off on this tirade. I have no idea what he is talking about. After a few minutes, I call his name, and he is focused again.

"I'm sorry," he says as he waves for the waiter to come back over. "I'll just take the liberty and order for the both of us. I'm hungry as shit!" He colorfully adds, "The best chefs in town work right here, you know."

"No, I didn't know that."

"We'll have the salmon in the butter herb sauce with potato au gratin and asparagus. Oh, and the house salads for the both of us please," he tells the waiter and hands him back the menus.

I don't utter a word. I just sit there and listen to him talk and make more of a jackass of himself than he already has. He starts and ends every sentence and conversation with you know. "You know, this is an exclusive club. It's for members only, you know." He talks nonstop through the whole meal, and I want to scream. He is acting like he is some big shot around here, giving orders to everyone. "Anybody who is somebody comes here. It's the hottest spot in Philly, you know.

Have you been to the club upstairs?" he asks and actually shuts up long enough for me to answer.

"Yes, a few weeks ago," I tell him.

"I bet you didn't know there was a restaurant down here," he says. "Do you know of any other place that serves seafood, French and Italian cuisine, and soul food?" He once again licks his lips as if it's turning me on. "Everyone comes here."

The waiter brings our plates. "Can I get you anything else, Mr. Taylor?"

"You need anything?" Russell asks me.

I turn in the waiter's direction. "I'm fine. Thank you."

"That'll be all," he says laughingly toward the waiter in a dismissive tone and manner.

"So you're a carpenter?" I ask while he has his mouth stuffed with a piece of butter roll. He nods yes and then takes a sip of wine.

"And you can afford to eat here?" I state more as question than a compliment.

"Well, it helps when your brother is part owner," he says and then snaps his fingers toward the waiter for him to come back.

"Yes, sir," the waiter asks.

"Can I have some fresh pepper?" he orders. Russell is ordering the staff around like slaves, and I'm not impressed one bit. I hated asking Rose to do anything for me, although she didn't mind, but as I got older, I did it for myself. Russell is nothing but a scrub. A pompous, arrogant wannabe riding on his brother's coattail. I don't know who this Alex person is, but it seems like he's done okay for himself, and it's sad as hell that he has such a leech for a brother. If there's one thing my father instilled in me at an early age, it's the value of your labor not being in vain, and Russell is the complete opposite of a man who works hard for the finer things in life.

"Right away, sir."

His narcissistic behavior is making me sick to my stomach, and I can't eat my food. I'm not hungry anyway. He finally stops talking long enough to realize I'm not eating.

"Something wrong with your food?" He points to my plate with his fork.

I'm about to say it isn't the food, it's the company, but decline. "No," I say.

"Don't get me wrong," he continues out of the blue, "I could have opened up my own restaurant too if I pushed a shitload of drugs into my community like my brother did."

"What is it they say, don't hate the player, hate the game," I respond.

Two hours later, we are still here and most of my time is spent me trying to deflect and ignore all of his rude behavior and sexual comments. It takes all I have in me not to slap him across his face. The waiter watches me from the corner of the room. I want to scream "Help!" I manage to eat a little something, and it is delicious.

Finally he is ready to leave. "Hope to see you again," the waiter whispers to me as he smiles and hands me my doggie bag.

"Likewise," I reply and smile back.

It is 9:00 p.m. before we finally leave the restaurant. "Alex lives ten minutes away," he tells me walking toward his car, but two hours after that, we still haven't arrived. He keeps making all these little incidental stops, which annoys me, getting in and out of the car talking to people. He even brings a couple of them to the car and introduces them to me, which for the life of me I can't figure out why.

It is well after 11:00 p.m. before he pulls in front of Alex's house as he lays on the car's horn. The blatant cacophony of the car's horn brings Alex as well as his neighbors running out their houses and onto their front porch.

"Damn you, Russell, cut the shit!" Alex yells at him while apologizing to his neighbors for his brother's rude behavior.

Russell laughs. "Wait here," he says and hops out the car.

I wait for a few minutes. I watch as Alex and Russell do a lot of talking and pointing toward the car. Finally he motions me to get out. I step out of the passenger's side and walk toward the house. Alex's mouth drops wide open.

"Hi, my name is Jessica," I say and extend my hand. "And I'm looking for Robyn."

The look on Russell's face is priceless, and I don't feel bad for deceiving him.

"I tried to tell you my name wasn't Robyn, but you wouldn't shut up long enough for me to say anything. Besides, I really needed to find Robyn," I say to Russell.

Now Alex is laughing and then opens the door. "Oh, how sweet it is. That sounds just like my brother. Never knows when to shut the fuck up," he says as he escorts me in the house and stops Russell from following.

"Is he going to be all right?" I ask Alex as I peek at Russell through the window. He is standing there with his mouth half-open.

"Don't worry about him, he is going to be just fine," Alex says, "So you said your name is Jessica. This is so unbelievable, triplets, my god. Robyn is going to be so surprised but happy to see you. How did you find Russell?" he asks as I make myself comfortable on his living room couch, and from the moment I step inside, I feel a familiarity in his home, a warm, caring atmosphere just like my home. I know someone put a lot of love into turning this house into a home.

"You have a beautiful home," I tell him.

"Thank you. So I take it you've met Raylene," he says.

I nod my head yes. "She didn't believe me at first either when I told her my name was Jessica."

"Wow, this is just so, it's just so incredible," he says over and over again. "I'm sorry, can I get you something to eat or drink? I know it's late but . . . ," he says excitedly.

"No, I'm fine. As a matter of fact, we just finished having dinner at your club."

"Oh, I hope—" he starts to say.

"Everything was delicious, excluding the present company at that time," I tell him. We both laugh.

"My condolences for that, but this is so amazing," he says as he shakes his head in disbelief. "Robyn is going to be so surprised to see you. She's right upstairs asleep. Let me get her for you," he says as he starts up the stairs.

"Wait," I blurt out as he turns and walks back toward me.

"You're shaking. Are you all right?" he asks.

"I'm just not sure how she's going to react. I mean, this is all happening so fast, and I'm sure she's going to have a thousand questions that I don't have any answers for. My first encounter with Raylene wasn't the best, and I don't have the strength to go fifteen rounds with anyone else," I tell him through my nerves.

He smiles. "I completely understand where you're coming from. Look, it's late anyway, and I'm sure you're tired, both mentally and physically. There's no rush. After all, it's been twenty years, what's one more night? I can tell you one thing, you have nothing to worry about with Robyn because she always wondered about her biological parents," he says to me.

I like Alex, he is easy to talk to. I sleep in the guest bedroom. Early the next morning, I hear a knock on the bedroom door.

"Good morning," he says. "How did you sleep? Robyn is already downstairs in the kitchen. I didn't mention anything to her, and I'm making breakfast."

I follow closely behind him as the muscles in my stomach start to constrict and tighten. I feel like I'm going to throw up. I take deep breaths.

He turns toward me. "Relax, everything is going to be just fine," he reassures me once again. "Robyn," he calls. "Someone is here to see you." I can see her reflection off the glass cabinets. Her hair is in two ponytails, and she looks exactly like me as he moves to the side. I step forward.

She takes one look at me and then blurts, "You bailed her out of jail?"

"No, no, no you don't understand! I'm not Raylene!" I exclaim as I slowly walk closer toward her. I can't take my eyes off her—another exact duplicate.

"I understand just fine, but what I can't understand is why the hell Alex would bail you out of jail."

"Robyn, this isn't Raylene, and I didn't bail her out of jail," Alex begins to explain.

"Yeah right, Alex," she says. "If she isn't Raylene, then who the hell is she?"

"My name is Jessica, Jessica Lovejoy," I answer.

"Holy shit," she says and then faints.

"Robyn!" Alex calls as he runs to her aid. "Get me a cold rag!" he screams toward me.

After a few minutes, she opens her eyes. "What happened?" she says, still slightly dazed.

"You fainted," he tells her. "Why?"

"I don't know. I am feeling light-headed. I just need something to eat and I'll be fine," she tells him as she tries to stand to her feet. She hit her head extremely hard, and I think she should at least be examined by a doctor.

"I'm so sorry, Alex," she apologizes again.

"Are you sure you're all right?" Alex asks her. "And stop apologizing. You have nothing to be sorry for," he tells her.

I can see he is very caring and loving towards her. I suggest again for her to be examined, "Just to be on the safe side," I add, Alex agrees.

"I don't need a doctor," she refutes. "Nothing like this has ever happened to me before." Her skin is flushed, and she is sweating.

"No, Jessica is right. I'm taking you to the hospital," Alex insists as he runs upstairs to get dressed.

"I'm fine!" she yells. "Besides, I don't have any insurance. It was just the shock of seeing her!" she yells up the stairs.

Within in twenty minutes, we are sitting in the emergency room. "My friend needs to be seen," he says to the triage nurse.

"Okay, sir, what seems to be the problem?"

"Nothing!" Robyn yells.

"Look, she passed out. Out of the blue," he tells her.

"And she hit her head pretty hard," I add, which causes her to stare me down.

The nurse motions Robyn to come with her as she directs Alex to the register desk. There is a look of worry that engulfs his face, and I don't have any words of comfort for him.

"She doesn't have any insurance," I hear him say. "Just use this," he says and throws his credit card on the desk. Alex and I take a seat in the waiting area.

Thirty minutes later, the triage nurse retrieves us from the lobby. "You may see your friend now, and the doctor will be in shortly."

"Thank you," Alex says as he rushes by Robyn's side. Alex reminds me of a slightly younger version my father. His caring and protective ways is exact duplicate of Matthew Lovejoy.

"Robyn, are you okay?" he says as he sits at her bedside and holds her hand.

A moment later the doctor walks in. "Mr. Richards . . ."

"Taylor," Alex corrects him.

"Okay, well, we were able to narrow down the source of what's ailing her. I'm afraid she's pregnant," the doctor announces. Alex's eyes bulge to the size of golf balls as he looks at Robyn. She drops her head and doesn't say a word.

"I'll give you a moment," the doctor says as he exits the room. I don't know if I should follow him or stay put.

After a few minutes, Alex says, "Were you going to tell me, Robyn?"

"There's nothing to tell. I just assumed my period would have been here by the end of the month. It's not like I've never been late before."

I clear my throat. "I should wait outside," I offer because I'm not sure what the hell is going on between those two, nor do I want to know.

"Yes," Alex says. "No," Robyn says simultaneously. I look toward Alex. He is annoyed but then agrees with Robyn, "No, Robyn is right. This is not the time or place to have this conversation. We'll talk about this later."

Seconds later, the doctor enters. "Everything okay?" he says as he looks at each one of us and then continues, "My nurse here has some pamphlets for your options."

"Options?" Alex quickly retorts. "What fucking options are you talking about, Doc?" he says as he snatches the brochures from the nurse's hands. They are pamphlets on abortion and adoption. Alex quickly becomes enraged.

"Get this shit out of here!" he yells. "What do I look like, some punk-ass nigga that can't take care of his responsibilities? If she was white, would you have given her the same literature, or would you have been edifying her on some prenatal and breastfeeding shit? Look, the best thing you can do right now is discharge her and get the fuck out of my way!" Alex screams and then storms out the room.

The doctor gives the nurse instructions and then leaves. The nurse tells Robyn to get dressed as she gives her, her discharge papers. Alex is waiting for us in the car, and we're on our way back to his house. No one utters one word the whole way there.

Alex
Your Ass Committed Adultery

What the hell is going on? Momma is dead, Jacqueline is gone, Robyn has twin sisters, and she's pregnant! How the hell did I fuck up my life this bad? Finding out Robyn is pregnant just takes me over the edge. I'm thirty-eight years old, and the one and only child that I had is dead and gone. I'm not prepared to do this baby thing all over again. I thought Robyn was on the pill or on some type of protection. How can she do this to me? She is the one person I trusted unconditionally, and the thought of Robyn getting pregnant on purpose is not setting well with me, or my soul, and the only other person who I would have confided in, my mother, is dead as well. I fall to my knees and scream as loud as I can.

I've never stopped loving my wife, and I don't want her to leave me, but ever since Alexis died, she changed. She withdrew from me when I needed her most. I tried to explain about Robyn, and I begged and pleaded with her to stay.

We've been married for fifteen years, and we've had our share of trials and tribulations, but we've always worked them out in the past. Jacqueline already had one daughter, Sharon, when we met, and she left too. I haven't spoken to Robyn or Jessica in two days since we've come home from the hospital, but I need to collect myself and find out what is going on. I walk toward Lexie's room where I last left the girls. I press my ear against the door, but I do not hear any voices. I go downstairs and look around and do not see them. I grab my phone and start to dial when they come walking through the front door.

"Hey," Robyn says.

"Hey," I respond back. "You girls all right?" I ask out of concern. Robyn continues upstairs without saying another word.

"Yeah, we're fine," Jessica tells me as she follows after her.

I know Robyn and I must talk but I have no idea where to start or what to say. I pick up my phone and call Jacqueline, there is no answer, so I leave a message. I call again and my mother-in-law refuses to let me speak with her as well.

Later on that evening, I smell a pot of fresh brewed coffee being brewed. I go into the kitchen, and Robyn is there making something to eat. "We need to talk," I say to her.

"There's nothing for us to talk about," she responds.

"Robyn, please," I say as I grab for her hand. She pulls away.

"No, Alex, you blame me. You think I got pregnant on purpose, don't you? Don't you?"

I nod my head yes. "But I thought you were on the pill."

"And I thought you had a vasectomy?" she retorts.

"Why would you assume that?" I ask, offended by her candid comment.

"The same reason you assumed I was on the pill, stupidity," she says.

She snickered as she starts to go back upstairs and then retreats back towards the kitchen.

"Well you please stop running away from me and talk to me!" I insist.

"Then talk," she says as she places her drink and sandwich on the countertop and folds her arms.

"Okay, yes, I believe you got pregnant on purpose," I confess.

"On purpose? Did I fuck myself, Alex?" she responds with her slick-ass mouth.

"It's just that I did the baby thing already and now she's dead, not to mention I'm thirty-eight years old and married."

"Alex, were you thinking about your wife when you were fucking me in that hotel, huh? Because from where I was lying, it looked like you didn't give a shit about Jacqueline. But now, all of sudden, you're bucking to be husband of the year, really? Why, Alex? What changed? Oh, the fact that I'm pregnant, that's what changed! When I first met you, what, I was thirteen. You wanted to be my hero, Alex. You wanted to rescue me, and I was excited because you seemed to genuinely care about my black ass. I remember the first time you ever made love to me, I was what, seventeen, and I was like damn, and Hakeem was nothing like that. And yeah, you always check in on me whenever you came into town after that; and I never forgot that night. Now, here we are, damn near three years later, and I run into at a bank, of all places, closing out my account, and you give me this pep talk about being my own person. What was it you said, 'Stop listening and giving dumbass motherfuckers who don't give two shits about you, or the horse you rode in on, your energy!' My only problem is, I did not think that you would be, one of those dumb- ass -mother- fuckers! Damn- it Alex, I trusted you!" she retorts. Do you recall all the things you said to me while you were eating my pussy and fucking my brains out in that hotel room? Do you, Alex? And now you are trying to act brand new, on me, of all people!" Those were the last words she utters to me before she goes back upstairs.

My phone rings. It's Jacqueline. She's returning my call.

"Hello . . . yeah, sure. I can do that." I pick up my keys and head out the front door. A half hour later, I'm standing on my mother-in-law's front porch. Jacqueline opens the front door, and there's my wife looking as lovely as ever.

"Hi," I say.

She grunts a soft "Hello." Her defenses are still up as well. She has on the royal-blue satin nightgown I bought for her, which literally takes my breath away. She is more beautiful than I remember.

"I know it's getting late, but I really need to talk to you."

"Is your bitch-ass girlfriend still in my house?" she asks.

"Jackie."

"Jackie my ass. Answer my question, Alex!" she yells.

"Yes, yes, she's still there."

"Then there isn't anything for us to talk about, Alex," she says as she starts to close the door in my face. I have to think quickly.

"But she's leaving and I miss you and I want you to come back home. I've been a jerk and—"

"And that's an understatement," she says and holds her hand up so I'll stop talking.

"What are you doing, Alex? What the hell are you doing? What kind of mind games are you trying to play with me? Did you think I was kidding when I told you I would not allow you or that girl to disrespect me any longer? Damn it, Alex, you know how to love me! Why would you even put yourself out there like that? You let this girl make a fool of you, and for what? Some tight pussy?" my wife says to me without a blink of an eye.

In our fifteen years of marriage, this is the first time she is so resolute in her decision. I used to be able to sweet talk her, and she would always give in. Not this time. I've noticed this inner strength in her. I've never seen that before. This is a turning point in our marriage, and to be quite frank, it is turning me on, and I respect it.

"'You Know How to Love Me' by Phyllis Hyman," I blurt out in desperation.

"What?" she says.

"That was the song that was playing when we first met, remember?" I say.

She smiles and nods her head yes. "But what does that have to do with anything?" she asks as she begins to soften.

"A lot, because you should know that I'll never love anyone the way I love you," I say to her as I grab her hands. "You've got to believe me, I was just trying to help her. Yes, I may have overstepped my boundaries, and I see that now."

"She's practically half your age, for God's sake!"

"Okay, I'm sorry. I made a mistake. I'll send her to Verdine's house like I had planned on doing from the beginning."

"A mistake is putting too much salt on your fries. Your black ass committed adultery! That's a sin!" Jacqueline yells and then looks around to see if anyone is behind her.

"Babe, please . . ."

"No . . . no, I can't do this right now. I thought I could, but I'm standing in my pajamas, talking to my husband, at my mother's house. How pathetic is that? You just don't get it. You've humiliated me. You were my world, and I've given you my best, and it wasn't good enough. You threw it right back in my face. I have nothing left. Lexie is dead, your mother is dead, and the only man I've ever loved is sleeping with a girl young enough to be his daughter! You've done something to me that I've never ever thought you, you of all people, would do to me. You hurt me! How am I supposed to recover from that?" she asks while pounding on her chest with her fist, which brings tears to my eyes.

"Baby, honey, please, I'm begging you, you have to give me a chance to make things right because I need you and I love you," I say. I step closer toward my wife, and I gently grab her face with both my hands. I look deep into her eyes and slowly start to kiss her.

She starts to resist. "Stop," she says.

"I was stupid." I kiss her left cheek. "I'm a damn fool." I kiss her right cheek. "But losing you is something I'm not prepared for," I say as I finalize it with a long, hard passionate kiss on her luscious lips. She is just as turned on as I am. We stand there for a moment panting and looking at each other.

She pulls away. "If you truly love me, like you claim you do, then you know what to do. I'm your wife, Alex, and somewhere along the way, you've seemed to have forgotten that," she tells me in this soft but surreal tone as she slowly closes the door in my face.

Jessica
Approved for Visitation

Part 1

I talked to Tamara, and she tell me that my mother has been by my place several times looking for me and she's worried. "Well, she doesn't have to worry about me. I'm fine," I tell her.

"Where are you, Jessica?" she asks as well. "We don't talk anymore, and I'm beginning to feel like…" and then she stops talking.

She is right, I have changed. These past few days, I have learned so much about myself and the truth is, Tamara isn't an essential part, to this part of my life, but she still is important to me. This is personal for me, and it's something I need to do. I just wish she can understand that there are other matters that need my undivided attention now.

"Look, I'll be home soon, and we'll talk then," I tell her, hoping that will satisfy her concern and curiosity.

The past couple of days have been pure chaos here, but it has given Robyn and I time to talk, which is good for us. When Alex comes back home, I ask him if he'll take us to see Raylene again.

"That's a good idea." He calls his warden buddy, and within a matter of seconds, we're in the car. Alex never says a word the whole drive down. It seems as though he is preoccupied about something because he literally drops us off in front of the prison. "I'll be back around four," he says before he speeds away. I look at Robyn she drops her head and doesn't say a word. We stand there a minute longer looking at one another, and after a few more minutes of awkwardness, we head in.

"We're here to see Raylene Chambers," Robyn says to the guard as we approach the front desk.

"Yes, your all clear for visitation. She's already in the visitors' center waiting for you."

I don't know what Alex said to the warden, but this time Robyn and I are given red carpet treatment, and I wasn't treated anything like before.

She is sitting there just like the guard said, and every time I see her, she looks different. She has an inner glow about her, which seems peaceful, and she is actually smiling.

"Well, ain't this a pleasant surprise," she says.

"I think so, and that's why we came to see you again. You know, talk, maybe try and figure this out," I say to the both of them. I look toward Robyn as she sits there with her arms and legs folded.

"Speak for yourself," she says and then mumbles something else that I can't hear. Robyn isn't as enthused about our reunion as I am, and I realize she has other issues she's dealing with, but this is important too. I hope her disposition doesn't rub off on Raylene either because they both have a little more attitude than I like to put up with. I find it best not to feed into either one of them anymore than I have to.

"Anyway," I sigh as I continue, focusing all my attention towards Raylene. "I was hoping by now, once we have met and since we are here… maybe, the three of us could try and figure what happened to us. Why and how we got separated. I mean, aren't you even curious? Wouldn't you like to know?

"And how do you propose we do that?" Raylene asks while keeping her eyes locked on Robyn as well.

"Well, I was thinking I would just ask my parents," I tell them both.

"What the hell is wrong with her?" Raylene finally asks.

"I don't know, lack of fiber I guess," I say and then laugh at my own joke. Raylene laughs too, which helps break some of the tension that seems to be lingering in the room.

Robyn
Approved for Visitation

Part 2

Jessica thinks her little fiber joke is funny. I do not. My world has been turned upside fucking down, and she's worried about having a family reunion, twenty years too late.

I'm scared and I'm alone, and the one person whom I trust with my very life has now flipped the script. Truth is, I haven't been feeling well for the past couple of days. Besides the fact that my period was late did have me a little concerned, but never in my wildest dreams would I have thought I was pregnant. Hakeem and I had done it plenty of times without protection, and I never got pregnant.

Alex isn't talking to me, and I have no idea what he's thinking or plans to do. Jessica is right as well, this is important too, and although the three of us may look exactly alike, we are as different as morning, noon, and night.

"So do you think they're going to tell you the truth?" I finally say as they stop laughing.

"Of course. Why wouldn't they?" Jessica responds.

"Well, they lied to you for the past twenty years, as you can see. Why should they start telling the truth now?" I say, which wipes the rest of the smirk from her face.

"She has a point," Raylene interjects.

"You and Raylene may have some grand illusions about talking to your parents, who evidently didn't want us in the first place, and then what? What's supposed to happen after that? Are we going to be reunited like Peaches and fucking Herb? No thanks, I'll pass, plus the fact I have more important things to worry about now," I blatantly tell the both of them.

Mixed emotions take over every part of my being. How could I have let myself get played like this again? Why would Alex, of all people, do this to me? What am I going to do now? Where am I going to live now, ugh! I'm trying to hold it together; I'm screaming internally because these two are staring me down. "What?" I finally scream at them. "What the hell are you staring at?"

Raylene
Approved for Visitation

Part 3

These past six months have been mad crazy for me, and this entire concept of being a triplet is foreign as hell. It's going to take some time for me to adjust to the fact that there are two other people on this earth that looks exactly like me. I've never been an emotional person because Big Daddy has instilled in me that emotions are a sign of weakness. I'm not a weak person, but my eyes begin to fill with tears with the thought that I have real blood relatives out here. I fight hard to hold back my tears because I don't like being vulnerable, especially in front of people.

I can see Robyn is dealing with her own demons as well, although I can't imagine what is more troublesome than this.

"You're probably right," I say. "Our past is our past, and this is my future now," I say to them. "This is my reality now, and I'm in this hellhole for something that wasn't my fault," I say as the floodgates begin to open, but I intercept them with my sleeve.

"He always said crying was for suckers and it's a sign of weakness," I tell them as I begin to quote every despicable thing Big Daddy has ever said to me, then I catch myself.

"What happened?" is the only thing she needs to say, and the race is on. Once I start talking, I can't stop. I start from day 1, my first recollection. "I was seven years old the first time I laid eyes on him, and from that moment on, my life has been a living hell."

I start recalling memories I thought I buried. Memories I never shared with my therapist, and there is no turning back now. I open up to my unknown siblings like flowers blooming in springtime. Their mouths stay wide open. That's how I know I have their undivided attention. They sit there and listen to every word that comes out of my mouth without interruption or judgment.

"He was a ruthless bastard and I was so scared of him." I smirked. "Wow, that's the first time I've ever said that. But nonetheless, he was there. He loved to read, and he didn't read junk either. He only read business articles and autobiographies. You'll never believe that I've read the autobiographies of Ms. Jane Pittman and Harriet Tubman and the Miseducation of the Black Man," I tell them.

"They're really good books," Jessica adds.

"I was the first girl he brought home and it wasn't long after that, that he started bringing in other girls, that he had taken from local shelters, and before you knew it, we were…we were…" I can't form the words. "Prostituting," finally spews from my mouth. I hate that terminology with a passion, and I'll beat a bitch's ass for calling me one, but the truth is, I am one.

"Is that why you killed him?" Jessica asks.

"I killed him because he was going to kill me. It was self-defense," I tell them.

"I'm so sorry for all the shit you had to endure," Jessica offers but the more I speak the more disturbed I become which is beginning to trigger some type of feelings that I'm not sure I can control. "It makes no sense to me that my parents would give two out of three babies away like that, but trust and believe, I am going to find out!" Jessica emphatically announces with conviction and rage in her tone and demeanor. It makes no sense to me that my parents would give two of their own babies away like that but trust and believe I am going to find out why," Jessica says emphatically. There is rage in her tone; as if, she is about to start something.

I continue. "Other than that, I'll be fine as long as this big-ass dike bitch stays away from me and these nightmares stop," I announce. Their voices sound similar, and if I haven't been facing them, I won't know which one is talking.

"Nightmares, what nightmares?" they say simultaneously, which piques my interest.

"They're just some recurring dream that I've been having for as long as I can remember, and they have become more prevalent since I've been here," I say in a dismissive manner, for which I'm sorry I bring it up.

"Do they sound like loud, sharp, piercing screams?" Jessica asks.

"Like someone being tortured?" Robyn adds.

"How the hell could you know that?" I say. The fear in both their eyes and in their voices is the same as mine, terrifying and horrifying.

"Because I've been having the same dream for as long as I can remember," Robyn says.

"Me too," Jessica adds.

There's our connection as triplets, another common dominator the three of us share besides our looks. I've never shared that part of my life with anyone before, not even with the family, because they can never understand what I'm going through. Not even Big Daddy knew I suffered from these dreams, which plagues my conscious state of mind on a daily basis.

Finally after twenty years, there is this sense of complacency that falls over me, and for the first time in my life, I don't feel alone. The three of us sit there and talk for hours.

Jessica tells Robyn and me all about her best friend, Tamara. "She's the sister I never had." I can tell that this Tamara person is very special to Jessica. When she finishes, Robyn tells Jessica and me about the time she walked in on her boyfriend and her sister in bed together, which has me laughing so hard.

"So you beat her ass, right?"

And I tell them about the night Carly, Amanda, and I got into the fight at the club. Today is a good day for me, I don't recall ever laughing so hard, so long, and so loud, and that is something I've never thought I'd do again: laugh.

Jessica

Tony, It's Me

Our visit was convivial and jovial, and I have a better understanding about both my siblings now… Raylene is strong-willed, a natural born leader. She doesn't like to appear weak or vulnerable in front of others. Robyn, on the other hand, is obstinate but driven, and her first response is to fight when she feels pressured. Where, I'm more laid-back and to trusting to a fault.

Raylene details her life story, which leave me at a total loss for words. She talks about all the physical, sexual, mental, and emotional abuse she endured at the hands of Big Daddy, which left me speechless. I'm glad he's dead. You have to be a strong willed -person to have gone through the shit she's been through and survived.

I have not been home in a week but I'm ready to get back now. Especially, so I can talk to my parents.

Alex is waiting for us in the parking lot and drives us back to Philly.

"Drop us off in Center City, Jessica wants to go shopping," Robyn tells Alex, which is a complete lie. I look at Robyn in astonishment, and before I can say a word, she adds, "Here's fine, we'll take the bus back!" Robyn yells as she's forcefully pushing me out of the car on the passenger's side. "Robyn!" I yell. "What the hell?" I scream as Alex speeds away.

"Jessica, please, this is hard enough, and I don't need any shit from you right now," she tells me.

"Hard enough? Robyn, what are you talking about?" I say as she takes two steps and looks up. We're standing in front of a Women's Clinic. "What have you done?" I ask her.

"Just exploring my options," she says and walks in.

I follow. "Will you please just stop and talk to me for a minute without all of the melodrama?" I say to her. She press the button to the elevator as we watch it come from the top floor.

"Robyn, please just talk to me. What are you doing? You can't be serious about this. I know Alex is acting like a major asshole right now, but I'm sure if you two just take some time out and talk to one another, I'm sure you'll be fine." I'm rambling and say anything that sounds good. I don't know if any of what I'm saying is even registering with her. As the elevator door opens, she steps in and pushes the button to the eighth floor. "Well, at least you should see what Alex thinks about this. After all, he is the father!" I yell in desperation.

Robyn stops and turns around. "Oh, Alex made his intentions very clear to me already, so I really don't give a flying fuck what he thinks now. You see, Jessica, what you don't seem to understand is that I am on this ledge all alone. There's no one out here with me, and I'm scared as shit!"

"I know—" I start to say before she shuts me down.

"No, you don't know! You can't possibly know how I'm feeling because your pussy is still tight! I gave Alex my heart and my essences, and he threw it right back in my face, and now you think I'm going to bring a child into a half-assed situation like this, and on top of that, I don't even know who the fuck I am!" Robyn so poignantly tells me and then starts to cry uncontrollably. I grab her and take her to the side. The receptionist asks if everything is all right.

"We're fine," I say so she would go back to her seat. I turn towards Robyn, "And you are wrong about a couple of things but mostly about you being in this by yourself. I'm here if you let me help you and stop trying to push me away and alienate me out of your life. I'm not Amber, Robyn, and I wouldn't do the things to you or Raylene that others have done. I promise you, we can and will get through this together, all of this. Look, you don't have to stay with Alex. I have a condo in Jersey. You can move in with me and really give yourself some time to find out what you want to do, and if you really decide that you don't want to keep the baby, then we can look into adoption, okay?" I say to her, which leaves a bad taste in my mouth.

She wipes her nose and her eyes. "Okay," she agrees. "But what do I do about Alex? I'm in love with him," she finally confesses. "What am I going to do if he decides to reconcile with his wife? Then what?"

"One problem at a time," I tell her. "Can we just get out of here for now?"

Robyn is blinded when it comes to Alex. She's confusing admiration, trust, and kindness for love, which is very easy to do. Her hormones and emotions are all over the place now, and it's clouding her judgment.

"How can you be so certain that it's love you're feeling for Alex and not just some deep-rooted affection?" I ask her.

"You're still a virgin, aren't you?" she asks me.

"And what does my virginity have to do with any of this?" I retort, offended by her question. "Love is action, love is a sacrifice, and love is kind, patience, and unconditional. Love does not hurt," I tell her. "Love is the way my father looks at my mother," I reminisce. "Now that's love."

"And we had all that," she states. "Look, all I know is what he told me. They've been having major problems in their marriage since Alexis died, and if there's a chance, I can give him back a little piece of something he lost, then what's wrong with that?" she asks with a straight face. I'm flabbergasted after I hear that.

"At least that's what I thought, but I guess I was wrong," she solemnly adds. Robyn doesn't utter another word after we leave the clinic. I get the feeling she's upset with me, but it doesn't matter. We get back to the house around seven, and she goes straight upstairs to lie down. I ask Alex if it will be all right if I make a call.

"Hello, Tony, it's me."

"Who's me?" he says. Tony can be a real jerk at times. He reminds me of Russell.

"It's me, Jessica. Just let me speak with Tamara," I demand.

"What do you want with Jessica?" he asks.

"Let me speak to Tamara!" I yell into the receiver.

"Boy, give me the phone!" I hear Tamara shout in the background. "Jessica, have you called your mother yet? I told you she's worried about you, and she's been calling me at least four or five times a day wondering if I've heard from you. Will you call her, please?"

"Tamara, I didn't call you to talk about my mother," I say to her.

"Jessica, what's going on? This doesn't sound like you," she tells me, and she is right. After the shit I've been through this past week, I'm not the same. I've learned new things about myself that I never knew, and I won't expect Tamara to understand. "Well, it is me, I'm calling you because I need your help."

"Help? What help can I give you? Because from where I'm standing, it looks like you don't need a damn thing from me anymore," she says in this downtrodden tone.

"What's wrong with you?"

I hear a sigh. "Nothing," she says. "What is it you want, Jessica?"

I continue, "Robyn will be staying with me for a while, and I'm gonna need the space in the second bedroom," I tell her.

"So basically, you want me to come and get my shit out of your house," she retorts.

"Well, I wouldn't have put it exactly like that, but yes," I say, detecting a hint of jealousy.

"Fine," she says in this dry, monotone voice. "Anything else?" she adds. It's quiet on both ends for a minute, then she says, "Look, Jessica, it's late, and unlike you, I have to go to work in the morning."

"Tamara!" I yell. "Am I bothering you?" I ask because her lackadaisical attitude is pissing me off and I can't understand why she just can't be happy for me. She doesn't even ask me who Robyn is.

"What do you want me to say, Jessica? You left here a week ago, and you haven't bothered to call anyone to let them know you're all right. We didn't know if you were dead or alive. You could have at least had the decency to call me, of all people. I mean, when I told you your mother was worried about you, you acted like you don't even care. And now you want me to be happy for you because you found a long-lost sister, well, hip, hip, hooray because I'm still trying to figure out what was so bad about your life before," Tamara so eloquently says to me.

I'm speechless as revelation set in. Tamara Mitchell is jealous.

"Just call your mother, Jessica," she strongly suggests and then hangs up the phone without saying goodbye.

With Robyn resting peacefully, I think this will be the perfect opportunity to talk to Alex. I walk into the kitchen, where he is invading the refrigerator. He practically pulls everything out that is in there. "Hey, thanks for the usage of the phone."

"Anytime," he says with his upper torso in the fridge and his backside sticking out. He is in so deep I can barely hear what he is saying. "Where's Robyn?" he yells as he manages to bring mounds and mounds of food out without dropping anything.

"She went upstairs to lie down," I say in astonishment of his balancing skills. I watch him make this massive sandwich on rye bread with turkey, ham, roast beef, cheese, coleslaw, lettuce, onions, and tomatoes and thousand island dressing.

I shake my head in disbelief. "What are you making?" I ask.

"Oh, this? This is my secret creation, and I normally don't let anyone see me make it. I call it the O-kee-doe-kee," he tells me and then winks and smiles at me before taking this humongous bite. "Hmmm," he says as he offers me a bite. I respectfully decline.

I wave him off. "I'm good," I say and then pause. I take a deep breath to collect my thoughts, "So, what are you going to do about Robyn and the baby?" I say as boldly as I can.

He looks at me for a moment and then wipes his mouth with the napkin. "No offense, Jessica, but what's going on with Robyn and me is none of your business," he lets me know with a mouthful of food.

"I beg to differ. Did you know she thinks she's in love with you? Why would you lead her on like that? Why would you give her such a false sense of reality, especially since you're still married?" I say to Alex as I watch him stuff the last piece of this oversize sandwich into his mouth, which I don't recall ever seeing him masticate.

He swallows and then washes it down with an ice-cold glass of beer. "Jessica, please don't take this the wrong way, and believe me, I respect and completely understand your concern for your sister, but whatever is going on with Robyn and myself, is between Robyn and myself," he repeats and then releases a loud burp as he proceeds to clean up his area.

He continues, "Because what you don't understand is that Robyn and I have a somewhat of an unorthodox relationship, which works for us, granted we're at a crossroad now, but we understand one another." He may have been trying to convince himself of that, but I'm not buying anything he is saying. He has this laid-back persona and aura about him, which is smooth like butter and it can suck you in without you even knowing it if you're not careful, which is what happened to Robyn.

"And can you actually believe that she was thinking about keeping the baby because she thought she could give you back a little of something you lost, but now she's getting an abortion," I enlighten him.

"What? An abortion! What the hell are you talking about, Jessica? Is that where you two went after I dropped you off? God, she better not have done anything that stupid!" He yells as he jumps to his feet and bolts upstairs, taking two steps at a time. It wasn't my intention to upset him, and I tried to stop him, but he was too fast.

He burst into the room nearly taking the door off their hinges and yells, "You better not kill my baby, Robyn!"

Robyn

I'm Done

I'm exhausted. I did not realize how physically drained I really am. When we get back to the house, I head straight to the room to lie down. I know Jessica is just trying to help but I need Alex.

Alex bust into the room nearly pulling the door off its hinges. "You better not kill my baby!" he yells at me.

I head in Jessica's direction. "You fucking bitch!" I scream as Alex blocks my way. "Why would you tell him that?" Jessica steps behind Alex. "Don't be mad at her. It's not like you were going to tell me, besides, this is between you and I!" he yells as he continues to block my path.

I back up. "Don't touch me!" I shout as my eyes began to fill with tears. I look at Jessica as she turns and walks out the room. It's just me and Alex alone again and I should be mad, but I'm relieved because I didn't know how I was going to tell him I was pregnant. I guess, it could have been worse and could not have wanted the baby at all.

"I'm so sorry," he says softly. "I messed up, and I brought you into my shit, which I should not have done. I have to fix this," he whispers. "I just don't have a clue how to," he adds. "Come here," he finally says to me.

"No," I say through my tears.

"Come here, closer," he commands as I slowly give in to his command. "Listen, I'm sorry. I'm so sorry for everything but can you please stop being mad at me long enough so we can talk. Please just talk to me, Robyn." he begs as he grabs my hand and lead me to the bed where we sit and talk for hours.

"You're right, it was wrong of me to assume you were on the pill and I should have used protection, and when Alexis died…well, that just about destroyed me, and then Momma.Robyn, you've got to believe that it was never my intention to hurt you. I'm, I'm just dealing with a lot right now, and I need time to figure things out. But when Jessica said you went to the clinic, well…I about lost it! I saw red. I do not want you to kill my baby, Robyn. I'm a man, but I cannot take another hit like that! I am not strong enough to endure or survive that kind of pain again. It will literally kill me," Alex says to me through tears in his eyes.

I stand to my feet as confusion, doubt, and disbelief creep in. Alex is the only person I've ever trusted, and in two short days I've seen a side of him I've never seen in all the years I've known him.

I feel relieved that we're talking, and he opens up, and he apologizes for the way he acted. I'm not hurt or mad anymore, but I have clarity. I know what I'm going to do. I drop my head and think about the time I went to summer camp and broke my leg, how that didn't hurt that much. The time I found out I was adopted, how that didn't hurt that much. Hell, not even the time I walked in on Amber and Hakeem didn't hurt as much as the words that come out of my mouth.

"I'm done."

I don't have any strength left in my body, but I manage to walk out of the bedroom and not look back. I hear Jessica calling my name, but I'm numb from head to toe.

Alex is my world. This man could tell me the sky isn't blue and my stupid ass would have believed him. He once called me a survivor, and I didn't know what that meant, but now I do. It's time for me to be on my own.

The next day, I'm moving my belongings into Jessica's spare bedroom. "This is your condo?" I say as I walk around.

"Yeah, make yourself at home," she tells me. "Don't mind those things in there. Tamara will be here tomorrow to pick them up."

"Oh, Tamara. That's your best friend?" I yell from the spare bedroom. "She lives here too?" I ask, feeling apprehensive and uncomfortable.

"No, well, she just stayed here a lot, and it was just easier for her to have some stuff here as well, but don't worry about that, it's all good. I can't wait for you to meet her though," Jessica says as I look into her eyes, and I can see that she is happy, which makes me happy. I like Jessica, and I can see that she has a really good heart. I tease her. I often say to her that she was born in the wrong era. She has the personality and the spirit of a love child from the sixties or seventies because she just wants everyone to get along and sing "Happy" by Pharrell.

I'm up early the next morning because I have to check my account. I'm down to $2,800, and my free ride is basically over. I'm pregnant and jobless, which is a recipe for disaster.

Time is flying because I have been here for three months now and I'm beginning to feel homesick. It's so ironic, I use to dream about getting out of here; and now, I'm dying to go back.

Upper Montclair is nice but there's no familiarity here for me. I have so many things I need to do and I to do it in my comfort zone but the only probably is, I can see how happy Jessica is by my being here.

I go out most morning getting familiar with the area or at the library. I've filled out dozens of job applications online with no luck. When I get back, Jessica tells me a package and some flowers have arrived for me. They are from Alex. I contemplate opening it, but after several minutes of smelling the roses, I give in. I open the box and seen an envelope with my name on it. It reads as follows:

> *My dearest Robyn,*
>
> *I pray this note finds you in the best of mental, physical, emotional, and spiritual health by the time it reaches your hands. My incessant thoughts of you keep me from resting comfortably at night. It pains me deeply to know that I am the cause of your anguish. I've been thinking a lot about how we got to this point, and please know it was never my intention to hurt you in anyway. I don't fully understand your decision, but I respect it, but as you know, we still have another matter at hand, and I would appreciate it, when you're ready, of course, if you would call me. I need to speak with you because I don't like the way we left things between us.*
>
> *You know my intentions about the baby, but I don't know yours. That baby was conceived out of love, and it deserves a chance to live a happy and healthy life. Please don't abort my baby because you're mad at me. I'm here for you, Robyn, and I hope you can find it in your heart one day to forgive me for the pain I have caused you. Hoping to hear from you soon.*
>
> *Love,*
>
> *Alex*

I'm now more distraught and confused than before. What is he trying to say? Is he saying he wants to be together if I keep the baby? What about his wife? Does he still plan on being with her or not? He doesn't clarify any of that in his letter. And why did he sign it "Love, Alex"?

I finally get the strength to walk away from him, and now he pulls this crap, and why didn't he say all this before? And what the hell, what's with this "Love, Alex"? He would have been better off signing "Yours truly" or "Sincerely yours."

His words don't help or comfort me one bit. Why the hell did he even write me this stupid letter, and what's with the roses and bottles of perfume? He used to tell me stories about how he used to send his mother and his wife roses and perfume.

"It's a testament of my love," he told me. I scroll through my cell phone and look at all the pictures we took when we were in Chicago, and I try to feel that feeling again, but it's gone. That's the night I got pregnant. "Damn, you Alex!" I cry out in anguish.

Living here for the past three months has been a major adjustment for me. I have no intentions of ever getting an abortion, but I don't tell Alex that. I'm three months pregnant, and my baby bump is just starting to form, and this morning sickness is kicking my ass. In addition, I forget how annoying it is to live with females because every little thing gets on my nerves, or is it the pregnancy?

After all the applications I put in, I finally find a part-time job at IHOP, which only lasts one week. The manager fires me after one of the customers leaves me a dollar and fifty tip.

"Was something wrong with your service?" I ask the man as I follow him into the parking lot.

"No."

"Then what's up with this bitch-ass tip! Fifteen percent is the minimum acceptable allowance which is to be left nowadays! Don't bring your cheap ass back in here if you can't afford it!" I yell at the customer and throw his money back at him. After that, I know I need a change of scenery.

"Where are you going?" Jessica asks with concern.

"I'm going to go back home for a while. I need balance," I tell her as I'm packing my bags. I caught the Greyhound from Penn Station in Newark that very night.

Jessica
They're Not My Parents

I must admit it feels good to finally be asleep back in my own bed. I'm worried about Robyn because she's having a hard time adjusting. She gets a part-time job at IHOP, which I think will help, but unfortunately it only lasts one week. She says the manager fired her because she threw money at a customer or something like that. When I ask her what happened, she just says she doesn't want to talk about it, and the next thing I know, she's telling me she's going back to California to find balance, whatever that means.

I finally call my mother and tell her that I want to come by and talk with her and Daddy.

"Oh, Jessica, we've been so worried about you. Where have you been?" she says.

"I was out of town on business," I say sarcastically because I've heard those words thousands of times from my father's mouth. "When will be a good time for me to come by? I need you and Daddy there," I say.

"Well, we're having dinner on Saturday with Francis and Patricia Millhouse. You remember them, don't you? And on Sunday maybe you can come to church with us," my mother says.

"Maybe I'll see," I say. Right before I hang up the receiver, she yells, "Oh, Jessica! Your cousin Brenda returned your call. She said something about you needing her services. Is everything all right?" my mother ask inquisitively. I didn't dare feed into her curiosity. "I'll see you Sunday" was the only response she get from me.

"Yes, Sunday, and Jessica, it's really good to hear from you," Vivian says quickly before she hears the click of the phone disconnecting. With Robyn out of town, this is a good time to confront my parents. Brenda is my older cousin and seven years my senior. She recently graduated from law school. Her mother and Vivian are sisters. After Brenda's twin brother, Brandon, was murdered and no one ever charged with his murder, Brenda decided if she wanted justice, she would have to be the one to pursue it. I ask if she could represent Raylene, pro-bono of course. Although she was as shocked as I was to hear about Robyn and Raylene, Brenda said she would be happy to help any way she can.

"Sunday cannot get here fast enough because all this idle time and not hearing from Robyn, I am driving myself crazy. I can barely sleep. All these mixed emotions keep running rampant through my mind, and I am about to lose all self-control. I cannot believe Robyn does not have the decency to at least call me to let me know she has arrived safely, how rude." I can hear the sorrow and sadness in Vivian's voice when we spoke on the phone, but one thing Matthew Lovejoy taught and instilled in me was never let your emotions guide and or affect your decision-making process. I make sure to arrive on time because time is of the essences, mine. When I arrive, I can see Vivian is very ecstatic to see me and Matthew is as obstinate as ever. "Good, keep that same energy."

I go straight toward the living room and take a seat. My mother follows behind as she hands me a small wrapped box. "Although we didn't make it to your graduation ceremony, we wanted to congratulate you on your accomplishment."

"Thank you," I say as I set the box on the table and then jump right in. "I need to ask you two something, and no matter how bad you think it is, I need you to be completely truthful with me, okay?" I say.

"Truthful? We've always been truthful with you," my father retorts.

"Do you know where I've been this past week?" I continue. I'm smug, confident, and in control. I'm determined to give them a piece of my mind.

"I was in Philadelphia with Robyn and Raylene," I say to them and then pause to see their reaction. Nothing, so I say their names again.

"Robyn and Raylene. Well, don't you have anything to say?"

"Like what?" my father asks. "Who are Robyn and Raylene?" he continues. I can't believe he wants to play it this way. I retrieve the Times Magazine from my bag and throw it on the coffee table. My father picks up the magazine, and they both stare aimlessly at the image on the cover. My mother's mouth drops open. She cover it with her right hand as they both look at each other in bewilderment and confusion.

"Well?" I say again demanding an answer. I wasn't buying this phony act of bewilderment or surprise.

"Matthew!" My mother cries out as she falls into his arms. He catches her and escort her to the couch.

"Is this some kind of joke because it isn't funny!" he bellows.

Although I was expecting some type of theatrics, I wasn't expecting this. I assumed they would have been very apologetic and filled with guilt, shame, and embarrassment, but instead they seemed genuinely surprised and taken aback as well.

"What's going on?" I ask skeptically as a lump begins to form in my throat. Their over-the-top reaction isn't what I expected from them and it's beginning to scare me even more. My father begins to slowly walk toward me and grabs my hand. "Pumpkin, there's something we need to tell you." His tone is different, and there is fear in his voice, as he drops my hand and grabs onto his wife. "It's time."He clears his throat and turn toward me and simply utters the words,

"You're adopted." In his patriarchate voice, tone, and manner. Now, any kind of feelings, care, compassion, or empathy he should have had is gone. He had more concern and compassion the time he had to fire fifteen employees than the words he just utters to me.

Although I hear the words that come out of his mouth, I don't understand what he just said to me, and I speak two different languages. I remain still for a moment longer, praying he would clarify what he just said. No more words are uttered as he continues to console his weeping wife. For a second time, I'm met with mixed emotions that start to build up deep inside of me. I feel like a volcano that is about to erupt.

He begins, "Your mother and I tried everything physically possible to have a baby, but by the second trimester, she would miscarry, two, three, four times. It was just too much. I guess it was God's way of telling us to try other options. We investigated surrogacy but wasn't completely comfortable with that either, so Francis introduced us to this attorney he knew, Eli Weinberg. He told us he could help us adopt a beautiful, healthy, well-bred African American baby girl."

"That's right, honey," she interjects. "And from the moment we laid eyes on you, we knew you were the one," adds as she manages to gain control of her crying. "We thought about telling you several times, especially as you got older, but one thing leads to another, and time simply ran out."

I sat there for hours, listening with my ears and my heart to every explanation they could think of to make me understand. I'm calm, and I'm keeping my emotions intact and under control. Finally, I ask, "So why didn't you just adopt all of us? Why would you split up triplets?"

"Excuse me," Matthew says. "What triplets?"

I am determined to show him my inner strength. I am not as delicate as he thinks I am. I refuse to fall for any more of his lies because the fact that they could have lied to me all these years isn't sitting well with me. They are strangers to me and no longer worthy of being called Mom and Dad.

"What do you mean 'What triplets?' My sisters, Raylene and Robyn!" I yell again because their ignorance is really starting to irritate me to no end.

"Pumpkin, I can promise you we knew nothing, absolutely nothing, about triplets. They only told us about you, but I can assure you if we knew there were three of you, we would have most certainly adopted all of you," he says, which sounds plausible but doesn't change how I'm feeling.

The anger that is building inside me is uncontrollable, and I've never experienced anything so intense before. "Pumpkin," he calls me and steps toward my direction.

I pull back. "Don't touch me!" I announce as I stand there beginning to shake.

Vivian is in the corner consumed with this uncontrollable grief. "We didn't know, we just didn't know," she repeats over and over again.

"Well, now you do," I say as I stand up from the couch, pick up the little box with the red ribbon, and walk out of my adoptive parents' house without uttering another word.

The time I went to summer camp when I was nine and broke my leg didn't hurt as much. Not even the time when Tamara and I fought over Joseph didn't hurt as much as the cold words, "You're adopted" that came from his mouth.

I'm extremely worried because I still haven't heard from Robyn. I told her to take the plane, but she decides to catch the bus, "It's going to take forever to get there," I add, and she gives me one of her I-don't- give-a-fuck looks. "Take the plane," I suggest as a final attempt.

Alex sent her a big bouquet of flowers, which she just left on her bed. I found a vase and put them in her room. I read the note Alex wrote her. He signs it "Love, Alex,: which I thought was kind of ironic.

I'm completely jaded by the time I get home, and I don't know what to do. I'm all cried out, and my entire body feels numb. I want to call Tamara but we haven't been on the best of speaking terms since Robyn moved in. I call Brenda again.

"Hello," I hear the voice on the other end say and that was all I needed for the flood gates to open. I don't even ask her how she's doing because I don't have any time for bullshit pleasantries.

"Everything alright?" she quickly ask. I didn't mean to take my frustration out on her.

"No, everything is not alright. My whole life is one big lie, messed up from the floor up and nothing makes sense to me anymore," I finally break. "My entire life has been nothing but on big ass lie; and I do not under how things got so messed up!" Once the flood gates opened the tears were nonstop and I am out of control.

"My entire life has been nothing but one big ass lie; and I do not understand how things got so messed up." Once flood gates open the tears start, nonstop. I am no longer in control.

"None of this make sense," Brenda adds. "Wait, wait, Jessica, just calm down. I need you to relax and just start from beginning."

I take deep breathes and try to calm down but a massive wave of hiccups bombard my body and takes control. "Oh great!" I say as I fight my way through them. I tell Brenda the whole ugly story from start to finish.

"Hello," I finally say because I didn't hear a word from her the whole time, and I wondered if she was still there.

Finally, she says, "Jess, I don't know what to say. Mommy has never told me that you were adopted because you know I would have told you something like that," she says. "Are you sure? Who told you this?"

"Matthew did," I reply in this cold distant manner.

"Uncle Mattie?" she says in disbelief, "When and why?"

"Because I was confronting them about my sisters, Raylene and Robyn, and I was asking them why they didn't adopt them as well. Why would they separate triplets, and that's when he blurts that I was adopted!"

Brenda is just as disturb by this as I am, and I know if Raylene is ever going to have any kind of freedom again, Brenda is her best bet. After Brandon was murdered, Matthew offered a million-dollar reward for the capture and arrest of his killer or killers, and two years later, no arrest have been made. I've always looked up to Brenda ever since I was a little girl. Besides the fact I thought she was beautiful, I love her strong will and her spirit.

"You know Raylene has that same strong will and energy like you have," I say to Brenda.

"That's good. Tell her to keep it because she is going to need it," Brenda says to me which lifts a hundred pounds of worry off my shoulders.

I exhale slowly and graciously and thank Brenda over and over.

"Jessica, relax. We're family, and you know there's nothing I won't do for family. Just give me some time, and let me look into the details of her case and let me see what I can do for your friend."

"My sister," I remind her.

"Oh, right, my bad…your sister. Jess, girl, everything is going to be all right; and a world of advice, don't be too hard on Uncle Mattie and Aunt Viv because I can bet my life, if they had known about triplets, they would have adopted all three of you. Brenda ensures me which is food for thought. I reach back out to Detective Sosa for some help.

It's getting late and I am mentally exhausted, drained, and depleted, I try call Robyn one more time, voicemail. I hang up and go straight to bed because if one more thought run across my mind, I am going to scream.

Robyn
California

This is one of the longest and worst trips I've ever taken, and maybe I should have listened to Jessica and flew. It takes four days, twenty hours, forty-eight minutes, and twenty-two seconds to get to LA. I'm mentally and physically exhausted, and after seeing all the shit that people do on public transportation, I feel like I need to bathe in a vat of antiseptic just to get the stench of dirt off me. I'm finally able to charge my phone, seven missed calls from Jessica, and not once does she leave a message which just drives me crazy. What is her issue with leaving messages? It's late. I'm tired. I'll call her in the morning.

I check into the Motel Six because no one is expecting me and I doubt I'm going to be greeted with open arms, especially since I left without saying goodbye.

After my HAZMAT bath, I order some food and relax for the rest of the evening watching television, or should I say the television watches me.

Early the next morning, I call for a Lyft and go back to the neighborhood. It's been close to three months since the last time I was here, and from the looks of things, nothing has changed. I'm not looking forward to seeing my parents, but I'm excited about seeing Autumn.

I see the old gang, and they are still hanging in the same spot, still doing the same things. I shake my head.

"What the fuck was my dumb ass thinking?" I verbally express out loud. "Excuse me," the driver says, assuming I was talking to him as he pulls in front of my house. I tip him and hop out the car. There is a car parked in the driveway. I see two people sitting on the front porch.

"Look what the cat dragged in," I hear one of the voices say as I step onto the porch. Its Amber's friends Peaches and Chyna.

"What the hell are you doing here?" I ask them both. They look at me from head to toe and roll their eyes. I'm not in the mood for their nonsense, so I just walk by them and go inside.

They still don't lock the front door when they leave. "Mom, Dad . . . Autumn," I call.

"Your parents aren't here," Peaches enlightens.

"Then why are you?" I say to them. Seconds later, I see Autumn taken the steps by two coming down the stairs. She stops and looks at me while she tries to catch her breath.

"Robyn, is that you?" she says as she gives me a big hug and then quickly takes a step backward.

"Oh my god, are you pregnant?" she shouts in excitement and then starts to laugh and rub my belly at the same time. I push her hand away. Damn, I didn't think I was showing yet.

"And how the hell did you know?" I say, giving her confirmation.

"I was just kidding." She laughs as she continues acting giddy and gay. "But you really are!" she exclaims. "That's awesome! I'm going to be an aunt!"

I just shake my head, and I really need her to calm down so we can talk. "Where's mom and dad?" I ask.

"At the hospital," she tells me. "I just came home to pick up a few things."

"Hospital? For who, for what?" I yell.

"For Amber and Hakeem beat her up pretty bad, this time," my baby sister says to me which makes my heart skip a beat or two.

"This time? What the hell you mean this time?" I scream.

"Well, things got pretty ugly between the two of them after you left. Hakeem's temper escalated. He's been out of control. His own father threw him out and doesn't want to have anything to do with him."

"And what did Daddy do?" I ask her.

"You mean besides drink more? Nothing," Autumn tells me. "It's been hell around here since you left. What are you doing here? Why did you come back?" she asks as she continues walking toward Peaches' car, open the rear door, and slips in the backseat. I quickly follow so I don't get left behind.

Autumn tells me everything from A to Z since the day I left. I'm speechless, and I feel ashamed. I don't know what to say.

Twenty minutes later, we're at the hospital. Autumn brings me straight to Amber's room. I walk in and see my parents sitting by her side. No greetings are given. I can't believe my eyes when I walk in and see my sister lying there with tubes running in and out of her. I'm horrified. She looks like a side of spoiled beef. Her caramel-colored complexion is gone. She's just as dark as me.

"That pussy-ass motherfucker," I say to no one in particular. I'm pissed, and I'm resolute Hakeem is going to pay for what he's done to my sister. My parents look at me and start to say something as Amber begins to moan.

"Robyn," she struggles to release the word from her mouth.

"Shh, it's me. I'm here," I say as I stroke her hair.

"What are you doing here?" she forces herself to say as she grasps for air.

"Well, who else is going to be a pain in your ass?" I say with levity while fighting to hold back my tears.

She tries to smile. "Ouch, you're glowing and you're pregnant?"

What the fuck is with their clairvoyant ass. My mother's face lights up as she looks at me.

"What, I'm worried about you," I say as I wipe my nose and my tears, which I'm unsuccessful in holding back. My mother hands me a Kleenex from the box that's sitting on the table next to her. "Thanks. What happened?"

"You really don't want to know," she says as she lets out a big sigh. "I wasn't you."

"Amber . . ." I start to say as she lifts her hand and wave me away, but I'm not going anywhere.

"What are you doing here acting like you care? You left, remember?" She starts coughing uncontrollably. I watch her struggle as my mother pours her some water and tries to help her drink some. Amber pushes her away. "Why did you leave? You weren't supposed to leave, Robyn. You weren't supposed to leave," she says as she readjusts her position in the bed.

"You're right, it was selfish of me to leave the way I did, especially without saying goodbye, and I'm so sorry for that."

"It was always you, Robyn. I've always admired you," she slurs as she fights to keep her eyes open.

I'm shocked and I wasn't expecting her to say anything like that. Only eleven months separate Amber and I and we fought constantly as kids. She made everything a competition between the two of us, and I never could understand why.

She continues, "You never cared about what people thought or said about you, and I love that about you, your confidence," which nearly knocks me off my feet. I wasn't aware she felt this way. All this sisterly bonding is beginning to take its toll on me, and I'm overwhelmed as I excuse myself and step out the room.

I don't dare fall apart in front of them. Amber is not the same girl I grew up with and left three months ago. She looks like hell. Her natural beauty is covered with bumps, bruises, and broken bones.

Hakeem single-handedly destroyed her self-esteem, self-confidence, and self-worth. Once I return, I stay by her side for the rest of the night. I grab her hand. "I'm here for as long as you need me," I assure her.

My parents look exhausted as well. I tell them to go home and get some rest. "I'll stay by her side."

I watch as she drifts in and out of sleep. Finally she is resting peacefully and I decide to step out.

"Robyn," she calls.

I walk back to her side. "You're supposed to be resting."

"Can I ask you something?"

"Anything."

"Is that Hakeem's baby?"

Her question makes me smile. "You're unbelievable," I say to her. "This boy beats your ass to bear recognition, and all you can think about if this is his baby or not."

She smiles and mumbles "divine justice" as she fights through the pain.

"More like divine suicide," I rebut defensively. "Now get some rest. I'm just running to the café to get something to eat," I assure her.

The next morning, my father brings me back to the motel so I can get my things and check out. I'm back in my old house and in my old room, which is just the way I left it three months ago. "I thought this would have been turned into your man cave by now."

He shakes his head. "Nope, we left everything just the way you left it. I was hoping you would be back someday." Sometimes they can be loving and caring toward me. "You know, something has to be done about Hakeem's black ass," I tell my father.

He looks at me.

"She refuses to press charges," he enlightens me.

"Desperate measures calls for desperate actions," I say out loud. Although I've liberated myself from Alex, I need his help one more time. I suck up my pride and call him.

"Hello," the voice on the other end of the phone says.

"It's me," I say after a couple of minutes of silence.

"Robyn," he whispers. Jackie must have been there, but as soon as I heard his voice, I lost it.

"I need your help," I cry.

"What is it, baby girl? Talk to me." He still cares. I explain the whole situation to him, and as always, he calms me down.

"Okay," he says. "I'll take care of it. I don't want you worrying about a damn thing." After a few minutes, he asks, "How are you doing? Did you get my note?"

A warm feeling is still burning deep inside me for this man. "Yes, I did, and I'm fine, Alex. I didn't get an abortion," I finally say.

He exhales. "Good, I'm glad. I want my baby, Robyn, and I want you too," he says. "But I'll understand if you don't feel the same way anymore," he adds.

"I haven't decided if I'm coming back, Alex," I volunteered. "I need to find a happy medium after everything that happened and all."

He is silent. I hear Jackie calling his name in the background.

"Thanks, Alex," I say.

"Who are you talking to?" she says.

"I'll take care of everything," he says and then abruptly hangs up the phone.

Autumn is up early cooking breakfast the next morning. "Where are you going so early in the morning?"

"To work."

"Work? You got a job? Damn, how long have I been gone?"

She smiles. "Yes, I got a job, and I graduate this year, you know?"

"Yes, I know. You think I would forget my baby sister's graduation from high school?" I'm flabbergasted. I can't believe how much she has grown in three short months, and she isn't the quiet, innocent, introverted girl I left.

I find Hakeem in the same place doing the same thing. He is so damn predictable. As a matter of fact, the whole crew is there.

"Robyn, is that you?" KiKi asks.

She looks like the typical hood rat as she walks toward me and reaches out to touch me. I step back. "Don't touch me!" I shout.

"Oh, you too good for us now?" she yells. I was about to say, "I've always been too good for you," but I reserve my comment. I have no time to entertain her or her stupidity.

"Where's Hakeem?"

She points toward the back room. I walk back and see him sitting on the chair.

"How dare you put your filthy hands on my sister!" I yell at him. "What's the matter, Hakeem, your dick isn't big enough for you?" I yell so everyone can hear me.

He looks around and jumps up. "What the fuck are you talking about, Robyn, and what the hell are you doing back here?" he says, acting like he isn't embarrassed in front of his homies but his bitch ass forgot, I know him.

"You know damn well what I'm talking about because you used to try that hitting shit with me!" I announce as his homies look at me sideways. All his dirty little secrets are going to be revealed today.

"Yo, Robyn, what's up?" Ricky asks. "Why you coming in here and blacking out on my boy?"

"Your boy put his hands on my sister!"

"Yo dog, she's half cracked! I ain't do a damn thing to her or her sister!" Hakeem refutes.

"He told us she was in the hospital for some appendix shit," Ricky says.

"Appendix, my ass. Did you see her, Ricky?"

"Look, Robyn, you need to kill all of that noise," Hakeem interjects because he knows how Ricky and the others feel about men hitting women.

"Yo, Robyn, you can't be coming here after all this time and saying some foul shit like that to my boy. You know and Hakeem knows we don't roll like that."

I turn toward Ricky. "Go see for yourself Ricky!" I tell him.

Hakeem stands there holding onto his crouch with this half-ass grin on his face. "Look at you, I haven't seen you for a minute, and this is how you greet your man? Look atcha running back to me pregnant and shit. Is it?" were the only words he was able to get out of his mouth before I say, "Nigga, don't flatter yourself. Your black ass couldn't cum if I called you. And hell no, this ain't your baby!"

Ricky is still coming to his defense. "Yo, Hakeem, you need to handle this shit, son!" As he turns toward me and says, "You think you're just gonna come back here starting all this shit about my boy! Hell, you're not even welcome here anymore!"

Hakeem has always been a coward, and I know for a fact that I've embarrassed his ass in front of everyone, and he doesn't like it, but I don't give two shits.

I turn toward Ricky. "No disrespect, Rick, but this ain't about you. Hakeem's dry ass knows what he did, and he's going to pay," I tell him and anyone else who is being nosy. Ricky looks at Hakeem one more time.

"Look, man, I ain't touch that girl!" Hakeem shouts as he jumps toward me like he is trying to scare me. Hakeem puts no fear in my heart. I don't flinch.

"Yeah, Amber and I got into a little something, something, and that's all!"

I'm so mad my hands are shaking. I hold my stomach and look for a seat but don't see one, "You see that's that bullshit I'm talking about. A little something, something you say, well, I got a little something, something for your ass!" I say to Hakeem and then start to walk away as I hear Ricky say, "Yo dog, you're right, Robyn is straight up tripping. She is on some jealousy trip or something!" as they all start laughing.

Alex is a man of his word. An hour later, I receive a call from a man by the name of Street Justice and Six Fingers, and I let them get acquainted with Hakeem's ass.

"Which one of you motherfuckers is Hakeem?" Street Justice shouts.

"I am. Who the hell are you?" his stupid ass asks.

"Your worst enemy," they both say.

Street Justice and Six Fingers commenced to beating his ass like a runaway slave.

"That's fucked up, Robyn," Ricky says as he and the rest of the lackeys start to leave.

Every one of them motherfuckers knew they were out of their league and no one dare to jump in.

I've been in Cali for four days now, and I thought about calling Jessica back, but with all the bullshit that is going on, it slips my mind.

I catch a Lyft back to the hospital. As I'm walking in, the nurse advises me that they are discharging Amber today.

"Are you sure she's ready? She still looks pretty bad to me."

"Look, there isn't anything left for us to do. Her physical wounds will heal over time. It's her emotional and mental state you need to be concerned with," she tells me.

"And what does that mean?" I ask her.

There was a look of confusion and contemplation on her face, she shakes her head and continues to walk way. What's wrong with her mental and emotional state? I figured she would be fine once she heals as long as she stays away from his dumb ass.

My parents walk in. "Did you know they're releasing her today?" I say to my father.

"Yeah, I'm signing the discharge papers," my father tells me.

My mouth falls wide open. "And why the hell would you do that? She's not ready to come home. Look at her, Dad!"

"Robyn, please, she's our daughter, and we know what's best for her," my mother says to me like I'm some fucking stranger.

"And what the fuck am I, chop liver? You know what, I'm not even surprised. I don't know what I was thinking. You're still the same, and you'll never change," I say, shaking my head is disgust.

"Change?" my father picks up on. "We're not the ones who need to change." This opens the door for me. All the anger and frustration I've held in for years comes out. The night they argued and I overhear that I was adopted, I was going to confront them then, but I didn't.

"Do you even know why I left?" I ask my father out of curiosity and wait for a response.

"Yeah, you were upset about Amber and Hakeem," he has the nerve to say to me.

"Fuck Hakeem," I quickly respond. "This isn't about Hakeem's lame ass."

"Then what?" my mother asks with a straight face.

"You're really going to sit there and act like you don't know?" I shout.

"Robyn, what the hell are you talking about?" she shouts back.

"Sterile my ass, they couldn't figure that shit out before we adopted Robyn!" I blurt and then stand there to watch their reaction.

"Adopted? Robyn is adopted?" Amber moans as complete silence fills the room. You can hear a fucking pin drop.

"So how long have you known?" my father asks with his head held down staring at the floor. He didn't have the decency to even look me in my eyes. "Pathetic," I utter.

"Since I was thirteen," I tell him.

"So why didn't you ever say anything?" he says.

"Why didn't you?" I respond.

"You're fucking adopted," Amber mumbles again in disbelief and pain as the nurse walks in with the discharge papers in her hands and explain specific instructions for her remaining recovery at home.

"This script here is for pain take only as needed," she stresses. "They can be addictive. Did you ever call any of these places from the last time?" she turns and asks Amber.

"The last time? What last time?" I ask.

My father walks over and grabs the papers out of her hands and crumbles them up and stuffs them in his back pocket. "Look, she won't need any of that stuff," he says to the nurse. "She's going to stay away from that boy," he says in his authoritative tone.

I'm floored, and from the look on the nurse's face, she is too and then walks out.

"The last time?" I yell at the top of my lungs. "How long has this been going on?" I ask Amber.

"Robyn, it's not what you think," Amber groans.

"What I'm thinking is Hakeem has been beating your ass for a while, and Mom and Dad have been too drunk to even care!" I say.

"Where the hell do you get off!" my father screams. "You haven't the slightest idea about the shit we've been through concerning you or your sisters! It's been one thing after another with you from the moment we brought you home!"

"Like what?" I reply because I would love to know what I did to them that would make them hate me so much. "Humor me, what the hell have you been through?" I say with as much sarcasm as I can muster up.

He slowly begins to walk in my direction which paralyzes me with fear because I'm not sure what he is going to do, but I stand my ground anyway. He stands within inches of my face, and we stare at each other for what seems like an eternity.

"We have too much to deal with right now, and I'm not going to let you put your mother through any more of your nonsense. It's bad enough you showed up here unannounced, pregnant, and unwed, but this is more than I'm willing to put your mother through," he says in this cold, monotone voice.

His words cut to the core of my soul, but I'm not going to give him the satisfaction of letting him know that.

"Honey, let's go," my mother says as she grabs his arm and pulls him away from me. He looks at Amber. "We're leaving! We'll see you at home" was the last words they say to us before they leave.

"Damn it, Robyn, you just got back here, and you're still causing trouble! Now, how am I getting home?" Amber cries in agony.

I thought coming back home would help me find balance, but all it did was confirm why I left in the first place. This past week help me put my life into prospective and what's important. It also makes me realize that I may have overreacted with Alex, and I should give him the time he needs to figure things out about me and what he is going to do with his marriage. Amber and I take a Lyft home, and I help get her settled into her room. Afterward, I have lunch with

Autumn, and we talk for hours. Autumn had me laughing so hard with all her jokes. I don't recall her being this funny.

"Well, living with you and Amber, you two gave me a lot of material," she adds.

I apologize to her for leaving the way I did. She tells me her plan on going to a community college, but her last two will be at Stanford and then onto med school. I love seeing her so excited, and the confidence she is emitting eases my mind.

"That's great, Autumn, and I am so proud and so happy for you," I tell my baby sister.

The word on the street is Hakeem hasn't been seen in three days and his father is looking for him. Ricky stops by my parents' and asks me where he is.

"How the hell would I know, and why the hell would I care?" I say to Ricky.

"That's fucked up, Robyn, that's really fucked up," he tells me as he speeds away. I try to convince Amber to come back to Jersey with me.

"Jersey? I don't know a damn thing about Jersey," she says. "I'm still stuck on the fact of you being adopted," she retorts.

Adopted or not, I love Amber, but she's never going to change. I smile. "Well, if you ever change your mind . . ." I say as I give her my address and telephone number in Jersey. "Make sure you keep in touch and use those numbers the nurse gave you," I say meekly.

"You know, I had this dream about you last night." I contemplate telling her about but then change my mind.

"Yeah, what was it about?"

"I was at this real fancy gathering, and everyone was there laughing, singing, dancing, and having a really good time, except you."

"Why? What was I doing?" she asks.

"Lying in a coffin, and then I woke up."

After a few seconds, she says, "Yeah, well, you know, you were always having those crazy-ass dreams when we were growing up. Do you still have them? I remember you waking up in the middle of the night, kicking, crying and screaming. What the hell were you dreaming about anyway?"

I continued packing and chose not to answer her question because it's personal and that's something I share with Jessica and Raylene. I may not have had the happiest of childhood and the nightmares didn't help, but I can't help believe I wouldn't be as "f'd" up as I am, if my adoptive parents didn't make me feel like a freak most of my life.

My relationship with Amber have always been tumultuous and filled with strife, but the fact is, I love this girl with every fiber of my being, and I know she feels the same. Life sure is funny. It takes me leaving and Amber getting beat to bare recognition for us to find a common ground, and for the first time in my life, it didn't feel like a competition. Moments later, my Lyft arrives in front of the house. I was ready now. I'm ready to be a mom, and hopefully a wife. I can't blame Alex for everything because I knew from day one that he was married, but our bond is strong, and I know he will chose me over his wife. It was nice coming back to Cali, but I'm ready to go home now.

Jessica
My Appetite's Officially Gone

It is good speaking with Brenda, and knowing that she's willing to look into Raylene's case is a relief. I call Detective Sosa, and he agrees to meet with me over lunch.

"Jessica, I'm glad you called because I want to share some new developments in the case with you," he tells me. Robyn finally calls and asks if I could pick her up from the airport this evening. I just shake my head. "Sure, what time?"

I call Tamara because I miss her and I want things to be just like old times, but she seems distant as well. "How's your dad doing?"

"Fine," she gives her one-word answers.

"That's good."

"So how are Claudia and the gang at work?"

"Good," she says. It's like pulling teeth with her, and I know that I pushed her away before, but I just needed time to figure things out, and she isn't making things any easier.

"You'll never guess who I heard was pregnant," I continue thinking that will help break the ice.

She is silent. "Myra Perkins," I say and then start to laugh.

"Oh," she says dryly.

"Tamara," I call.

"What?" she says abruptly.

"Never mind," I say. "Good night."

"Good night" is her cold flat response. I cannot believe that my thirteen-year sistership with Tamara Mitchell is over. I'm mad and glad at the same time, mad because of her piss-ass attitude; I'm glad because I don't let it affect me. In the past, I would have coddled her and tried to make her understand, but not today. I do not have the time, energy, or the crayons to try to appease a grown-ass woman.

It takes everything I have in me to get up and walk out of my adoptive parents' house that night without saying a word because now, I'm just like Robyn and Raylene, discarded, not wanted, thrown away like a piece of trash, and that knowledge tears me to pieces. The agony of living a lie is more than I can bear, so I open a bottle of '86 chateau, which Vivian left here, and commence to drinking myself into a state of oblivion.

I hear the key in the door, I jump to my feet. "Nice of you to show up!" Robyn yells as she enters the living room with her, kiss-my-ass-attitude.

"Nice of you to call," I respond and then quickly apologize. "Look, I'm really sorry for not picking you up from the airport.

Robyn sees an empty bottle on the floor. "Have you been drinking?" she asks in disbelief. She picks the empty bottle up and places it on the coffee table.

I stretch my body as far as it will go and let out a big sigh. "Well, you'll be happy to know, they're not my parents either," I announce. I'm waiting for her to give some type of sarcastic remark but she doesn't say a word. I can see her curiosity is piqued as she shakes her head.

After a few minutes, "Huh, well what did Mommy and Daddy Dearest have to say for themselves?"

"They claim they were never told that there were triplets up for adoption, and if they had known, they would have adopted all three of us," I tell her as I try to keep a brave front.

"You sound like you don't believe them."

"I don't know who to believe anymore," I tell her.

"I see," she says as she picks up the bottle again. "And that's why you finished off a whole bottle of '86 chateau? Hell, I didn't even know you drink."

"I don't," I say as I sprint towards the bathroom.

She follows closely behind. "Jessica, you're going to be alright. We're going to be alright and you're not alone anymore. I truly appreciate Robyn's efforts in trying to comfort me. I didn't allow myself to grieve with the loss of my best friend and now with finding out that I was adopted too, has me questioning, everything.

I'm awakened by the smell of bacon, which Robyn has sizzling in the kitchen. Robyn is a really good cook. She's told me one time that she did most of the cooking because her mother was often passed out somewhere.

"You're up early," I say to her.

"Yeah, will I got people to see and places to go. How are you feeling?" she asks laughingly.

I just look at her as she places a plate of food in front of me, which I push away.

"Number one rule to drinking is to coat your stomach, and since you didn't, you need to put something on your stomach to absorb it, you know, soak it up like a sponge," she says as she slides the plate back in my direction. "Now eat."

I need to get myself together. I'm supposed to be meeting with Detective Sosa by noon. Before I get to the shower, Robyn is already dressed and nearly ready to go. Plus, she has a boat load of energy, and I'm baffled where it all comes from.

"I'll take two of what you had," I say as I watch her dance around the place gathering her things. Where are you going," I ask out of curiosity.

"I'm going to see a man about a horse," she says as she reaches for her coat.

I smile, "You never told me how your trip went and, did you find your balance?" I inquire.

Robyn stops for a moment, stands still as a small smile creeps across her face, "Maybe I won't call it balance. It's more like a revelation, a reality check," she adds. Robyn's demeanor is different as she continues and says, "It doesn't make sense, Amber would go fifteen rounds with me, but let this fraction of a man beat her beyond recognition. Two plus two is four, and this isn't adding up for me. I will say one thing though, she's not the pain in the ass, I left three months ago. She is lost, defeated, and depressed. You should have seen her Jessica; her competitiveness is gone. I couldn't stand seeing her like that. Put a fork in me because I'm done. Besides, I have my own shit o worry about. I cannot live my life and hers too."

She turns in my direction, "Why, Jessica? Why do you think she stayed with him?" Her question is a double edge sword because Alex is just as mentally and emotionally abusive towards her, and she stayed, I wanted to say to but I reserved my comment because there was a sparkle in her eyes.

Two plus two is four, and this isn't adding up for me, which leaves me speechless. I will say one thing, though, she's not the pain in the ass I left three months ago. Amber is defeated and depressed as if she is lost. Her competitiveness is gone. I cannot stand seeing her like this. I'm done. I have my own shit to worry about. I cannot live my life and her life too."

"What doesn't make sense, Robyn?"

"That she stayed. Why, Jessica? Why would Amber stay with someone who was so abusive towards her?" my twin had the nerve to ask me. Her question was completely ironic because Alex is just as mentally and emotionally abusive towards her as Hakeem is towards Amber. I reserve any comment I may have had because I can see how excited she is.

She continues, "Jessica, I'm telling you, when I walked into that hospital room and seen my sister lying in that hospital bed looking like a side of spoil beef, I wanted to die." She pulls a picture out of her pocketbook and shows me a picture of this beautiful girl with similar features to Christina Milian.

"She's gorgeous," I say as I hand her back the photo.

"Yeah, she is. Amber takes pride in her appearance, but seeing her this past week, it was like she didn't care, and that's not even the worst part. Evidently, he has done this several times before, and my parents haven't done a damn thing about it," she tells me while standing near the front door with her hand on the doorknob. "But thanks to Alex!" she shouts.

"Alex, what does he have to do with anything?" I ask.

"He's amazing," she says gazingly. "He called two of his buddies to come down and talk to Hakeem," she says as she flashes a devilish smile.

"Talk?" I ask questionably.

"Yes, talk," she says and then opens the front door and exits.

I meet Detective Sosa at the corner luncheonette, and I remember to be on time.

"Jessica, over here," he yells as he see me walk through the door.

The waitress escort me in his direction. I like Detective Sosa a lot, and he's very pleasing on the eyes. I let him know that I got new counsel for Raylene.

"Well, actually she's my cousin," I tell him as the waitress places two menus on the table. He picks up his menu and proceeds to look through it.

"That's great," he replies. "Anything I can do to help, please tell her to call me. Did you have a chance to speak with your parents?" he ask as his head remain buried in the menu. "I'm so hungry I could eat a horse," he adds. I drop my head and take a deep breath without saying a word because I'm still in disbelief by the whole situation.

He clears his throat and looks up, "Jessica, are you alright?" I nod my head yes. "May I be frank? I need your consent for some DNA testing. I've already—" he stops as the waitress approach us with two glasses of water and takes our order. He continue speaking after she leaves. "As I was saying, I have known Ms. Chambers for a long time, and I've always been drawn to her. His vested interest in Raylene is identical to Alex's concern for Robyn. I believe that you and Ms. Chambers were part of some black-market baby smuggling ring which I've discovered. The DNA testing will help me determine who your biological parents are."

I was flabbergasted when he said that, and I immediately went from sugar to feeling like grade "A" shit, "Boy, this keeps getting better and better," I say as I sit back in my seat. The waitress approaches with our plates but my appetite is officially gone.

Detective Sosa tells me this elaborate tale of murder, betrayal, and human trafficking which completely blows my mind and leaves me speechless. After a while, his words become inaudible, and nothing he says makes sense. I hear words like Seattle, Jade and Jonathan, Charles, and Eli Weinberg. Detective Sosa is speaking so fast while never missing a bite of his food. The things he was saying sounds like some off-the-wall, clandestine operation that you would read in mystery books or see in movies.

"Wait, wait, wait," I finally say as I wave my hand in his direction so he would stop talking a mile a minute. "Human-trafficking, for babies? Are you serious because this kind of stuff doesn't happen, especially to someone like me. Are you sure it's me, us?"

"Are you aware of another sister?" he continues.

"Yes, but you didn't answer my question."

"That's good because I'm going to need her to submit DNA for testing as well. Although I'm pretty sure once we have confirmation of you or Raylene, hers will be the same. After all, your identical triplets for godsake!" I can see he was excited as he continues enjoying his meal while rambling at the same time.

His excitement now becomes my misery. "Answer my question!" I yell out of frustration.

He stops and looks at me. Finally, he realizes that his excitement over practically solving a twenty years old case isn't as contagious as he thought it should be. I'm horrified.

I was expecting to come here and hear things about Matthew and Vivian not hear things about human-trafficking and baby smuggling. I thought I was going to get some answers to questions I've had my entire life, but the only thing Detective Sosa manage to do is confuse me even more.

"What makes you think we are the missing babies?" I ask. "And where and when did all this happen again?" He pulls a folder marked "Unsolved" from his jacket and proceeds to show me every piece of evidence that is in the folder. The more he speaks, the further I slump into the chair, hoping it swallows me whole. I carefully listen and analyze every word that come out his mouth. It is extremely disturbing to hear what he is saying. I get up and walk away from the table. "Jessica," he calls as he follows me. "In order to move forward, you need to know where you came from."

Alex

And There Lies My Dilemma

My marriage is back on track, and Jacqueline has never been happier. Almost losing my wife made me realize how much I really love her, and I will never take her or our marriage for granted again. Sharon will be graduating from college this year, and she is engaged to a nice young man named Jasper. He's from Atlanta, and his family owns a chain of Subway restaurants. I'm truly honored when she asks me if I won't mind giving her away at her wedding.

"I would be honored to, but are you sure you wouldn't want your father to?" I ask.

"I thought he would be on my right side while you're on my left," she says and then smiles. Sharon was five when I married her mom, and I should have been more of a presence in her life. I kiss her on the forehead. "I would like that a lot," I tell her.

It's early Saturday morning, and it is a beautiful day, and I want to surprise them with a fun-filled day. "Your mother is still in bed?" I turn and ask Sharon rhetorically. I'm excited and I want to get our day started because we have a lot to do. I run upstairs into our bedroom, where she's still in bed.

"Honey, come on, get up! Why are you still in bed? We've got a thousand things to do today," I say excitedly. She doesn't move. She doesn't say a word. "Jackie, come on, girl. Get up, let's go!" I say again and then smack her on her butt cheek. I pull back the covers, and my wife is convulsing and shaking uncontrollably as white saliva spews from her mouth. Her eyes roll back toward the top of her head. "Oh my god, no!" I yell out in anguish. "Sharon, call 911!"

The police and ambulance arrive in seven seconds flat. "What took you so long?" I scream. This can't be happening because our life is good again. Everything is perfect, and we're happy. This has to be a bad dream that I really need to wake up from. I'm livid and out of control. I'm yelling at the EMT workers because from where I'm standing, it looks like they aren't doing a damn thing. I even threaten them that if she dies, "I will kill you!" I tell them.

Two uniformed officers quickly intervene and strongly suggest that I get a grip of myself and clam down or they are going to arrest me. They won't let me ride in the ambulance with her, but Sharon can which is actually a good idea.

Stay with your mom, and I'll pick up your grandmother, and we'll meet you at the hospital," I tell her. I needed some time to collect my feelings and get a grip on my emotions. I'm not good in emergency type situations.

"Okay," she says. Ten minutes later, they're bringing Jacqueline down on the gurney.

"Jackie," I call she is unresponsive but breathing. The officer offers to take me in his squad car to the hospital as the ambulance pulls off. I head back into the house to retrieve my wallet and car keys. My mind is spinning in twenty different directions because for the life of me I cannot figure out what the hell is wrong with my wife. I skip the steps two at a time, and as I reach the bottom step, I look up and Robyn is standing in my doorway. The sight of her stops me dead in my tracks.

"Robyn," I call, "what are you doing here?" I say as the sun rays hit her face, which gives it an additional glow. I was powerless against her beauty. She has an inner glow that captivates me, and I couldn't stop staring at her.

"I needed to see you," she replies, "Is this a bad time? I'm sorry. I shouldn't have come here, this is clearly a mistake," as she turns and start to walk away.

I quickly come to her side grab her hand and escort her into the living room. I close the door behind her. We take a seat on the couch. It's been a little over three months since I last saw her.

"Alex, are you sure this isn't a bad time. Was that an ambulance I seen leaving? Is everything alright?"

I jump to my feet and yell, "Jackie! What are you doing here? Look, I really want to talk to you, but this just isn't a good time for me right now, I'm sorry." I say apologetically as she jumps to her feet.

"This was a mistake, and I should go."

"No, wait!" I exclaim. I've never been at a loss for words before when it came to Robyn, but today I'm speechless. "Did you get my note, the flowers, and the perfume?" She nods her head yes. "Talk to me, Robyn, just talk to me," I plead.

She slowly opens her mouth. "First off, thank you. Your friends . . ."

I smile. "Good, I'm glad they were able to help," I say, but I can tell there is more she wants to say. "You have my undivided attention. Just talk to me. I'm listening," I reassure her.

Once Robyn opens her mouth, she opens her heart. She tells me that she's still in love with me and always has been. She confesses to me that she's scared about being a single mother and how she doesn't want to do this alone. She tells me the real reason she initially went back home was to get as far away from me as possible but then realized that's that not what she really wanted. "I want you, Alex. Yes, I was mad and acted prematurely before, but I had time to think, and now I know what it is I want. I want you, and I want us to raise our child together like a real family," she confesses to me.

Her words are music to my ears because I thought I lost her and my baby. I love Robyn too, and there lies my dilemma: I'm in love with two women at the same time. Robyn and I talk and talk, and for as long as I have known her, this is my first time really seeing her. She opened her heart to me in that moment.

"I hope it's a boy, and I hope he has a smile like yours, and I've always loved the name Jeremiah. Do you like that name?" she asks. "Yes, that's a nice name. Whatever you want. I'm just so glad to see you," I add.

I can't stop looking at her. Robyn's beauty has always paralyzed me with one look. "Hello," I answer laughingly.

"Where are you?" the voice on the other end yells. It is Sharon, and they are at the hospital. "The doctor needs to speak with you! Why are you still at the house? You said you were leaving an hour ago and did you pick up Grandma yet?" Sharon screams. With Robyn professing her love for me catches me off guard. Her words threw me for a loop, and I got sidetracked from the issue at hand. I apologized to Sharon and assure her I'm on my way.

"Robyn, I'm so sorry, I have to go. Wait here for me, okay? I'll be back," I say and then run out the door.

I pick up my mother-in-law, and we make it to the hospital in thirteen minutes. "Alex, what were you doing? You said you were leaving right away." Sharon is relentless in her pursuit to get answers, and all I can do is apologize over and over again.

The doctor comes in and extends his hand. "Mr. Taylor, I presume."

"Doc, how's my wife?" I say as I reciprocate his actions.

"Mr. Taylor, your wife is very sick. Her condition has progressed as I thought it would, and the seizure is just another added complication," he says to me as if I know what he is talking about.

"Doc, what the hell are you talking about? What condition?"

There is a look of bewilderment on the doctor's face because of my ignorance.

He clears his throat. "Wow, this is awkward," the Doctor says, "I just assumed you and your wife discussed her condition.

My patience is gone. "Doc, what condition?" I yell again.

"Your wife has cancer," he solemnly says. "I'm so sorry, but I suggested she starts aggressive chemo treatment a while ago, but she told me you two discussed it and decided against it. Her cancer spread, and she's in stage 4 now. There's nothing left for us to do. I assumed you knew."

Total destruction and despair hit me like a bulldozer demolishing a building. I look toward Sharon and her grandmother as they stand in the corner horrified and sobbing at the same time. Anger ignites from inside out, and this incredible amount of pain just takes over my entire body.

I struggle to speak, and the words are hard to say. "Can you give us a moment please, Doc?" I finally release.

I pull myself together because I can't let my wife see me in such a state of destruction. She slowly begins to open her eyes and through her groggy voice says, "I'm so sorry, honey. I just didn't know how to tell you." She's apologizing to me, which I think is funny because if anyone should be apologizing to anyone, it's me.

"Mom," Sharon cries as she walks by her bedside.

"Hey, hey, now, you stop all the crying . . . both of you . . . all of you," she says as she looks at me. "I'm going to be just fine, and I'll start aggressive treatment now. I get it, I do. I'm ready to fight now because I know how much . . . how much I am loved," she says, still looking at me.

So many thoughts plague my mind, and for the first time in my life I question God. Within the past two years, I have experienced so much tribulation that it makes me wonder if he is real.

"It's not fair!" I manage to say. "It's just not fair!"

"It's all right, Alex," Jackie says.

But it isn't all right. "No, it's not all right, Jackie. First Alexis and then Mama and now you. What does he want? What do I have to do? Why am I surrounded by so much death?" I yell out of anguish.

"Alex, stop it!" my mother-in-law demands. "Just stop with all that blasphemy because the Lord don't owe you a damn thing, and get off that pity soap box of yours and be the man my daughter needs you to be right now!" My mother-in-law scowls at me in her matriarchic voice just like my mother used to do. I stand there for a moment longer looking at my wife. I kiss her on the forehead and then leave. Although my mother-in-law is right, I can't deal with this now, and I just want to be alone.

Raylene
I Think They Call It Peace

They transfer me to the Edna Mahan Correctional Facility in Hunterdon County, and the good thing about that is it gets me away from Leslie. So much for our sisterly bond because I haven't seen or heard from Jessica or Robyn in months, but Detective Sosa comes by and let me know he's still waiting on the results of my DNA and then proceeds to fill me in on his findings and theories as what may have happened to me twenty years ago.

"And Eli and his firm were involved because they were the ones who manufactured all the illegal documents, and desperate couples paid them thousands and thousands of dollars to get them well-bred, healthy African American babies," he tells me.

I sit and listen to this whole other story which he claims is my life. From the moment he opens his mouth, I watch and listen to every word that comes out. He tells me a story of lies, betrayal, and murder. As bad as this all sounds, it's still better than the life I've lived.

I finally see the article that Times Magazine did on me and Big Daddy. For once in my life, I wish they would get their story straight. They wrote, "Raylene Chambers is a long-time resident of Camden, New Jersey, and has been brought up on previous charges of embezzlement and fraud in other cases . . ." Where the hell do they get this shit from? Being stupid should be against the law too. I finished my GED, and now I'm enrolled in their college prep classes. They have a fully accredited college program through their reentry program. I've always thought about going to college, and now that I have the opportunity, why not, especially if it's on someone else's dime.

I've started a journal, writing down all my feelings of hurt, disgust, shame, pain, disappointments, and fear. I write about anything and everything. I have calculated all the time I was facing, 7,322 days, ain't that a bitch! Although writing has become very therapeutic for me, I must keep my guard up so I don't become too complacent here. I'm told I have a visitor, and my first thought is, It's about time they brought their ass back to see me. As I walk into the visitor's center, I do not see anyone who resembles me. As I turn to leave, I hear a voice say, "Oh my god, it's true! Jessica really does have a twin."

"Excuse me, who the hell are you?"

"I'm sorry, my name is Brenda, Brenda Jackson, and Jessica asked me to look at your case."

"Jessica . . . you know Jessica?" I ask her.

"Yeah, she's my cousin," she tells me.

"And you're an attorney?" I repeat as I turn back, sit down, and graciously smile because there's hope again. I immediately go into defense mode and tell her my whole life story, and once I open my mouth, I'm nonstop. I start telling Brenda everything that has happened to me starting from day one, up until the day I killed Big Daddy; and she listens to every word I utter without interruption, condemnation, judgment, or reproach. "Your reality is your truth! My reality is my truth! Our choices don't define us, our character does! You know what's in your heart and you did your best with the circumstances you were faced with at that time. What more does anyone want from you? In other words, fuck them!"

Brenda talks about the loves of her life, Gregg and her son, Marcus. Next, she tells me about her father and her sister, Savannah. Lastly, she speaks with such passion about her twin brother, Brandon, who was murdered out west a little over two years ago. "And after that, that's what made me go into law," she says. "There's just so much injustice going on, and no one is being held accountable for it!" I got the feeling she was speaking from a personal experience. "Awhile back, I was one of five finalists for this very prestigious job with a Fortune 500 Company, or so I thought. Anyway, they narrowed it down to five finalists between myself, African-American, a Caucasian, a Hispanic, Native American, and an Asian."

I laugh. "You're kidding, right? Where you working the UN?"

"I wish, and get this: we find out there was no position this was more about this white man trying to blackmail each one of us and use us for his own personal and illegal gain," she says.

"Oh my god, what did you do?"

"We had to learn to put our differences aside and work together. Was it easy? Hell no. Was it worth it? Hell yes because we beat this bastard at his own twisted, sick game. I had no intention of letting this fraction of a man beat me, especially since he was the bastard that killed Brandon! Can you imagine how hard it was for me to go through all that and then come back and lie to my father's face about what really happened to his only son?"

She stops and stares into space before she continues, "It hurt me, but it didn't stop me, but I say that to say this: I need you to stay strong. I need for you to dig deep down in you and find that same energy you had all these years. I need you in survival mode. I know you had to have made some very difficult decisions in your past in certain situations. That's the energy I'm looking for from you today and going forward. I'm not here to judge you, Raylene. I'm here to help you because through the good, bad, or indifference, this here, doesn't define you, your character does."

I automatically like Brenda. She is down to earth, passionate, and educated, which makes her a triple threat. She gives me a quick rundown of her background, personal and professional, and her education. "This girl is on fire!" I sing because she thinks like I think as we laugh. "And the first thing I am going to do. is apply for a new trial due to inadequate representation," she explains as she stands to her feet. "Okay, Raylene, I'll be back I touch with you as well as Jessica."

"Jessica, you're gonna see Jessica?" I ask her.

"Well, most likely I'm just gonna call her. Why?"

"It's just that I haven't heard from her in a while, and I was wondering if . . . well, if she isn't too . . ."

She smiles. "You want her come by and see you?" she finishes my thought. There is a great sense of complacency and pride that falls over me, and for the first time, my mind and heart are at rest. I think they call this peace.

Robyn

Is This a Bad Time?

Maybe it is wrong of me to come, but I need clarity on his letter. As the Lyft pulls in front of Alex's house, I see an ambulance driving away and another squad car parked across the street. I just assume it's for the neighbor. It's 9:30 a.m., and Alex is an early riser and probably not home, but his truck is still in the driveway, which is a good sign.

I ask the driver to wait one moment. I want to make sure he is home first. The front door is wide open, and as I approach it, I see Alex coming down the stairs, two at a time. He looks at me and then stops dead in his tracks. "Robyn," he calls as I turn and see the driver speed away.

My heart is pounding, and my palms are sweating, and then it hits me: I don't know if Jackie is here or not, and it is too late to retreat. Alex is calm and so serene, and he has this angelic look in his eyes as he looks at me. I feel it too, which is why it is so easy for me to open up to him and tell him that I love him and how I want us to be a family and raise our child together.

He invites me in, and we sit, talk, and laugh just like old times. Alex still takes my breath away with his caring and gentle nature toward me, and the look in his eyes is priceless when he looks at me. "What are you doing here?" he finally ask me.

"Is this a bad time?" I say after I realize the ambulance left from his house.

Alex starts to fumble over his words. "Yes, no, I mean yes. Jackie, that was Jackie . . . and I need to, but I want to . . . What are you doing here? I should be going, but I want to talk to you," he tells me. I feel like the biggest idiot on the earth, and I try to leave, but he stops me, which is confirmation that he still loves me.

His wife is on her way to the hospital, and he chooses to stay and talk to me. I'm on cloud nine until the telephone rings.

"Robyn, I'm so sorry! I must go! Wait here for me, please, okay? I'll be right back!" Alex sounds excited to see me. Knowing that he still cares is all I need, and it makes me feel good. I hate this inner struggle I'm dealing with, my heart feeling one way and my mind saying something different, but now my heart and mind are in complete unison with each other.

Knowing that he still cares is all I need, and it makes me feel good. I hate this inner struggle I'm dealing with, my heart feeling one way and my mind saying something different, but now my heart and mind are in complete unison with each other. I think they call this peace. I look around the living room, and it has changed. The centerpiece is gone, and the china cabinet that was sitting in the kitchen is now in the dining room.

I left abruptly this morning because I wanted to avoid the interrogation I would have gotten from Jessica.

"Where are you going? Are you sure you want to keep putting yourself out there knowing he's a married man? You do realize nothing good is going to come from this."

Now I can let Jessica know how wrong she is about Alex now that I've seen him. I call her to let her know I've arrived safely so she does not have to worry.

"Hello," she says dryly.

"What's the matter with you?" I ask.

"What isn't wrong?" She sighs, but I'm not beat for any of this because I'm too excited. I came to see and he still loves me. We are finally going to be a family. Now Jessica will have to eat her words about him being a married man because he is going to be my husband. "Anyway, am just calling to let you know I'm here in Philly. I came to see Alex, and by the way, he still loves me, and we are going to be together," I say to her as smugly as I can. "I get you do not understand our love, but I will show you how wrong you were about his feelings for me and his baby," I say to Jessica with conviction in my voice. I wait a few seconds for some type of response, but she does not say a word. After a few more moments of silence, I add, "Maybe you can call your best friend, Tamara and have her come over tonight," I say and the next thing I hear is the sound of dial tone.

Twenty minutes later, Alex is back home. I run into the living room to give him a big hug, but he's pacing back and forth. That peaceful and serene feeling that we shared earlier is gone. Rage, anger, and a cold blank stare is all over his face.

"Alex," I say softly, "what's wrong?" He's silent for what seems like forever. I approach with caution, taking one baby step closer to him. "Alex, you're beginning to scare me. What's wrong? What happened?" I beg and plead for him to talk to me, just talk to me. Alex walks toward the china cabinet in the dining room and knocks it completely over. All his mother's fine china shatters onto the floor into a gazillion pieces.

"Get out!" He turns and yells to me, "Leave and don't come back! I don't love you, Robyn. I can't love you because everything I love dies! How could I've been so stupid to think that something like this could work! Not again, damn it! Not again! What the fuck do I have to do?" Alex was ranting and raving like a mad man, and he was scaring the hell out of me because I have no idea who he was talking to. He stops and looks me straight into my eyes and says, "Get the hell out of my house and my life and don't ever come back here again!" Alex turns around and proceeds upstairs into his bedroom. He slams the bedroom door so hard the pictures fall off the wall. I'm left standing in his living room in the dark for hours. I'm numb from head to toe and moving was just not an option.

Jessica
My New Partner

I assure Detective Sosa that I will stay in touch with him even with all the personal shit I have going on. Robyn have officially lost her mind, and if she is content with being Alex's doormat, then there's nothing left for me to say. She and Tamara have become amazingly comfortable with thinking they can talk to me anyway they want to. "You should call your girl, Tamara and see what's she's up to." Robyn says me before I hit the disconnect button on my phone. I'm just about sick of their shit.

It was 2:00 a.m. when I hear the key being turned in the door. I turn on the light and walk into the living room. Robyn is standing there. She looks beat up and emotionally drained, and the look on her face tells me everything I need to know. I watch her as she goes into her room and closes the door behind her. I turn and go back to bed.

I meet my new partner today. Her name is Sage Williams, and I've seen her around the academy several times before, but we were never formally introduced until now.

"Hi, I'm Jessica Lovejoy," I say as I extend my hand.

She looks at me and slowly extends her hand back in my direction. Sage has this tough exterior, which I think is a front.

The other day, while waking our beat, this homely-looking man approaches us.

"Um, um, um . . . I just love a woman in uniform," he slurs to her through some missing teeth.

"Um, um, um . . . I just love a man with teeth," she replies to him as we laugh.

"You know you're so wrong for that," I say. "So, what made you go into law enforcement, Williams?" We address each other by our surnames.

"Being a police officer is in my blood. It's all I've ever wanted to be since I was a little girl. To me this is more than just wanting to play cops and robbers, Lovejoy. It's about making sure the lines of justice don't become blurred. Not to mention I have a six-year-old son who I need to make this world a safe place for," she says. There's determination in her voice, and I can respect the fact that she wants to make sure the lines of justice don't become blurred because it's blurry as hell from where I'm standing.

"A son? What's his name?" I ask because she is close to my age. She must have been a kid when she had him. "How old?" I start to say and then stop.

"He's six going on 26. His name is Swayer and he's the love of my life!" she says emphatically.

"He seems like a remarkable young man," I say as I see the look of pride in her eyes.

"He most definitely is." Sage opens up like spring flowers beginning to bloom. We share similar commonalities. She dropped out of law school six months prior to taking the bar exam, and her family was livid as well and plus the fact she had a baby out of wedlock, they disowned her as well, and the both of us were stupid enough to have dated the same cadet, Sean.

"Well, consider yourself lucky, Lovejoy. At least you didn't sleep with him," she admits to me. It's the unspoken commonalities we share the most that seals our partnership.

After three months on the job, Sage tells me she's getting bored and she's ready for some real action. She's a good cop, but she can be a bit impetuous at times, which worries me all the time. My workdays are long and arduous, and normally by the time I get home, I'm mentally and physically exhausted.

Robyn has been very sullen and mopey since she came back from Alex's. It's just best to leave her alone until she's ready to talk.

"You look like hell, Lovejoy. Not sleeping well?" Sage asks as we dress for roll call. We normally sit in the back row because Sage says she doesn't trust any of the men here and she wants to keep her eye on them. As we're listening to today's announcements, I hear the captain talk about an APB on an Anthony Mitchell and circulate a flyer.

"Oh my god, that's Tony," I say.

"Who's Tony, Lovejoy?"

"He's my best friend's brother," I whisper. The captain assigns us our normal details, but all I can think about is Tamara and why she hasn't called me and let me know Tony is in trouble. I know we haven't been on the best of speaking terms, but she should have called anyway.

I am in a state of shock as I stare at the APB.

"Lovejoy, Lovejoy you, all right?" I hear as Sage is calling my name. "So, let's do that?" is the last audible thing I hear her say. I agree, "Um, yeah, sure," I add, but in all honesty, I have no idea of what I am agreeing to.

"Wait! Do what?"

"Focus, Lovejoy. What is going on with you today?"

"It's just that I know this guy," I tell her.

"Good, let's go," she says as we head toward our squad car. "So since you know him, let's go and get him," she insists. "How else are we going to get any kind of respect around here? Come on, Lovejoy, half of these assholes here probably think we should be home barefoot and pregnant anyway, including the captain, but if we bring him in," she says as she waves the flyer in the air, "the captain will have no choice but to give us some real police work. You know I'm right. If we want it, we're going to have to take it!"

Sage is hyped like she is on some women's rights freedom march.

"Lovejoy!" she shouts. "Where's your loyalty? Didn't you take an oath to protect and serve the public and not your best friend's brother?" she says to me.

Our patrol is going well, and it is like any other normal night, a couple of minor traffic stops and partygoers being too loud. It's close to midnight, and our shift is coming to an end. We start to head back toward the station when the call comes in.

"All units, all units, robbery in progress at the corner of Birch and Main. Suspects are described as black males, wearing white tees, blue jeans, and baseball caps. They were last seen running southbound on Main," the dispatcher announces. Sage throws on the siren and speeds in that direction. I spot Tony and the other suspect walking down the street. I jump out the car. "Tony!" I yell. They turn, look at me, and take off running. Sage follows in the squad car and calls for backup. I pursue after them on foot. I follow Tony into a dead-end alley as his partner goes the other way.

"Tony, it's me, Jessica!" I say as I slowly approach him with my gun drawn on him. "Don't do this!" I beg and plead with him.

"Lovejoy, where are you?" Sage calls as she rushes to catch up with me.

"I'm over here!"

"Leave me alone, Jessica!" Tony shouts, "Just tell them I was too fast and I got away."

"Lovejoy, what are you doing?" Sage yells at me with her gun drawn and pointed at Tony.

"Williams, stop! Back off. Let me handle this. I know him. He's not going to hurt me!" I try to reason with her. Everyone is yelling and screaming at one another, and emotions are high.

"Lovejoy, step aside! Police! Drop your gun and put your hands up!" she orders Tony.

Tony is unstable, shaking, and scared. I need Sage to stop yelling at him and let me handle it. I turn in her direction. "Williams, stop, back off, and let me handle it!"

"Lovejoy, don't be a fool! He has a gun!"

"I'm well aware of that, and he won't hurt me, if you just let me handle this," I tell her and slowly turn back in his direction. "Tony, I'm putting my gun down," I say as I slowly place my gun on the ground. "Tony, whatever is going on, we can work through it together, and I'll help you any way I can, but I'm going to need for you to put your gun down and come with me so no one gets hurts," I say, and I'm making progress.

"Lovejoy, move!" Sage yells again.

"No, I'm not going to let you shoot him, Sage! Where's backup?" I ask.

That is the last thing I remember saying because the next thing I hear are the sounds of shots being fired and returned.

Raylene
7,322 Days

Word on the street is Amanda is hardcore now and she's picking up where Big Daddy left off, which is downright crazy. She is going to get herself killed. Nobody from the family keeps in touch with me anymore, and that's fine with me because I don't have the time or energy to worry about anyone else but myself.

My mornings are pretty much routine and mundane. I'm up at 5:30 a.m., and I do some jumping jacks and sit-ups in my room. I'm the first one in the shower by 6:15 a.m. because I want to get the hot water. They start serving chow by 7:15 a.m. and by 8:00 a.m. I'm in class until 10:45 a.m. I get one hour of mandatory recreation time in the courtyard. Otherwise, I'm in my cell reading, writing, and studying.

Brenda tells me she has spoken with Jessica and wants me to add her name to my list of visitors. "And the first thing to do is get a new trial due to inadequate representation." "I'll keep you posted when it's gets approved," Brenda tells me before she hangs up the phone.

When they first transferred me, I used to mark off each day that passed on my calendar. I add up all the time. I'm looking at 7,322 days, which knocks me off my seat, and to make matters worse, I am having those nightmares more often.

I am summoned to the warden's office just before lights-out.

"Chambers, I just want to let you know that Leslie is being transferred here, and I'm counting on you to stay far away from her because I don't want any trouble in my house," he scolds me. Ain't that a bitch!

There's so much foul shit going on in this place that I start keeping two journals, one for my personal protection and the other filled with some of my personal thoughts, poems, and short stories I've started to write. I find writing to be very therapeutic, and as fucked up as my has been, there has got to be a best-selling book or movie in here. Learning how to adjust to this environment has become a daily task for me as well. I am numb from head to toe twenty-three out of twenty-four hours of the day. I've never experienced so much solitude in my life.

Big Daddy had always controlled my thoughts, actions, and feelings, and now that I am in control of myself again, it just feels so mechanical and fake to me. This is new territory for me, and I don't know how to handle it. My hour in the courtyard schools me on a lot of shit I don't want to see or hear. I quickly begin to understand this thing called segregation because 61 percent of the inmates are African American, who basically stay together, 22 percent are Caucasians, and the other 18 percent are of Hispanic descent, including Mexicans, Puerto Ricans, Cubans, and South Americans, and each group only socializes with their own, which is fine with me because I'm not trying to socialize with any of these bitches.

"I heard about you. You're the one who checked Leslie in the county," this unidentified woman says to me.

"So what of it?" I say.

"That makes you top dog around here," she continues. I look around at my surroundings, and since I'm not too impressed with my current situation, I decline. "No, thank you."

"No woman is an island, especially in a place like this. We can all use a friend," she says as she brushes the hair from my face, which makes me uncomfortable. This is all a little too familiar again.

"It's my friends who got me here in the first place," I reply to her as I step backward because I don't want her touching me.

"My name is Charlie," she smiles.

"And?" I say.

"And I'll be seeing you again," she says and then walks away. What the fuck is it about me that attracts females? I wonder if Jessica and Robyn have the same problem. If my reputation precedes me like she heard, then she should know not to fuck with me either.

I'm called to the visitors' center, which I'm glad of because it gets me out of the courtyard and away from that girl. When I get there, I see Detective Sosa, which surprises me.

"What do you want?"

"How are things going?"

"Fine, until I heard Leslie is being transferred here," I tell him. "So what do you want?" I say again.

"I have your result from your DNA," he says. I just stand there and look at him. He continues, "And it confirms that you are the biological daughter of Jade and Jonathan Armstrong, and your given birth name is Jordan Armstrong," he tells me. His words literally blows me away and stops me in my tracks. It's one thing for me and Robyn to have been adopted, but for Jessica too, I drop my head as tears fills my eyes, and my body begins to shake. I can feel the pressure building again, and I almost flip out again, but Sosa catches me. He wraps his arms tightly around me and vows that to help me get through this. No other words are spoken after that.

After a couple of minutes, "Did you tell Jessica yet?" I ask.

"No, not yet," he response. He stops in his tracks. "Jessica isn't built like you, Raylene. Finding out she was part of some kind of human-trafficking-smuggling ring hit her extremely hard. It's going to take her some time to come to grips with all of this."

"Wow, you're really full of surprises," I say to Sosa.

"Why is that?"

"Why did you do all of this? Go through all this act like you care or something?" I say.

"Because it's not an act. I've always cared about you," he replies.

I shake my head. "People just don't do nice things for people without expecting something in return. That is something Big Daddy has instilled in me all my life," I tell Sosa. There is a look of confusion and disbelief that engulfs his face. "Do me a favor, please? Don't ever mention that man's name around me again. I find out Sosa has used his influence or connections with the warden to give me some special privileges and protection. The Warden tells him that I have become one of their model inmates, which was a surprise to me because I was under the impression he did not like me."

"Wow, he really did a number on you," Sosa says to me. I do not know who I can trust or believe anymore. I want to believe him, but I cannot allow myself to get sucked into another man's web of lies and deceit. I thought about all of my past encounters and experiences I've had with him—some were good, some were bad, and some were indifferent, but the fact still remains he's just another man who will eventually only want one thing, one day. I finally say to him.

He stands to his feet and places his hands over mine. "Stop selling yourself short and stop thinking all men are like Cornell. You have always been a diamond in the rough. You see, a person of your caliber does not need a lot of nurturing, you just need truth! You were never allowed to think for yourself because you were too busy trying to survive!" Cornell has dictated every part of your life! You have no idea who you really are, do you? But let me tell you what I see. I see a warrior, someone who is strong, independent, vibrant, young, beautifully made, and beautifully black, who, unfortunately, had to fight her entire life! Was it fair? Of course not! Did it defeat you? Of course not! Was it necessary? I do not know, but you have won, and you are still winning because you are still here! You are not alone, Raylene, and yes, everyone could use a break, occasionally."

I hear Sosa loud and clear, and I'm speechless, but more importantly, I believe him, and for the first time in my life, I feel validated and vindicated as a human being. I'm in control, and I'm making my own decisions now, without repercussion or fear, and the only person I am responsible for is me, myself, and I. My physical body may be locked down, but my mind and my conscious are free, and that makes today a good day!

Robyn
Next of Kin

I'd tossed and turned the whole night and this heartburn is adding more aggravation to an already fucked up situation. I get up to get some Tums when I notice the time. It is well after midnight, and Jessica should have been home by now. I get a funny feeling in my gut but dismiss it because I've been in a foul mood ever since I got back from Alex's house.

I take two Tums and head back to bed when there is a knock on the door. I stand still for a moment thinking they'll go away when they knocked again.

"Who is it?" I yelled.

"It's Officer Johnson, ma'am. Please open the door."

I look through the peephole and see a uniformed officer standing there. "Can I help you?" I say with suspicion in my voice as I crack open the door.

"Are you Robyn Richards?" he asks me.

I nod my head yes because I'm still confused as to why he is here at 4:00 a.m.

"I'm sorry to inform you that your sister, Officer Lovejoy, has been injured in the line of duty," he says.

"What? What injury are you talking about?" I say still with a great amount of skepticism topped with fear in my voice.

"Ma'am, if you don't mind coming with me!"

"Stop calling me ma'am!" I shout. "What injury?" I ask because the fear was becoming real as I grab and hold my stomach. I can feel the baby getting just as anxious as I am.

He stands there and looks into my eyes and then softly says, "I'm afraid she's been shot. Please ma'am, if you don't mine, we really need to get going," he continues to say as am grasping for air.

I slowly acquiesce to his request and reach for my coat and my purse. Nausea starts to set in as we head toward his squad car. Thousands of thought run through my mind nonstop.

"She' at University Hospital, "he informs me. I'm escorted into the back of his squad car with sirens blaring. I do not dare say a word the whole ride because I am afraid to open my mouth for fear that I may vomit.

At the hospital, I'm met by her captain and her partner.

"Hi, I'm Officer Sage Williams," she says to me. "You must be Robyn. I've heard so many great things about you." I vaguely remember hearing her name once or twice before, but I've just been wrapped up into my own shit to care. I feel like a total ass right now. I continue looking at Sage as she speaks and nod my head in agreement with whatever she says.

"Did anyone notify her parents?" I ask.

Her captain approaches me, "You're the only name listed as next of kin," he informs me. Your parents are here?" he asks skeptically.

"She's adopted, as was I," I tell him. "I think you should call them. I'm sure they would want to be here."

I tell her Captain everything I know about them. He sends another officer to go and pick them up. The doctor finally comes into the lobby where we're anxiously waiting.

The doctor approaches her captain, "This is her sister," he immediately tells the doctor.

"This is her sister," he says to the doctor.

All of his attention is now focused on me, "Your sister is still in surgery, and at this point, it's still too early to access one way or the other because of where the bullet is lodged," the doctor says and just as quickly as he appeared, he disappears. I'm about to faint after he said that. I look for the first seat closet to me. Sage comes and sits next me.

"Can I get you anything?" she asks me.

After two deep breathes, I ask, "What happened?" but before she can open her mouth, her captain instructs her not to say a word and to go back to the station and start writing her report. The look on her face looks like regret. She turns and walks away.

Two hours later a well-dressed, stocky man and finely dressed, attractive lady come running into the emergency room. "We were told our daughter is here," his baritone voice booms. As soon as I see them, I know. I slowly rise from my seat and cautiously walk toward the receptionist's desk. It isn't my intention to frighten them any further. "Excuse me," I say as they turn and look in my direction. Time stops and they just stare at me for what seems like forever. I can see tears forming in her eyes, and he clears his throat two to three times before he begins to speak.

"Pumpkin," he whispers softly as he clings tightly to his wife.

I stretch my hand in his direction. "My name is Robyn, and I'm Jessica's twin sister," I say, but before another word can be spoken, the doctor comes back out. "It's critical. She slipped into a coma," he announces, which causes Mrs. Lovejoy to pass out, and Mr. Lovejoy shuts down completely, and for a second time my whole world has been turned completely upside down.

For days and days on end, I watch as they sit by their daughter's bedside praying, and I feel like I'm heading toward a nervous breakdown myself, and I'm scared because Jessica is all the family I have left now. Alex has made it is perfectly clear this time that he does not want to have anything to do with me ever again, which I still do not understand why. What did I do?

I cannot stand looking at Jessica lying in that hospital bed so lifeless, and it makes me feel just as useless when Amber was in the hospital because there wasn't a damn thing I could do then and there isn't a damn thing I can do now.

I cannot believe my eyes when Tamara walks through the door. Best friend my ass; they have not spoken to one another in months, and now she has the audacity to sashay her ass in here. I try to hold my peace given the current situation, but I can't because I've seen how it affected Jessica the last time they argued, it cut her to her core, and that's my only discontent with her. I don't want Jessica upset.

"What the hell are you doing here?" I say.

"Robyn, please, I'm not in the mood for your nonsense," Tamara says and pushes me to one side and goes and stands next to Mr. Lovejoy. He looks at her and welcomes her with open arms. It's going to be a long night.

I watch as the tears fall from her eyes, which I don't think much about at first. "How did you know she was here?" I ask out of curiosity because I doubt anyone from the hospital called her.

She is quiet, so I repeat the question, "How did you know Jessica was here, Tamara?" as Mr. Lovejoy turns to look in her direction, waiting for a response. She is mortified, and she immediately starts to apologize over and over again to Mr. Lovejoy.

"I am so, so sorry," she says, sounding like a scratched CD disc. She babbles on about how he didn't mean it and it was an accident. "You know, Jessica is like a sister to him, and he would never do anything intentionally to hurt her," she says voluntarily. The door opens, and the nurses are escorting Mrs. Lovejoy in after checking her out. They assist her into a seat. Mr. Lovejoy walks toward his wife and grabs her hand, but the look on his face is the same as mine—confused.

"Tamara, what are you talking about? What do you mean do anything to hurt her?" he asks calmly but inquisitively.

Through her runny nose and bloodshot eyes, she says, "Tony shot Jessica!" She sobs uncontrollably. Well, if there is ever a moment in time when the earth will stand still, it is now. It's a good thing Mrs. Lovejoy is already sitting because it would have been a repeat performance. It's official. I was skeptical about her before but now its personal, and I do not like Tamara Mitchell one bit. Before she could say another word, this giant voice booms like thunder after lightning strikes and yells, "Get the hell out!"

"I'm so—" is the only thing she can get out of her mouth as she drops her head and walks out of the room. No one speaks another word.

It is going on 10:00 a.m., and my scheduled doctor's appointment is right upstairs. Jessica was supposed to come with me. I excuse myself but assure them that I will be back. I press the elevator button, and as the doors opens, this man runs into me and nearly knocks me over. "Excuse me, Jessica. Oh, thank goodness, they told me you were shot. Are you okay? What happened?" he says in one breath and doesn't give me a chance to respond.

"Excuse me," I say, annoyed.

"Jessica," he abruptly says again and then stops and stares at me. "Wait, you're not Jessica?"

I shake my head. "No shit, Sherlock," I say as sarcastically as I possibly can because I'm tired, hungry, and annoyed, which is never a good combination for me. I proceed to go around him and step into the elevator. Before the door closes, he turns around and comes back into the elevator as well.

"Sosa," he says.

"What?"

"You called me Sherlock. My name is Detective Sosa, Lawrence Sosa," he says as he tries to apologize, but I am in a funk and I'm not in the mood to socialize.

"Whatever," I say as I step off the elevator and head toward the receptionist's desk.

"Robyn," he calls. "Your name is Robyn, right?"

I stop and turn around and walk back in his direction. "How the hell do you know my name, and who the hell are you?" I say again in my don't-fuck-with-me voice. He quickly confesses and smirks at the same time. I don't see anything funny.

"Like I said, my name is Detective Sosa, and I've been working with your sister Jessica on your case, and I stopped by the station to see her, but they told me she was shot last night, and that's why I'm here. How's she doing?"

"Not good. She fell into a coma as they were operating on her," I say and then literally fall into his arms, which I don't mean to, but I'm mentally and physically exhausted.

He grabs me and escorts me into the nearby waiting room, where he gives me a cup of water. "You're pregnant," he says.

I take a sip. "Boy, you really are a detective," I rebut and then smile. I point to the receptionist's desk. "I have an appointment today, and Jessica . . ." I start to say and then stop because I'm sure he can't care less about my problems. "Anyway, you said something about my case. What case is that?"

There is a look of surprise when I say that, and the more and more I look at this guy, the more attracted he becomes. His hazel-colored eyes and that smooth olive complexion is actually beginning to turn me on. I'm becoming sexually aroused without having sex. This can't be normal. Something must be wrong. I'll check with the doctor about this because this can't be good for the baby.

As I wait to be seen, we sit, and he tells me everything. I'm in complete shock, and I have no idea any of this is happening.

"I'm surprised she hasn't mentioned anything to you about this because she knows I need your DNA as well to confirm. I made that very clear to her."

"Well, it's probably not entirely her fault. I haven't been the most approachable person these past few days, and now this. I mean, everything is happening so fast it's hard to take it all in," I say.

"I can imagine, and you're right, everything is happening so fast, but now that I've met you and know you're pregnant, well . . . we can slow it down a bit," he says to me and flashes me a smile.

"Oh, wait, we have another twin sister," I say.

"Yes, I know. Raylene," he says, which surprises me even more. He smirks again. "I've known Raylene for years," he confesses. He sits there with me, and we talk until my name is called. I go into my doctor's office with a smile on my face, and to my surprise, he is still waiting there when I come out.

"You waited for me?" I ask.

"Uh, yeah . . . I hope you don't mind," he says. "How are you?" he asks. "I mean, is everything good with the baby and all?" he says as he stumbles over his words.

I'm impressed. "Yes, everything is just fine," I tell him.

We head back toward Jessica's room, where Mr. and Mrs. Lovejoy are still sitting by her bedside. I introduce Detective Sosa to them.

"It's a pleasure to meet you, sir. Sorry it's under these circumstances," Detective Sosa says.

Mrs. Lovejoy nods her head and does not say anything. Detective Sosa looks at me. "How's she doing?" he starts and gets no responses. He continues, "I know this isn't the best time, but it is imperative that I speak with the both of you.

Mrs. Lovejoy looks up. "About what? What could possibly be so important that you need to speak to us about, especially at a time like this?" Mrs. Lovejoy is beside herself as she speaks so lovingly and eloquently about Jessica.

"She's a fighter, you know, a survivor. The first time I'd seen her, I knew, we both knew. And they didn't have to tell me anything else about her because it didn't matter." She looks at me, "And they never mentioned anything about twins to us," she adds emphatically. "All they said was she was put up for adoption by a teenage, unwed mother. Her passion is genuine that she loves her daughter, while Mr. Lovejoy stands in the corner crying like a newborn baby. I'm speechless as I watch this man crumble and cry. It is clear they love Jessica very much.

"Can we please just do this some other time," as he hands Sosa his business card in this defeated voice. I get up and walk over to Mr. Lovejoy and hug him as tight as I can.

Detective Sosa

No Strings, Issues, Rebounds, or Regrets

The news of Officer Lovejoy being shot disturbs me greatly, and by the time I arrive at the hospital, I'm advised that she has already slipped into a coma.

I truly enjoy meeting Robyn and immediately feel a connection with her, which I like. I call Sully and tell him that I'm due to talk with the Lovejoys within the next few days. "Any luck with finding him?" I ask.

"Still searching," he says, but I know if anyone can do it, Sully can.

After leaving the hospital, I go directly to the station to speak to Officer Williams. I need to know the details as to what really happened because I assured Robyn that I would get to the bottom of things. I have her repeat her story to me and then request a copy of her report as well. Her captain advises me that she would be temporarily assigned to desk duty until a full investigation is completed.

"Is there a problem?" I ask the captain.

He seems hesitant. "There shouldn't be, ballistics will determine if the bullet came from her gun or his," the captain says. "If you don't mind, what's your interest with Officer Lovejoy, Detective?"

"I'm in the middle of an investigation which is directly related to her and her sisters, and this just complicates things further," I inform him.

"I can imagine, especially when you have an overzealous rookie who wants to prove herself," he adds. I know what he is saying.

"Well, let's pray she has the strength to pull through this because she's going to need it," I say. I thank the captain and ask him to keep me posted.

My every thought is of Robyn, and for whatever reason, I find myself being drawn to her from the moment I first laid eyes on her, and I want to see her again. She has this inner glow about her, and even though she is an exact copy of Raylene and Jessica, she is different. Her vibe pulls me in, and although I'm aroused by it, this is more than just another sexual feeling. No woman has ever had that kind of effect on me so quickly, not even Lita, and I'm not about to ignore it.

Two days later, I go back to the hospital to check on Officer Lovejoy. When I get to her room, no one is there. I stand by her bedside and say a prayer. After a few seconds, I turn to leave as Mrs. Lovejoy enters.

"Detective," she says. "What are you doing here?"

"I just wanted to see how she's doing," I tell her. "I first met Jessica at graduation, and I've come to know her quite well over these past few months, and I just wanted to stop by to see how she's doing and see if there's anything I could do," I offer.

Mrs. Lovejoy didn't respond nor did she take her eyes off Jessica. I quietly start to walk away. "Detective," she calls.

I turn. "Yes?"

"Have you ever loved someone so much that when they're not breathing, you aren't either?"

"Ma'am?"

She smirks. "Oh, please call me Vivian. My mother-in-law was the madam in this family. From the moment we brought her home, I knew that I couldn't love her any more than if I had given birth to her myself," she says in this heartbreaking tone. This probably isn't the best time, but if she's willing to talk, I'm compelled to listen to whatever it is she has to say.

"Which adoption agency did you use?" I ask.

"Oh, we didn't use an agency. We went through a private law firm out of Seattle. Goldman, Goldman, and something . . ."

"Weinberg . . . ," I add.

"Um, yeah, that's it. Carl Goldman Sr. handled all of the documents and logistics for us. He was heaven-sent at that time because Matthew and I have been trying for so long but I kept miscarrying over and over again. We even went to a Southside Fertility Clinic that he suggested, but I wasn't chosen for one of their studies because I didn't medically qualify. After that, Mr. Goldman contacted us and told us about a baby girl that was up for adoption. He told us the mother was an unwed teenager and all she wanted was to give her daughter a decent life, something she couldn't provide. We paid five hundred thousand dollars in three separate installments, and three days later we received a call and went to pick up our daughter. All paperwork seemed to be in order, and it was literally that simple. Detective, you must believe me, we knew nothing about a black-market ring. We would have never been a part of something as shady and heinous as that," she says, and I believe her. She is an open book, and without knowing, she has answered questions I haven't asked.

"Would you mind my coming by to take a look at all of your paperwork?" I ask before I leave.

"Anytime," she says.

I finally find the courage to call Robyn and invite her out to dinner. I like her because she isn't pretentious and she doesn't act like a porcelain doll either.

"With Jessica still in the hospital, I assume you wouldn't want to eat alone," I say in a failed attempt to ask her out.

"I guess," she says as if she is contemplating my offer. "I don't like eating alone," she confirms. "Okay, where do you wanna go?"

"We can decide that after I pick you up. I'll see you in twenty minutes," I say and then hang up the phone.

Robyn intrigues me, and I am going to do everything in my power not to blow this. When Lita called off the wedding for a second time, I was distraught and was on a temporary path of self-destruction.

"You get ass thrown at you every minute of every day. I hope you're being smart about it," Sully says, which makes me stop and think about how reckless my behavior has been over the past several months.

When I arrive at her place, she is already standing at the front gate in the guard's house. "I thought it would just be easier if I met you down here," she says.

Robyn tells me she is craving Italian, so I bring her to one of my favorite restaurants. She is just so easy to talk to, and I find it refreshing that we have such an amazing connection with each other. It doesn't feel forced when we talk, and Robyn challenges me on everything, from politics to religion. Normally they are taboo topics to discuss with anyone and especially on a date, but I just enjoy the fact that she is talking. She tells me all about her adoptive family in California, and she even confesses to being a co-conspirator in crime to have her ex-boyfriend beat up.

"So you're confessing to me that you were a conspirator in assault crime," I say, which causes her quickly to change her story. I laugh. She has this off-the-cuff sense of humor, which is simply adorable. She talks about the time Amber and her stole candy from their corner store when they were nine and tried to hide the candy in their training bras, which ended up falling out because they both were too flat chested.

By the time we reach the restaurant, I know her life story. I help Robyn into her seat.

"Wow, I never thought I would laugh like that again," she states as she makes herself comfortable.

"With a smile like yours, you should smile all the time," I tell her.

She stops. "What do you want from me, Detective?" she finally asks as she opens her menu.

"Excuse me?"

"Look, you seem like a really nice guy, and I appreciate the fact that you're willing to help us find out about our past, but I'm pregnant, and not once have you asked me anything about the baby or the father," she says to me.

"I figured you would tell me when you're ready," I tell her. "And what do I want from you? For now, your friendship, just your friendship. Is that a crime?"

She smiles and shakes her head no.

"Besides what's the worst thing that could possibly happen? I mean, you could fall madly in love with me, and after we're married, have six or seven babies of our own?" I say jokingly as I keep my eyes on my menu. I feel her eyes on me.

The waiter approaches our table. "May I take your order?" he asks. We give our orders, and I hand him both of the menus still with no eye contact.

"So what about the baby's father? Are you two still together?" I finally ask as I refill both of our glasses with water.

"Well, so much for me telling you when I'm ready," she responds.

I shrug my shoulders. "Time's up," I say with direct eye contact.

She fumbles with her napkin and her silverware for a moment. She takes a long sip of water and clears her throat. I can see this is hard for her, and it isn't my intention to make her feel uncomfortable,

"Listen, I didn't . . ."

"No, no, I want to talk about Alex. I need to talk about him because I don't understand what happened myself. I don't even know where to start."

"The beginning always works for me."

"Alex is a trucker and was always coming to LA on business. That's where I first met him."

"How old were you?"

"Thirteen when I first met him, but over the years, we've became fast friends. I was always running away from home and Alex would look out for me. You know, talk to me and protected me. He would tell me how beautiful and smart I was, and he just basically believed in me, you know what I'm saying. My family made me feel like an outcast most of my life, and then I found out why. But Alex was different. He accepted me for me, and I'm not going to lie, it made me feel good. You can believe that before he left out of LA, my black ass was back at home."

"So he looked out for you."

"Yeah, he did. He really cared for me, at least I thought he did."

"Well, what changed?"

"That's just it, I honestly don't know! I mean, he was mad at me at first because he thought I got pregnant on purpose, which I didn't. I know he has been having problems dealing with his mother and his daughter's deaths, and he and his wife—"

"Wife!" I shout and then stop her. "He's married?" I yell, which startles the other patrons as well. I look around and nod my head. I need to regroup and pull back. "I'm sorry, it's just that I wasn't expecting . . ."

She doesn't say a word for a while, and I'm beginning to feel like a jackass because I break my own rule. I prejudge her before I know all the facts. There is a moment of awkwardness that lingers in the air. I need to say something, but I don't know what to say.

"Jessica told me the same thing," she says after a while. "And I didn't believe it. I didn't want to believe it! Alex always said that their marriage was over and he made me believe that he was going to leave her and be with me, and I believed him. I believed everything that man has ever told me, and now I don't know if any of it was ever real. I feel like the stupidest person on this earth," she says.

"You're not stupid, Robyn, and you shouldn't feel that way. You let your feelings dictate your actions, which is always a dangerous thing to do because your feelings and emotions change. We all do it, but he misled you with his feelings too," I try to explain to her.

"But he told me he loved me. Was he lying?"

"Robyn, think about it, can you honestly say you can love two people at the same time?" I ask her. "You can't give 100 percent of your time and attention to two different people at the same time. It's physically impossible, and someone is always going to get the shorter end of the stick, plus you don't know what he was telling his wife about you, do you?" She shakes her head no.

We finish our dinner, and I take her home because it is getting late and she needs to rest. I'm convinced, and it is official for me. I love the way she makes me feel. She gives me this sense of invincibility like I can fly. I'm digging this girl, and I don't want to scare her off because this man has done such major damage to her self-esteem and self-worth that I am going to have to take baby steps with her. I'm physically attracted to her as well, and I have to control and suppress these overpowering sexual urges that have been running through my body.

I drive Robyn back home and pass the guard's gate this time. As we approach the front door, she turns around, and we are face-to-face when she leans in to kiss me. I stop her.

"No, not like this," I say. "I'm not confused, and I'm not on the rebound. I like you, Robyn, a lot, but I need the feelings to be mutual with no strings, issues, rebounds, or regrets attached. You understand what I'm saying?" I open the door and wait for her to go in and then turn and walk away.

It's been three weeks, and Jessica is still in a coma. Robyn and I have been spending a lot of time together, and every day my feelings grow stronger and stronger. When I look at her, it calms my world, and I know she feels the same way, but she insists on keeping this wall of defense up, which makes me work harder to penetrate through it. She has to be able to trust herself again before she can trust me, which I completely understand. But I need her to know that I am not Alex and I will not do anything to hurt her because my love is real.

With Jessica in the hospital, I'm not comfortable with the idea of Robyn staying here by herself.

Sully can see I'm truly happy. "Wow, she might actually be the one," he says tome and then laughs.

I smile. "You're right, she jus might be. With Lovejoy still in a coma, I'm thinking about asking her to come and stay with me for the time being. I uncomfortable with her being by herself at night but before I do that, I have to get my spare key from Lita first," I add.

Sully is hysterical with laughter and anticipation. "I'll bet . . . I'll have better luck finding Charles Lambert before you get your spare key from her," he says.

I stand and extend my hand. "It's a bet," I say. Sully knows I never walk away from a challenge, but deep down he is probably right because she has yet to return my grandmother's engagement ring, but I don't dare tell him that.

The next morning I call Lita and ask if we could meet for lunch.

"I knew it would be a matter of time before you came to your senses. Yes, Lawrence, yes, I'll meet you at our special place and same time," she says.

"Fine, I agree and hang up the phone. I immediately call Robyn to check on her and see how she is feeling.

"I had a great time last night."

"Me too," she adds.

"So, what are your plans for today?" I continue.

"Going to the hospital to see Jessica, then I'll be back here later," she tells me.

"Okay, do you mind if I stop by after work? There's something I want to ask you," I tell her.

"I'll see you later," she says and then hangs up the receiver.

Lita is late as usual, which solidifies that things are never going to change with her. She likes the idea that I'm somewhere waiting for her, which gives me more time to think. How could I have ever been so in love with someone so selfish? I had more than my share of arguments with my family behind her, defending her, and they were not disappointed when I called and told them the wedding is off. "Lita, over here!"

She is stunning as usual, and she is still wearing my ring. "Baby, I am so glad you called, and I don't like the way we left things. I really, really missed you. You know, I was thinking we should forgo the whole church scene and fly to Vegas and have a quick sermon and then vacay in the Bahamas or Jamaica. We can do the whole church thing on our one-year anniversary. What do you think?"

She talks at the speed of light. I try several times to stop her, but she just keeps going on and on. Finally I yell, "Lita!" Everyone in the restaurant turns and looks in our direction.

"I didn't call you here so we could discuss wedding plans! We're not getting back together! I just need my spare key back and, while you're at it, my grandmother's engagement ring too!"

She is calm. "Lawrence, baby, please, I know we had some problems in the past, and I know I can be a bit . . ." She stops. Hell, she can't even say it. "And I know I can be trying at times, but I've been there for you, loving you and supporting you with your career and all. I mean, you have put your career before me several times, and I've accepted it," she cries.

"Accepted it? Lita you bitched and complained every chance you got, but that's beside the point, and there's way more problems than just my job, Lita! Look, you are a wonderful person, and I have no doubt that you're going to make some man very happy someday, but I'm not that man," I say to her as graciously as I can.

"There's someone else? Who is she, and what does she have that I don't?" Lita says. She is not listening to me, and I'm trying to be as cordial as possible with her, but it isn't working, and I'm beginning to lose my patience with her.

"Who is she, Lawrence? What's this bitch's name?"

"Hey, now, that's enough!" I yell back at her as I bang my fist on the table, which makes her jump in her seat. "You see, it's this shit right here, this is the kind of shit I don't want to put up with anymore!"

"What?" she asks like she's clueless.

"Your jealousy, Lita, it's out of control, and I can't deal with it, I won't deal with it anymore! I won't deal with it anymore!"

She doesn't say a word. She just sits there for a few minutes looking at me as tears began to form in her eyes. I'm not sure as to what she is going to do next because she is the type that loves to be the victim.

"I'm . . ." is the only thing I say as she lifts her hand and stops me. She stands up from her seat and adjusts her hair and clothing and then heads toward the front door without giving me my key or my ring. I thought about going after her but that is just going to make matters worse.

Robyn

Two Big Heaping Bowls of Chili

If it isn't for Elle, I don't know if I would have survived these last few weeks. He has been so attentive, patient, caring, helpful, and loving toward me, and at times I thought he would leave and never come back. I didn't realize I have so much pent-up anger toward Alex, and at times I find myself taking it out on him. I act like such a bitch, and he'll just step away for a while and return later. I'm not used to anything like that, and I don't know how to respond, but it is effective, and it gets my undivided attention. Even the way he looks at me sometimes just takes my breath away and melts away my pain and anguish. He calms my entire world. I don't believe that I'll ever be happy again, but he has proven me wrong every time. He calls this morning and wants to know if he can stop by later. "There's something I want to ask you," he says, which has my curiosity piqued.

I've been getting to know Mr. and Mrs. Lovejoy a lot better as well, and we are beginning to bond ourselves. They love the fact that Jessica and I have connected so well and appreciate that fact that I'm looking after her condo.

I tell them about my adoptive family and what my life was like growing up. "And, yes I was just as shocked and startled as you were when I first realized there was another sister. I passed out too," I say laughingly.

They ask about Raylene, and they want to know what she is like. I haven't had a strong connection to Raylene like I have with Jessica. As a matter of fact, I don't even know if she knows what happened to her.

"Would you like to meet her?" I ask them because they seem curious to know more about her. Mrs. Lovejoy seems hesitant, which makes Mr. Lovejoy say, "Maybe now is not the best time."

All morning long, I get the feeling Mrs. Lovejoy wants to ask me something but doesn't. I excuse myself because I have to go to the bathroom. Upon my return, she says, "May I inquire about the baby?"

I smile and nod my head yes.

What are your plans? Do you plan on giving the baby up for adoption" she asks as sensitive as she can, and then slowly exhales?

"Adoption? Heavens, no. Why would you think I was going to give my baby up for adoption, especially now what we're going through? I would never do that to my baby!" I tell her, which makes her seem relieved.

"And how are you going to support yourself and a baby?" Mr. Lovejoy asks, which is something that plagues my mind daily because I'm literally down to the end of my savings.

"That's something I'm still working on. I still have a little bit of my savings left, but I need to find a job, and I know no one is going to hire me now, not while I'm pregnant," I say.

"And what about the father?" he asks. "Does he know about the baby, and is he in a position to help?"

I smile and choose my words carefully. "Yes, Alex knows about the baby, and he is more than able to help financially," I say. "He owns several successful businesses in Philly," I tell them. Mr. Lovejoy seems pleased with that answer.

"But I don't want anything from him. He made it very clear that he doesn't want to have anything else to do with me or my baby," I say, which wipes the smile from his face. "But I know things are going to work itself out because I' a survivor and there's isn't a situation that I can't or won't overcome." I utter. Now, I just have to believe it myself.

For the rest of the afternoon, we sit and talk about Jessica. They tell me so many stories about her and what she was like growing up. We laugh, we cry, and we pray, but more importantly, we bond.

It's getting late, and I need to get back to the condo. "How did you get here?" Mr. Lovejoy asks.

"The bus. There's a bus stop right up the street from the condo," I say.

He picks up his cell, and within seconds, a gentleman comes into the room. "Take her to Jessica's condo," he instructs the driver.

"Yes, sir," he says.

Mr. Lovejoy hands me his business card. "In the morning, I want you to call this number. Ask for Lee and tell her that I want her to help you get started working on the Summer Jam project. She'll know what you're talking about."

I'm so overwhelmed that I can't find any words to say. For complete strangers to extend so much help and kindness to me is something I would have never thought of in a million years.

I'm on cloud nine, and I can't believe my luck because this is an opportunity to make something of myself and secure some type of future for my baby and me. I cannot stop smiling.

It is after six when the guardhouse calls. "There's a detective here to see you," he announces.

"Please let him through," I tell him.

Things between Elle and I are going great. Although we haven't officially said the words aloud, he's my boyfriend. I keep thinking a lot about what he said the other night when we were at dinner, and I don't know if he was joking or not.

What's the worst thing that can possibly happen? I can fall madly in love with him and, after we're married, have six or seven babies of our own. I shake my head, which brings me back into reality as I hear the knock on the door.

"Come in, it's open."

His face lights up when he sees me, and my face lights up when I see him.

"Hey," he says.

"Hey, back at cha," I say as he walks towards the kitchen and gives me a kiss on my cheek. He takes his jacket off and places it on the back of the chair and then takes a seat.

"It smells delish. What are you making?" he asks.

"I found this recipe on Facebook, and it looked so good, and I've been having a craving for chili that I just had to try it," I say excitedly. He laughs because everything I see, I say the same thing.

"And how was your visit with your sister and the Lovejoys?"

"Oh my god, you'll never believe what happened!" I scream.

"What, did Jessica wake up?" he asks.

"No, I wish she did, but no. I got a job! Mr. Lovejoy offered me a job today. Isn't that great!"

Once I start talking, my mouth is going a hundred miles a minute. I tell him everything we talked about and then some. Elle just sits there and listens to every word that comes out of my mouth no matter how stupid it sounds. After a few minutes, I notice how he is looking at me, so I stop talking.

"What's wrong? Why did you stop? I'm listening," he says.

"Because I sound like a bumbling idiot and I've been running my mouth from the moment you got here and I haven't even asked you about your day," I say to him.

"I don't want to talk about my day," he says, "because my days are normally filled with suspects, perpetrators, victims, prostitutes, and junkies, which I definitely don't want to discuss. So continue, please."

I place two big heaping bowls of chili on the table, two baked potatoes with sour cream and butter, plus salads. We say our grace and begin to eat.

"So you said you wanted to ask me something this morning," I remind him.

He nods his head as he takes a spoonful of the chili. "Not bad, not bad at all," he says with a smile and a wink.

Elle tells me that he does not like the idea of me staying here alone while Jessica is still in the hospital.

"I have a split-level townhouse, and you are more than welcome to stay on the second level, if you like, until Jessica is well enough to come home. What I'm trying to say is that I would feel more at ease if you weren't here by yourself."

I'm so flattered by his offer, and I want to accept it, but I can't. Mr. Lovejoy has offered me a job of a lifetime, and I'm not going to pass it up over some fantasy about being with a man again who is not my husband. Plus the fact the commute would kick my ass physically and mentally. Elle's townhouse is in South Jersey, and Hip-Hop Records is in New York City. I graciously and respectfully decline his offer. "Thank you, though," I say.

"For what?" he asks.

"For caring," I tell him and give him a kiss on his cheek. He hangs out for an hour or so and then leaves. I tell him to call me when he gets home.

I call Lee first thing in the morning. "I was expecting your call," she says. "When can you come into the office?"

"I can be there Thursday morning around 11:00 a.m.," I tell her.

"See you then."

Shortly after getting off the phone with Lee, Mrs. Lovejoy calls me and says they are on their way to the hospital. "The doctor called. He said that Jessica has showed some signs of improvement. Robyn, she moved her hands and her feet," she says. I can hear tears of joy in her voice.

"I'm on my way." I immediately call Elle's cell phone but don't get an answer, so I leave him a message telling him the good news. Ten minutes later, I'm dressed and heading out the door when my cell phone rings. "Elle," I say, but it is the guard at the guardhouse.

"Your car is here to pick you up," he informs me.

I'm surprised but grateful because I wasn't expecting for them to send a car service for me.

By the time I'm in the car and headed toward the hospital, Elle returns my call. "Morning, babe, I got your message. That's great news, and I'm so happy for you," he tells me.

"I can't believe it! Everything is just falling into place, and I am so happy!" I scream with excitement. "I mean . . . you, a new job, and now Jessica showing signs of improvement. I mean, what else could happen to top this?" I say rhetorically.

"Marry me," he says.

"What?"

"Did I stutter? Marry me! I love you, Robyn. I've loved you the first time I've seen you, and these past couple of months have been the happiest months than the past five years put together. I know . . . you think it's too soon and you still need time to figure things out or get over Alex or whatever else you can think of . . . and I've tried. I really did try to give you the time and space that you needed, but I can't do it anymore! When you didn't accept my offer to move in with me, I knew then, and it was wrong of me to even come at you like that. So I'm coming to you now, and I'm coming correct. Robyn, I'm dying here, and I need you to save my life. Let me be your hero. Will you please just tell me you will marry me?"

The word yes comes out of my mouth so fast and so loud that I scare the driver. He looks at me through the rearview mirror. I wave my hand to let him know I'm all right.

"I will do a better job at proposing when I see you tonight," he says and then hangs up the phone. The smile on my face can span across eight states and then some. Today is a good day.

Robyn
I Feel Conflicted

I run straight toward her room and, to my surprise, walk into a small crowd of people as well. Mrs. Lovejoy is excited and smiling at the same time. "Great, Robyn, you're here!" she says as she grabs my hand and begins to introduce me. "This is my niece Brenda and her fiancé, Gregg, and over there is my other niece Savannah. This is my brother-in-law, Richard, but he prefers to be called Rick, and this is Rose, our . . . lifeline basically. She raised Jessica too."

It is a full-fledged family reunion going on, and I feel like the guest of honor. Mr. Lovejoy has Jessica moved into her own private suite, and as the doctor enters, he's overwhelmed to see so many people in her room.

He turns in Mr. Lovejoy's direction. "Although this is a good sign, but we're not out of the woods yet," he tells him. "We will continue to monitor her closely and see if any more things develop," he says as he walks to her bedside and looks into the pupils of her eyes with his little light.

Mrs. Lovejoy approaches me. "How are you feeling, honey? Did you rest well, and did you eat any breakfast?"

I smile. "I'm fine, and yes, I did eat, but I'll be glad to get my body back because being pregnant—" I start to say and then stop. After the words leave my mouth, I wish I could have taken them back. I look at Mrs. Lovejoy and apologize because I can't imagine how she felt unable to have a baby.

She's a class act. "I'm fine. There's no need to ever apologize to me because God knows what's best for us all," she says, but I still feel like an idiot.

Within seconds, Elle walks through the door, and I'm so happy to see him. "What are you doing here?" I ask.

"Official business," he says and then turns and acknowledges everyone else. "Good morning. How's she's doing?" he asks Mr. Lovejoy.

"We're not out of the woods yet but she showed some signs of improvement." Mr. Lovejoy tells Elle.

Elle smiles. "That's good to hear. Listen, her captain asked me to update you on the investigation."

"What investigation?" I ask

"Into the shooting," he says. He clears his throat. "It seems Jessica and Officer Williams, her partner, were coming close to the end of their shift when they heard the call about a robbery in progress, and they responded. The two suspects were in connection with a string of robberies that were being committed. They were identified as Anthony Mitchell and Ryder Crews. Officer Lovejoy immediately gave chase after Mitchell on foot, while Officer William pursued the other suspect, Crews, in the squad car. Unfortunately, Crews got away, so Officer William went to assist Officer Lovejoy with suspect Anthony Mitchell. Lovejoy had suspect cornered into a dead-end alley, and at some point, Officer Lovejoy felt she was making progress with Mitchell, and she placed her gun on the ground as a sign of good faith. Mitchell did not. Officer Williams was trying to persuade Officer Lovejoy to move aside, but she was determined not to let Office Williams shoot her best friend's brother. Tensions and emotions were high, and there was a lot of yelling and screaming, and that's when Officer Williams said she thought she heard the sound of the suspect's gun being fired, and that is when she began to open fire in that same direction, Officer Lovejoy was caught in the crossfire between the two. They are waiting on ballistics to see which gun the actual bullet came from, Williams or the suspect, Mitchell.

It is quiet, and no one says a word. You can barely hear anyone breathing. After a few minutes, I say, "You said Officer Williams thought she heard the sound of the suspect's gun being fired."

He nods his head.

"Well, what do you mean if it wasn't a gun, what was it?" I ask because what he was saying is not making any sense.

The sound of a car backfiring," he says as he drops his head. The sounds of screams and cries that everyone let loose is piercing to the ears and our hearts.

"You mean to tell me my child is lying here in a coma because some overzealous, rookie-ass cop opened fired on the suspect, not to mention a family friend nonetheless, because she heard the sound of car backfiring, which she thought was a gun? Is that what you're standing here telling me and my family, Detective?" Mr. Lovejoy is livid, and I don't blame him. Elle is speechless. I feel for him, but I'm mad at the same time.

He tries to explain to Mr. Lovejoy, but he doesn't want to hear it. Mr. Lovejoy looks at his wife. "You see, this is why I didn't want her doing this cops and robbers shit and dealing with all this bureaucratic bullshit!" Mr. Lovejoy goes on a political tirade that criticizes everyone, from the Mayor's office on down.

"Uncle Mattie," Brenda hollers, "I fully understand your frustration, but the detective here had nothing to do with any of that! Now we need to stay focused, and the only thing that matters at this point is Jessica coming out of this coma and justice being served! Like the detective said, once ballistic confirms which gun the bullet came from there is nothing we can do. Let's just take one step at a time and stay calm.

"Well, I just wanted to come by and update you and to see how she was doing," Elle says as he looks at me. I just sit there and feel conflicted, and I don't know whom my loyalty should be to at that point, so I turn and look in the other direction.

He drops his head. "Well, I gotta go," he says and then walks out the room without looking back.

For the remainder of the night, we sit there and share more stories about Jessica and the things she used to do which makes her sound like a complete nerd to me.

"You should have seen her. I can only imagine what it took for her to stand up to me the way she did. She was so resolute and passionate in her decision, and she wasn't going to back down no matter what I said. No one ate dinner that night, did we, Rose?" Mr. Lovejoy says with a hearty laugh behind it.

"No, we didn't, and that was some of my best cooking," Rose confirms and laughs as well.

"Uncle Mattie and Auntie Viv, you two should be really proud of Jessica because I know it must have taken a lot for her to stand up to the both of you, especially you Uncle Mattie," Brenda laughs.

I jump in. "I remember when I first saw her, I thought she was Raylene and I thought Alex had bailed her out of jail, but then when I realized that there was three of us, oh my god!"

Each and every one of us shares a Jessica moment or story. The eight of us cry, pray, and laugh together, which is therapeutic and distressing at the same time.

"How is anyone supposed to get any rest with all of this noise?" she says. It is Jessica, and she is awake.

Jessica

My Memory Is a Blank Slate

All I hear are voices, laughing, crying, and praying. Plus, I have been having this same recurring nightmare repeatedly. It's the sounds of horrific, high-pitch screams, like someone being tortured. When I open my eyes, I see a bunch of strangers standing over me. I ask them to keep the noise down, and within seconds, a group of doctors and nurses are at my bedside poking and prodding me. I don't know what is going on, and I don't like it.

I see this finely dressed, slender lady standing there, and next to her is this well-toned, muscular man with his arms wrapped around her. She is crying. There are other people in the room that I've never seen before, but the one girl does look familiar because she looks just like me.

"Can everyone please wait outside, and I'll come and get you as soon as I can," the man in the white coat orders. I'm assuming he's the doctor as they follow his instructions in a single line out of the room. He immediately starts giving the nurses instructions, and I hear words like *evaluations*, *brain scan*, and *blood work up*. I'm scared, confused, and alone, and I don't want them touching me. I am restricted by the nurses around my bed. I try to sit up, but I'm denied as well.

"Jessica, I need you to be still," I hear him say.

My eyes widen. Jessica? My name isn't Jessica. Why is my mind playing tricks on me? How can I not remember my own name? Frustration sets in. They are smothering me, and I feel like I can't breathe. I start kicking and moving around with as much force as I can gather.

"Jessica, I need for you to be still," he says again, but it doesn't last long. I'm too weak and too tired, so I acquiesce and stay still.

"Okay, I'm going to slowly pull this feeding tube out. So I need you to take a deep breath in when I pull and then slowly exhale," he instructs. "Can you do that for me? I nod my head yes.

My throat is sore as I take a gulp of water. He then proceeds to give me a full examination. First he starts shining that light in my eyes, and then he orders every kind of test known to medical science on me. Immediately he starts bombarding me with the questions nonstop, two and three at a time. "Do you know where you are? Can you tell me your name? Do you know what today is? Do you recognize anyone? Do you know who the president is?"

"Try and talk," he tells me.

I swallowed and then say, "What do you want me to say?"

He smiles. "How do you feel, Jessica?"

"Fine, I guess, but it's . . ."

"It's what," he asks.

"Why do you keep calling me Jessica?" I ask him.

He looks at me and then at the two nurses. There is a look of concern that engulfs his entire face.

"Did you happen to recognize any of the people that were standing here a few minutes ago?"

I shake my head no.

"Umm, do you know where you're at?"

I scan the room. "Well, from the looks of things, I'm in the hospital. I just don't know why," I tell him. He nods his head.

"Do you know how old you are?" he continues.

"Nineteen or maybe twenty, I'm not sure," I say.

"Jessica, can you tell me what you do remember?" he says.

"It's kind of hard to explain because it feels more like a déjà vu than anything. I know it sounds funny, but I feel like a different person completely," I say and then start to become overwhelmed.

"Okay, okay, I don't want you to overexert yourself, so I want you to rest, and I'll be back later to check on you," the doctor tells me as he gets up to leave.

"Doc, who are all those people out there?"

"They're your family, Jessica," he tells me. "Do you want them to come in? Maybe it will help you to remember them," he tells me. I'm skeptical but agree.

The doctor instructs one of the nurses to open the door, and within seconds, it's like a flash flood. They all surround my bed with oohs and aahs. I'm quiet as I look at each face individually. I see tears of joy and pain in their eyes and on their faces. I try hard to remember them. I want to remember them but I don't.

"Hi," is the only audible thing I can utter because I didn't want to be rude. Visions of me sitting in an etiquette school flashes through my mind.

"How are you feeling?" the lady asks me.

"*Hi*" is the only thing I manage to say after a few seconds because I had a strong feeling of grace and etiquette being taught.

"How are you feeling?" the lady asks me.

I don't respond to her. I look toward the doctor for help as I shrug my shoulders. My memory is a blank slate. The doctor comes to my rescue. "Take your time," he says again as I take one more glance around the room. "Anything?" he asks. Sadly, I shake my head no as I curl into a fetal position into the bed.

"What's going on? What's happening?" the man's voice echoes throughout, which makes me jump. There is anger in his tone and everyone seems upset. The doctor tells everyone they have to leave now so his patient can rest. "I'll explain everything to you outside," he tells them as he sternly kicks them out.

It isn't my intention to hurt anyone's feeling, but I'm just as confused as they are, and I need to know what has happened to me before I can answer anyone's question. Who am I, and where did I come from? I don't even know how I got here or how long have I been here, and no one has yet to explain to me why me and this girl look alike.

Raylene
God Loves Me and He Cares

It's been weeks, and I haven't heard from Jessica or Brenda, and she promised to get back to me with my new court date. This is why I choose to stay by myself, because every time I open up and let people in, they always end up letting me down one way or another, and I'm sick of it. When the fuck am I going to learn?

They decide to send Leslie to another correctional facility, which I'm happy about, but I still have Charlie's ass to contend with. She approaches me at dinner the other night. "Payback is a bitch, Chambers," she says and then walks away. I'm not worried about her ass, but I know I better watch my back just in case.

I've signed up for this new weekly program they are implementing called Outreach, where a group of local pastors come to the prison once a week and offer Bible study classes to anyone interested. I go a couple of times and find it to be very interesting. I've never been much on religion before, but this one pastor and I become fast friends. Bishop Walker has a unique way of breaking down the scriptures without using a lot of biblical jargon or terminology, which I'm able to relate to. Last week's discussion talked about God's love for us and how he cares, which has me thinking a lot.

After class, I ask Bishop, "If God loves me and he cares, then why did he allow me to go through all of the hell I've been through my entire life? That isn't love."

My question must have thrown him off because he tells me he wants me to think about that question myself and we would talk again next week. "I'm not sure I'll be coming back next week," I tell him.

The very next morning is pure hell for me. Any and everything that can go wrong goes wrong! My room gets searched, and then I'm blamed for inciting a food fight in the café, which I have nothing to do with, and I'm accused of cheating on my final exam for my GED. What the fuck!

I come back. "It's good to see you again," Bishop says. "And I'm so glad you decided to come back. Did you find an answer to your question?"

"No," I say. "And this past week has been pure hell," I tell Bishop.

"And why is that?"

"Hell if I know." I then feel a sense of shame. "Sorry," I mumble. "I'm just so tired of fighting all of the time," I tell him.

He smiles. "God sees you, Raylene. He sees your trials and your tribulations, and God knows you. He knows your heart and your burdens are not in vain. He has a blessing with your name on it that you can't even imagine. You asked me last week if God loves you and he cares, then why did he allow you to go through all the things you've been through your entire life? But if not you, then who? Who will he use? He's not punishing you. He's using you," he says to me.

"Using me? For what?"

"His purpose, his will," he says. "Don't you see, out of all the people he could have chosen, he chose you. You are still here even after everything you've been though. He made you for a reason, and it's your duty to find what it is you were created to do. You weren't promised a golden road to travel on, but you were promised life and life more abundantly if you choose him."

I laugh because that is too hard of a concept for me to believe.

"I know it's hard for you to believe now, but God has a plan for you and your life as long as you don't give up, give in. You will make it, I promise. Trust him, Raylene, and surrender all, accept his love for you. Remain steadfast in all you do and then watch the power of God change your life!" he says passionately as I hang on to Bishop's every word.

We talk for hours after the other inmates and pastors leave, and I tell him my whole life story from the beginning up until the time I killed Big Daddy. I tell him about my twin sisters, and I even tell him about the whole black market smuggling ring Detective Sosa believes we come from. Bishop is intrigued, in disbelief, and disturbed all at the same time.

By the time I get back to my cell, I go straight to bed. I toss and turn most of the night because I still have this unnerving feeling that something is wrong, but I don't know what it could be. I finally get a good night's sleep when I'm awakened by the guard. "Chambers, get up. The warden wants to see you, now," he stresses.

He is on the phone when I walk into his office, and he motions me to sit down. I'm tired and pissed that I'm summoned to his office again. My first thought is Charlie, but I quickly dismiss that thought. "Okay . . . yes, I understand completely . . . Yes, I'll be sure to do that . . . Okay. No, thank you. Bye," he says and then hangs up the phone.

He turns to me. "Chambers, I'm sorry for dragging you here so late, but I'm afraid I have some bad news," he says and then pauses.

"Bad news? What is it?"

"That was Detective Sosa, and he informed me that your sister Jessica is in the hospital. She's been shot, and I'm afraid she's in a coma."

That is the straw the break the camel's back for me because I go ballistic. I scream, punch, hit, throw, kick, and break any and everything I get my hands on. I'm convinced now there is no God. There can't be! The warden calls in the guards, and I'm immediately subdued and transferred to the infirmary. I need a cooldown period.

Bishop Walker visits me every day, and most days we don't say one word. He just helps me cry. After two and half days, I say, "I need to understand why something like that happened. Why Jessica? She wouldn't hurt a fly," I say.

"You seem to have more questions than answers," Bishop says.

I nod my head in agreement with him. "That explains why I haven't seen or heard from her or Brenda in weeks," I tell Bishop Walker.

After being released from the infirmary, I'm transferred into a minimum-security unit. While lying in bed reading, she stops by.

"Hey, Chambers, I heard about your sister. That's fucked up. I hope she's okay," Charlie says, standing in my doorway. I don't respond. It looks as if she is going to say something else but ends up walking away.

I receive a letter from Carly today. She writes that they haven't seen or heard from Amanda in weeks. Bre met someone, and she moved in with him three weeks ago. She says that Brittany, Nikki, and she moved out of the penthouse, and they all live together, and no one is hooking any longer. "Do you, baby girl," I say and then crumple up her letter and throw it into the garbage can. They are part of my past, and Bishop Walker always says, "You can't move forward if you're always looking back."

I get up early the next morning and start my day as usual when I hear my name being called over the intercom. "Raylene Chambers, report to the visitors' center."

My first thought is why Bishop would go to the visitors' center. We always meet in the recreation room. As I walk in, I see Detective Sosa standing front and center.

"What the hell are you doing here?" I say out of frustration.

"I came to check on you to see how you're doing. The warden told me you didn't take the news to well."

I roll my eyes. "Yeah, well, I'm dealing with a lot of other issues right now, and that was the icing on the cake," I say to Sosa, "How's she doing? She's going to be all right?" I ask when his phone rings. He excuses himself as he turns his back toward me.

"Hey, you, what's up? Oh that's great news! Really? When? She doesn't remember anything? How long did the doctor say? Okay, babe, she's resilient, and she already made it through the toughest part. The rest is just going to take time, patience, and love . . . because I know. Really . . . what, no, no, I'm not mad . . . well, okay, a little disappointed. Why? Because I felt like you weren't on my side . . . I know it's not your fault, it's no one's, but I just need to know that the woman I marry is going to be in my corner and doesn't turn her head in the other direction when things start to get a little uncomfortable for her liking. Don't be silly, of course I still love you and of course we're going to be married, Okay . . . I'll see you later," I overhear Sosa say as he turns back in my direction.

"It seems she's awake but she has amnesia and has no recollection about anything or anyone prior to the shooting," Sosa tells me.

"Are you serious?" I say. "Wait, who was that on the phone?"

"Robyn," he says.

"You and my sister are getting married?" I echo throughout the visitors' center. I'm shocked because I've known Sosa close to seven years and I assumed the type of women he would be attracted to would be more of a model-like female. Plus the fact, I'm not sure I'm comfortable with having him as part of my family.

I'm dumbfounded, and all I can do is sit there with this stupid-ass look on my face. Robyn's and my connections aren't as strong as Jessica's, but she's still my sister, and this isn't an easy thing for me to accept. Sosa looks at me then just walks away without saying another word.

Robyn/Jessica
Coming Home

The entire room erupts with excitement and praise when Jessica speaks. I feel like ten thousand pounds of worry are lifted off my shoulders. The doctor and nurses rush in and immediately start examining her as they kick us out of her room. I'm so elated, and Elle isn't here so I can share the good news with him. I'm bothered by the way he left without saying goodbye, but that was my fault.

I don't know why I feel conflicted because although the situation is fucked up, Mr. Lovejoy should not have taken his frustration out on him. I'm mad too at the situation as well, but not at him. I knew when he looked at me for support or reassurance, I know he's doing the best he can. I didn't give it to him. I just looked in the other direction, and I feel like grade A shit for doing that, and I need to apologize to him. I call him.

"Elle."

"Hey, you, what's up?"

"Jessica is awake!"

"Oh, that's great news! Really? When?"

"Just about twenty minutes ago, but there's a problem. She lost her memory."

"She doesn't remember anything? How long did the doctor say?"

"He doesn't know. He can't say for certain if she will ever regain her memory."

"Okay, babe, she's resilient, and she already made it through the toughest part. The rest is just going to take time, patience, and love."

"How do you know?"

"Because I know."

"Really?" I say.

"Really," he confirms.

"Are you mad at me?"

"What, no, no, I'm not mad . . . well, okay, a little disappointed."

"Why?" I ask.

"Why? Because I felt like you weren't on my side . . . I know it's not your fault, it's no one's. But I just need to know that the woman I marry is going to be in my corner and doesn't turn her head in the other direction when things start to get a little uncomfortable for her liking," he says.

"I know, and I'm so sorry. I felt conflicted like I had to choose a side, and Mr. Lovejoy was just letting off steam because of the situation. But you're right, I shouldn't have felt that way, and I want you to know I am on your side always and forever. Do you still love me, and do you still want to marry me?"

"Don't be silly, of course I still love you and of course we're going to be married. Okay . . . I'll see you later," he says and then hangs up the phone. I feel better, and I'm so relieved that I forget to ask him where he is at.

The next couple of days are all in preparation for Jessica coming home. Mr. and Mrs. Lovejoy are concerned about Jessica coming back to condo with her memory still being the way it is.

"We think it would be better for her to come back home where she will get proper care around the clock and hopefully the familiarity will help jog her memory," he tells me.

I can understand their concern, and they are probably right, but I'm hesitant about being there alone now, but I don't let them know that. "Okay," I say.

I try calling Elle again because instead of me moving in with him, maybe he can move in with me. It goes straight to his voice mail, which I think is strange. I leave a message.

The doctors tell Mr. and Mrs. Lovejoy that they just want to keep Jessica one more night for final observation and then she will be discharged in the morning.

"All of her tests came back, and everything looks in order. There seems to be no permanent physical damage done to the brain, and all of cognitive and motor skills are improving daily. The only thing left is time. If she is ever to regain her memory again to its full capacity, it's going to take time. Just know there are no guarantees," the doctor says.

"Thank you, Doctor, we truly are grateful to you and your staff for everything you've done for our daughter," Mrs. Lovejoy says.

"I want to give a donation to the hospital's endowment fund for further research and study for people suffering from head injuries," Mr. Lovejoy tells him. The doctor's eyes widen and are truly appreciative of his generous donation of one hundred thousand dollars.

I call Lee and reschedule my interview for tomorrow. With Jessica being released, I want to be there.

"No worries, I completely understand. Monday will be just fine," she says.

I take the car service back home and try calling Elle again and again. No answer, it goes straight to his voice mail, and he hasn't returned my call from earlier. This isn't like him, and I'm beginning to worry.

The guard at the guardhouse tells me I had a visitor today. "Who was it?" I ask.

"I don't know. He refused to leave his name," he tells me.

"He?" I ask.

"Yeah, a middle-aged man, looks to be in his early forties, salt-and-pepper sideburns, medium height, medium built," he says. My mouth drops open, "Alex", I utter.

"What did he want? Did he say why he was here?"

"No, not really, but he's been here several times before. Usually, he just sits in his truck across the street, but today he actually came over and asked if you were here. I tell him no, and then he just walks away."

I thank the guard and I told the security guard to call the police if he shows his face around her again!

"Is everything okay?" he asks.

"Everything is fine as long as you call the police if you see him again," I say and then walk into the building. As if I don't have enough shit on my plate to worry about, and now Alex. What the fuck does he want? Why is he here? I haven't seen or heard from him in months, and I've finally gotten to the point where I got that nigga out of my system, and now he's back. Oh, hell no! The baby, maybe he's gonna try to take custody of my baby. I'm beginning to lose it. Where the hell is Elle when I need him, and why isn't he answering his damn phone? "Ugh!" I scream out of frustration.

The doctor is pleased with my rapid recovery, and they are releasing me this morning. He explains that it may take time for my memory to come back or it may never return to its full capacity, but we just have to wait and see.

Matthew and Vivian say they will feel better if I stay with them because I'll be better cared for and familiar surroundings might help to jog my memory faster. I'm cool with that.

I am trying hard to remember, and I observe and listen to everything that is being said and going on around me because the feeling of not knowing anything is scaring the hell out of me. I am vulnerable now, and anybody can tell me anything, and I would have no choice but to believe them.

Robyn and I finally talk, and she explains the whole story to me, which sounds like a movie plot or something. "And that's basically how we met," she says.

She says I was right about Alex too, but she assures me that he is out of her system for good.

"Good, I'm glad," I say because it sounds like the right thing to say. Besides, I do not know who this Alex is either. The one thing I am excited about and looking forward to is her baby. I just love babies. I'm going to be an awesome aunt.

"Do you have any names picked out?" I ask her the other day.

"I've always loved the name Jeremiah for a boy and haven't gotten a clue for a girl's name," she tells me.

I pick up on how close the three of them have become. The past couple of days while here with me, I've listened to them talk. They are concerned about her and her baby, and when Matthew offered her a job at his record company, I thought that was very admirable of him. It seems like they are very nice people, and if they chose me to adopt, then I guess I should be lucky.

"So why did I leave? Why would I leave a place where things were good?" I ask because from the way they are making things sound, I was a fool to leave.

"Pumpkin, we don't have to rehash all of that now. Besides it isn't important anyway," he says to me as we're leaving the hospital.

"Well, if my memory is never going to return, then it is," I rebut. The drive home is long and slow. Matthew tells me all about the argument we had that night. He expresses to me about how strongly he was against my decision and how adamant I was to pursue it. Then we both felt a sense of guilt for acting the way we did and doing the things we've done.

"I'm so sorry. I should have never pushed you away like that, and I was wrong, and I'm so sorry, pumpkin," he says.

It isn't my intention to make him feel bad. I'm just trying to fill in the blank spots from the last twenty years of my life because they both seem like very nice people. I nod my head. "Thank you, Matthew, for being so candid with me," I say.

"You know, feel free to call us Mom and Dad, if you like," he offers, but I respectfully decline because I'm not comfortable enough yet.

From the moment we step into the house, Vivian starts bombarding me with question after question. Do I remember this? Do I remember that? But nothing looks remotely familiar to me. I watch them as they watch me, hoping that something would trigger my memory, but it doesn't. They escort me into my old room. "We left your room just the way you left it," Vivian says.

I stand in the doorway and look around. I try to get a sense of who this Jessica person was and what she was like. The room is filled with a lot of antique porcelain dolls, which looks extremely expensive, as well as musical instruments. They look like violins or violas.

I start touching one of them. "I saved everyone from the moment you first started playing," she informs me. "Oh, Matthew, remember how she would run into our room so we could hear the new piece she learned how to play?" she reminisces. Her emotions are high, and I try to feel what she is feeling, but I don't. Am I incapable of feeling emotions?

Maybe my being shot damaged some major nerves or something that they missed.

"Come on, Vivian, let's give her some privacy. Some time to get used to her room again," Matthew says as he pulls her out.

He closes the door behind them. I stand in the middle of the room unable to move. I'm mentally exhausted, and the only thing I want to do is go to sleep.

Detective Sosa

Do You Believe in Karma, Detective?

After I leave Raylene, I head straight to see Lita. I want to propose to Robyn tonight, but I need my grandmother's ring back first, and she is being extremely difficult about it. Robyn's been calling me several times, but I just can't answer it now because I need to stay focused. Lita is really pissing me off, and I cannot afford to lose control, so I leave my gun and my badge in the glove compartment of my car as I go into her apartment.

"Lita!" I call as I knock on the door. "Open up, I know you're there!"

After a few seconds, I hear the sound of the dead bolt being unlocked, but the door remains closed. I turn the knob, and she's standing there in her nightgown, and she looks like hell. Her hair looks as if it hasn't been comb in weeks, she has on no makeup, and God only knows when was the last time she took a shower. I rush to her side.

"Lita, what's going on? Are you okay?" I ask her. She seems dazed, and her words are slurred. I escort her to the couch so she can sit down, but she is acting like a junkie on crack.

"Lita, did you take anything?" I ask as I look into her pupils. They are dilated. I slap her face. "What did you take?" I yell. She can barely keep her eyes open as her brother comes running in.

"What the fuck did you do to my sister?" he yells. "She called me and told me she took some pills because if she can't live with you, she doesn't want to live without you," Jose tells me. I'm shocked because I didn't know things have gotten this bad for her. I listen as Jose tells me the whole story. "What are you doing here?" he asks. "Are you trying to push her over the top?"

I've never had a problem with Jose, and I'm not about to start now. I explain to him that I've been trying to get my grandmother's engagement ring back from her for months and she hasn't given it to me.

"Do you know where it could be?"

He shakes his head no. "She needs a doctor now!" Jose yells. I pull out my cell and call 911. The squad car arrives within three minutes, and the ambulance is there four minutes after that. Lita is going in and out of consciousness as they begin to work on her.

"Does anyone know what she took?" the EMT asks. I look around and find an empty bottle of sleeping pills. I give them to the medic as they rush her out on the gurney. Jose and I follow in my car. As I'm driving, my phone rings again. I immediately hand it to Jose and tell him to answer it.

"No, this is Jose. He can't speak right now. He's driving. We're on our way to the hospital," I hear him say.

"Who is it?" I ask him, which he ignores and keep talking.

"What do mean why? His fiancée ODed . . . Who the hell is this?" he repeats as I snatch the phone out of his hand.

"Hello . . . Robyn, baby, no, I'm sorry for that, but I really can't talk know . . . Yeah, University Hospital, but I'll see you soon," I tell her and then hang up the phone as my sirens blare.

They take Lita straight into the room to pump her stomach. Jose and I sit in the lobby pacing back and forth. One by one her other family members begin to arrive. Her mother is frantic as she cries and prays at the same time as her father and two other brothers start blaming me. It isn't my intention to get into a pissing match with any of them, but I'm not going to let them attack me, especially without knowing all the facts.

"Kiss my ass . . . and that's not what happened!" I yell at the top of my lungs. It is brutal, and the hospital security has to be called. I walk away so I can calm down, and when I return, I see Robyn standing in the lobby.

"Babe, what are you doing here? Are you okay?"

"I'm fine . . . What's going on with you? I've called you several times today, which you haven't returned, and who the hell was that on your phone earlier?" she asks.

I know Robyn is miffed, and I really wish she hasn't come down here because this is a part of my life I don't want her to be part of. The doctor enters and starts to update her family. I walk over to listen as Robyn follows.

"Well, we successfully pumped her stomach, and she's resting comfortably now," he enlightens us.

"Can we see her now?" Jose asks.

"Well, she's only asking to see one person, her fiancé," the doctor says. "Is that you?"

Robyn looks at me. I drop my head and look back at her. I see fear in her eyes as I answer "Yes" to the doctor and follow him to her room. I stay by Lita's side for the remainder of the night. Earlier the next morning, she is awake.

"You didn't have to stay, but thank you," she says as she tries to sit up. I assist her.

"How are you feeling?"

"Besides embarrassed," she responds, "I'll live."

"Listen, Lita . . ."

"No, no, Lawrence, you listen. I'm sorry, and I was wrong. It's clear that you've moved on with your life, and I need to do the same. It wasn't fair of me to act so damn childish, and well . . . ," she says as she pulls her hand from under the covers and hands me my grandmother's ring. I stand to my feet and bend over and give her a kiss on her forehead. Lita is going to be all right now, and she's able to move on.

I go straight to Robyn's after leaving the hospital, but I stop at her favorite breakfast place first and get all her favorites. I know I will have to do a lot of begging and pleading to get her to stop being mad at me. I slip the guard one of the freshly made banana walnut muffins I just picked up, and he doesn't announce my visit. The element of surprise is my best defense. I can't give her a chance to say no. I knock on the door, and she opens it without even asking who it is. I block it with my foot before she has a chance to close it.

"Come on, babe, open the door. Besides, the food is getting cold. I stopped by Jay's Deli and got all of your favorites," I say as she pulls the door open.

"You have a fiancée! Really?" she yells. "What, you asking to marry me was some kind of sick joke or something? I can't believe I let myself get played again!" I let Robyn rant and rave because I know she has to get it all out of her system before I'll be able to say a word.

But once she stops, I ask, "Are you done? Yes, I was wrong for not telling you about Lita, and yes, we were engaged to be married last New Year's Eve, but I called it off. I didn't answer your call when you called because I went to see her, and when I got there, that's when I found out she had taken sleeping pills. I had no idea that she had taken it so badly, babe, and I'm not going to walk away from someone who is in distress, I don't care who they are. You should know this about me by now," I say to her.

"I know that, but what I don't know is why you went to see her in the first place. Do you want to get back with her?" Robyn asks me.

Her question makes me smile. My baby is jealous. "No, of course not. I went to see her because I had to get this," I say as I pull out the ring from my jacket pocket and kneel on one knee.

She drops the muffin in her hand onto the floor as she shouts, "Oh, hell yeah!"

After our congratulatory making up, she says, "Oh my god, you'll never guess who's been coming around here!"

"Who?" I ask as I sit down at the kitchen table and begin to eat some breakfast. She keeps staring at her ring and smiling from ear to ear. I love seeing her so happy.

"Alex," she says.

"Alex?" I repeat. I'm not a jealous person, but hearing his name cut me to my core because I witnessed firsthand how getting over him nearly destroyed her. "What does he want?"

"I don't know, and I don't care. I told the guard if he sees him hanging around here again to call the police," she says as she finishes eating her breakfast.

"I'm the police I remind her," she just gives me one of her sideways looks.

I'm restless all night long, and I don't like the fact that Alex has been hanging around. Robyn suggests since Jessica living back at home, I can come and stay with her which is not a hard sell.

Robyn is resting peacefully when I leave this morning. I leave a note next to her pillow telling her I'll be back later. As I'm leaving, the guard tells me the man is back and points toward the black SUV sitting across the street.

I step out of my vehicle and slowly walk in his direction. Our eyes meet and stay locked on one another until I reach his car. "Can I help you with something?" I ask.

He doesn't respond immediately as he sits there. His appearance is unkempt, and he's in need of a shower.

"Sir, can I help you with something? I'm Detective Sosa," I add as I extend my right hand, "And you are?"

"I know who you are," he sternly replies and without extending his hand back toward me. I snicker and retract my arm. After a few seconds of awkwardness, he tries to speak, clearing his throat over and over until his voice was not squeaky.

"Alex Taylor," he says, "So how's she doing? I mean, is she happy?" he asks.

"Do you really care?" I rebut in defense, but after careful consideration, I say, "Of course she is. She's extremely happy, and as long as I'm here, she will always be happy," I add. At first, it feels like two male lions fighting over their territory; except Robyn isn't a piece of property. I quickly assessed my competition and quickly realized, there isn't any. This man was damage, lost, and depleted. Any hopes and dreams of being with Robyn was a distant memory he was trying so desperately to remember or hold on to. No need to kick a man further when he's already is down.

"You know, Detective, I've done a lot of things in my life, some I'm not proud of, but through it all, I've always maintained a sense of compassion for people in general. I've never put anyone in jeopardy, and I've never forced anyone to do something they didn't want to do. I'm a firm believer what you put out in the universe, you get back. I think they call it karma. Do you believe in karma, Detective?"

I nod yes.

"But as time continued, things started happening, not to me, of course, but people I love. First my daughter, and then Mama, and now my wife," he says.

"And, I would like to know how every meaningful and significant female relationship I had, ended in their deaths? Can you please explain it to me, because for the past few months, I've been lost like a motherfucker." He screeches in pain. "The day I learned my wife had cancer was confirmation that I could not let any of my bad karma fall on Robyn or my baby. Don't you see? I had to tell her I didn't love her anymore. I had to save her life. I've already buried my daughter and my mother, and now my wife," this broken man explains to me through his tears. I do not blame him. I have a better understanding of Alex Taylor now, and I feel his pain. "She hates your guts, you know. She told the guard to call the police if you come around here again," I tell Alex as he continues to stare at whatever he was holding in his hand.

He smirks. "I would be surprised if she didn't. I won't be back unless you don't treat her right. I need you to do me a favor, Detective," he says.

"What's that?"

"Be the man I couldn't be for her. Don't let her down," he says to me before he drives away.

I call Robyn and tell her about our conversation, but she is indifferent and said I should have arrested him anyway.

"Robyn, can't you see every meaningful female relationship in his life has ended in death and he was scared for you?" I tell her, but she is indifferent and isn't trying to understand anything about Alex Taylor.

Sully does it! He's found and located Charles Lambert, who's been in deep seclusion with around-the-clock care and protection. He's been a resident for the past twenty years at Greystone's Memorial Physiatrist Hospital.

I speak with his doctors. "He has good days and bad, and he's been socially and emotionally withdrawn since he's been here. He has no real connection or concept of time or place," the doctor explains.

I want to check things out on my own before I say anything to Robyn and Raylene, so I go to the hospital. I walk into his room at a snail's pace because I don't want to startle the feeble, albino, gray-haired man. His room is immaculate. There is state-of-the-art equipment everywhere, and there is the gentle sound of Earth, Wind, and Fire coming through the speakers in his room. Mr. Lambert is sitting in the chair, which is facing out the window.

There are lots of pictures of Jonathan, Jade, and their babies. As I look at Jade, I can see where Robyn gets her beauty from. It's evident that the past twenty years has no mercy on the billionaire because it has robbed him of any vigor, vim, or vitality a man of his caliber should have.

"It's a two-hundred-year-old oak," the doctor informs me. "And most of his days, he just sits there staring at it. A family of baby raccoons moved in, and once in a while we take him outside because he likes to feed them," he adds.

From the moment I got this case, I knew it was going to be intriguing, unbelievable, and disturbing all wrapped into one. The one thing I've learned this past year is it's not how you get knocked down but how important it is to get up and stand on your feet. Raylene, Robyn, and Jessica are three young women who had the fortune or misfortune to go through some of life's most difficult times, but in each of their situations, they have preserved, and triumphs will always be victories as long as they don't quit.

www.ingramcontent.com/pod-product-compliance
Lightning Source LLC
Chambersburg PA
CBHW070515160726
48003CB00004B/1571